Ninety Percent Death Rate

By

Al Hagan

Chapter 1

Dani shoved her back against the passenger door and clutched her mother's butcher knife, breathing hard. She knew the next few minutes were going to determine the rest of her life. Or maybe the end of it.

The SUV was only going to offer a temporary refuge at best. It was never going to move again under its own power, and even if it would run and she had the key fob, it was blocked in front, behind, and on the sides by a wall of other dead cars, bumper to bumper in a massive, frozen gridlock that stretched for untold miles. There was probably an unending traffic jam all the way to Dallas, and then to Oklahoma City, to Wichita, to Kansas City, to... everywhere.

She had run as fast as possible but she could hear them gaining on her. They had longer legs than she did so they could run faster. It was only a matter of time, and not much of that. Their shoes slapped down on the pavement, coming closer and closer, gaining on her much too quickly.

Desperate, she skidded to a stop beside the big SUV and jerked the door handle, breaking a couple of nails. It opened, so she dove in and slapped the lock down. She pushed away from the driver's door to the passenger's side, forcing herself over the console with her heels dug into the seat while she slid her backpack off and pulled the knife out. She had no doubt that her pursuers could smash the windows and pull her out, but she was going to make them pay. Maybe even make them pay so much that they simply got frustrated and shot her and let her join her dead family. And almost everyone else.

Tears unexpectedly flooded her eyes, thinking of her family, followed immediately by anger at the world that had put her here and frustration at her own weakness in dealing with it. She furiously wiped her eyes, sniffled a little, and then drew a deep breath and gritted her teeth. She decided she would fight to the death. Suicide was a sin for a Catholic and a short, nasty, torturous life as a sex slave was not going to happen if she could prevent it.

Suddenly, there was a knock on the window that she was pressed up against. She jumped and swung the knife around at the face that loomed in the window, grinning in at her. The window was up and the door locked, but a man was there, just letting her know that she wasn't going to simply open the door and start running again once she caught her breath. No, that route was blocked.

Then the driver's side window exploded inwards with a shower of glass that peppered her with fragments. The surprise forced a little cry from her and she swung back to face this new threat.

There were two of them standing there. One stuck a rifle in far enough to use the barrel to clear away the remaining glass and then pointed it at her. She steeled herself for the shot, the knife held out in front of her, pointed at the gangbanger peering in at her. But he didn't shoot. His face creased in a smile, looking at her. He pulled the rifle back and placed it on the roof of the vehicle. He said something to the man beside him and they both laughed.

"Why don't you come out?" he asked. "Be my woman. I'll protect you."

His companion said something that she didn't catch and the thug laughed. "Naw, man. Shut up. I'm working here. Working."

He turned back to face her. "You come out now or there's going to be consequences." He said the last word slowly, as if each syllable was a separate word, as he reached in and unlocked and opened the door.

She growled back "I'll cut you!" and waved the knife around for emphasis. He shook his head, disappointed, and things went downhill from there. The two gangbangers started telling her what they were going to do to her. She didn't even understand some of the terms they used and laughed about.

I'm barely eighteen! I'm still in high school! I've only had two boyfriends! Jesus, Mother Mary, please! she thought. *I know suicide is wrong but surely there must be an exception in a case like this!* She turned her wrist over and looked at the blue veins just beneath the skin and considered that option while she prayed for a miracle to save her. *Whatever happens, I am not going to cry! Not! Not! Not!*

Chapter 2

Eric had slept in and gotten a late start. His muscles ached from riding a bike for the first time in years, but he figured that stretching them out was better than not. He could always take it easy, but at least he would be making progress.

He knew the onramp from State Highway 99 to Interstate 45 would be a beast for a guy on a bike. It went up and up, way higher than he wanted to pedal, before sweeping over and descending to dump traffic onto I-45 northbound. He took an earlier exit down to the ground-level service road before turning north and was faced with a long line of useless businesses full of dead machinery — body shop, car dealer, car repair, equipment rental. He figured no survivors would want anything at any of these places, so it was perfect for him to hang out a while. He chose one at random and put his hammer and pry bar to work.

My two-piece master key, he thought.

Noontime, the temperature was actually nice inside, still cool enough from the night without having yet turned to hot and airless from the afternoon sun. He found a small waiting area with drink and snack machines and a five-gallon water dispenser, exactly what he wanted. The first order of business was to secure the location, which meant dragging a three-person seat in front of the door he breached, and then stacking chairs on top of that. Anyone trying to get in would make a hell of a racket. And, just in case someone with a key came to the back door, he stacked some furniture in front of it, too.

Next, he filled his canteens and had a lunch that was a culinary delight of warm Coca-Cola and junk food. He felt pretty safe, so he laid his jacket and poncho liner on the floor and lay down for a rest, although he oriented himself so that his rifle lay across his body and pointed at the door. He could just flip the safety off and pull the trigger and the bullet would hit the door, without wasting any time on swinging the rifle onto the target or any of that nonsense.

After a little break to ease his aching muscles, he downed another tepid Coke as he packed up and dragged his barrier out of the doorway, then hit the road again. Almost as soon as he got going, he spotted trouble ahead.

There was an SUV with two men on the driver's side, thugs, obvious gangbangers, apparently having a conflict with someone inside. Eric was a hundred yards from them and he could have sneaked off quietly, detoured around them, and gone on about his business, but that option never even entered his mind. His instinct was just the opposite: they were predators, attacking someone weaker, and he needed to do something about it. He wasn't necessarily happy about it, but he had to do it.

Some people run away from danger, some run towards it.

The men were loud, oblivious to anything else but their prey, but he quietly dismounted, leaned his bike against a car, and slowly moved closer while unslinging his rifle. As he moved in, he zigged over to check out the other side of the SUV and sure enough, there was another banger there, watching through the window and serving as a roadblock to prevent anyone from bailing out that side of the vehicle.

He closed to within three car lengths and stopped behind a car to give him cover. Adrenaline was flooding into his system and his heart felt like it was thumping so hard it was going to crack ribs. In a few seconds, he was going to kill three men in cold blood. And he was going to shoot them with no warning. Just simply kill them. This wasn't a situation where he could confront them verbally and get them to go away. That would have been stupid. The odds were three to one and this wasn't a movie. There was no guarantee that he was the hero and was going to emerge unscathed. This situation would only be resolved in blood.

Hopefully, not his.

A voice inside him screamed *Are you crazy?!* His mind

flashed back briefly to what it had taken to get him this far, what he had lost, what he had done. He thought *No, not crazy. This is the world now. A lot has changed in a week.* He swung his rifle off of his shoulder and up into the low ready position, took a deep breath, and stepped forward towards the targets. That was all they were now, not men, just targets that he must shoot quickly and accurately.

One Hell *of a lot has changed.*

Eric aimed the M1A Scout at the first guy, took his time with the shot, let out half a breath and then held it, and slowly squeezed the trigger. He needed this one to be exact, since the following shots were going to be sloppier. He would be shooting faster, and at moving targets. If he was lucky, they wouldn't be targets that were shooting back.

The first shot was a nice heart-and-lungs hit, followed up by a rapid couple of others. The three bullets went through the first man and into the second, and they both collapsed in a heap.

Eric rapidly sidestepped to the other side of the vehicle to engage Thug number three. This one had ducked when he heard the gunfire, but also wanted to draw the pistol stuck in his pants. Unfortunately for him, he couldn't do both. He was trying to figure out what to do when he saw Eric step into view with a big rifle aimed at him. The thug straightened up to draw his pistol but he was way too late. Two bullets slammed into his chest and he went straight down to the pavement, game over.

Eric stepped back to his original spot to check on the first two bad guys. There was too much movement going on there, so he put two more rounds into the center of mass. The movement stopped.

Breathe, thought Eric. *Just like in martial arts. Breathe. Now scan 360, once fast, once slow and careful. Okay, no apparent threats. Reload.*

He pulled a fresh magazine out of a pouch left-handed and placed it on the trunk of the car in front of him, made sure it was ready, then did the swap. The partially-used mag went into the pouch and he scanned again, fast then slow, then moved up.

In TV and the movies, the good guys always know when all of the bad guys are down. There's nothing that tells them that, they just all know somehow, and then they drop their guard and cluster together to look at some clue or plan their next move. They don't reload, or check the wounded, or set up a perimeter or even pay the slightest attention to anything else.

Real life isn't like that.

You never, ever know if all of the bad guys are down, and ninety-nine times out of a hundred, they aren't. Some are wounded but can still fight, or some ran off to get more friends to come back and fight, or some are waiting to shoot you in the back when you aren't looking. You simply do not know, so you have to assume they are and act accordingly.

That being the reality, Eric's head was on a swivel, constantly looking for threats, like a fighter pilot. He closed in on the two bodies by the door but he went over to the shoulder of the highway to come at them from an angle where it would be awkward for them to turn and shoot at him if they were able to do so.

They seemed to be out of the fight. A .308 tends to do that, with about 1,950 foot-pounds of energy on tap. A hot 9mm load might go 500, a .44 Magnum 1,200 for comparison. Even more importantly, it delivers that massive hit all at once. It's like the difference between taking four jabs versus one roundhouse punch. The roundhouse may be no more powerful than all four jabs put together, but it hits all at once, and probably ends the fight.

***

Dani's first warning that her miracle had arrived on-scene was loud booms and some kind of meaty thumps. Her little brother had once stood on a chair and fallen, making a similar sound when he hit the floor. But these were bigger, more substantial, more violent.

The two men in front of her jumped and flailed and fell to the pavement in a tangled heap together, spouting blood and moaning. Then there were more booms and noise behind her. She looked around and could see a man moving out there, a few vehicles back. She lost sight of him and then there were two more booms and a couple more smacking sounds as more bullets hit the two men on the ground by the driver's side. Blood splattered up and hit the dashboard and she recoiled back to get away from it. One of the men's arms had been outstretched, reaching upwards for something. Now it dropped, the elbow hitting the pavement, and then the forearm slowly fell over to the side.

Everything seemed to go very quiet as the report of the shots faded away. The man came closer, cautiously, surveying the area, rifle up and ready to shoot again. She was frozen. She couldn't move a muscle except for her eyes, not even breathing. She didn't know if an angel or a devil was drawing near.

Chapter 3

Eric scanned the area again, then glanced into the SUV, a quick in-and-out as fast as he could, to see if there was a threat and then get out before they could react if there was. He saw a girl and a knife. She was pushed up hard against the opposite side of the vehicle, as far away from the two thugs as she could get. He peeked in again, slower this time but still ready to pull back.

"I have a knife!" she yelled, jabbing it in his direction even though he was too far away to cut.

He wordlessly turned and started back towards his bike. After a moment, "Hey, where are you going?" came from the SUV. He almost laughed, thinking that she couldn't threaten him with a knife and then complain when he walked away. That wasn't sending mixed signals, much!

Dani slapped a hand over her mouth but it was too late. She'd already said it. *Oh, my God! Why did I do that? Why did I yell at him? Did he save me, or, or what?*

She slid towards the open door, looked out, and went pale at the sight of the dead men and the blood. Five high-velocity hollow point rifle bullets do quite a bit of damage, and two bodies leak a lot of blood, even if it was just coming out by gravity and not being pumped out by the hearts. The world suddenly seemed a different place for her, more real than when the gangstas were taunting her, telling her how they were going to sexually assault her. That was talk, just talk. Words. This was real. *Really* real. Death and blood real.

There's so much blood. Oh, God, so much blood!

A confused blur of thoughts and emotions swept over her. A moment ago the best she could hope for was that they would gang-rape her and let her go. Highly unlikely, but a girl could dream. Now they were dead, completely and thoroughly. No restarting the game, no going back to a previous save. Dead.

Dead. *Dead.* She felt body-slammed.

There was no way she could get out of the SUV on that side without stepping on bodies so she scooted back to the other side of the vehicle and looked out that window. There was only one body there, and it was further from the door than the two on the other side. She hopped out with her backpack and stood for a moment, holding onto the vehicle because she didn't trust her unsteady legs right now.

From out of left field somewhere, she thought of the police. The idea almost made her laugh. *Yeah, there aren't any cops any more. There aren't going to be any questions or detectives or investigations or trials. Not that the police ever did us any good anyway.*

Feeling better, she started to walk around the SUV, then had a thought that caused her to spin nimbly around like a top and head straight for the body. The blood leaking from it was flowing off to the side so it looked like what she wanted was clear. She felt under it where a right-handed person would have a gun stuck into their waistband and found what she was looking for. She pulled it out by the handle, keeping away from the trigger, then stood and slid it into her back pocket and drew her shirt tail over it. Her blue jeans were tight, and the pistol made them tighter, but it wasn't going anywhere. It made a good holster for now.

I am NOT going to be a victim again! That guy knows how to shoot. I'll get him to teach me. Or I'll find someone else who will.

Then she thought *Jesus, I just watched that guy kill three men.* Her knees went weak again. *Maybe I need to run from him. But then, he killed them to save me. Or something.*

Just about then, "that guy" came back, wheeling a bicycle. He turned to look at her but never broke his stride, speaking as he walked: "We need to unass this AO. They might have friends. Or just some more like them. I'm heading north. Want to go?" He spoke rapidly and a little too loudly from the adrenaline.

She felt like her emotions were written on a wheel like in Wheel of Fortune, only it never stopped on one. It just kept spinning and she was experiencing each emotion as the wheel passed the marker, one right after the other, rapid fire. She was scared of this guy, then thankful, then surprised and irritated. She knew she wasn't drop-dead gorgeous, but she was hot and she got a lot of male attention all of the time. From all ages of males, not just the ones in her high sch —

WAIT! She thought. *This guy is older. I'd better say I'm older, too. Not that I'm going to jump into bed with him. But he did just protect me, so that is not outside of the realm of possibility.*

She felt a warm rush of sexual desire envelop her like stepping into a hot shower, surprising her so much that her jaw dropped. *Really? I'm* horny*? With dead bodies around me? Chica, get hold of yourself!*

The next instant she realized she had an ear-to-ear grin on her face and was lightheaded with euphoria. *Oh, thank God! Thank you, Jesus and Mary, that I am not being beaten and raped right now! Thank you that I'm still alive!* She put her fingers to the little gold cross on her necklace. *I will pray. I will do everything I can. But I think I have to go now.*

She peered around the SUV and looked at the guy. He was scanning back and forth and locked eyes with her momentarily. Everything she now owned was in her little backpack, and no one that she was related to was alive, as far as she knew. Then her personal little Wheel of Emotion spun again and grief and sorrow and loss flooded her, and she didn't know what she wanted or what she should do. Except for one thing - that was obvious, and she trotted off to catch up with "that guy."

***

Eric's first thought on getting a good look at the girl was *WOW!* followed by *Put that thought on hold and get out of here, horn dog.* He paused long enough to grab the AR rifle that one of the thugs had placed on the roof of the SUV in order to free his hands for the upcoming rape. He slung it across his shoulder but it was awkward carrying two rifles and pushing the bike.

The girl trotted up and matched pace with him, following behind. The road was so jammed with vehicles that there were few places they could walk side-by-side. "Can you push the bike?" he asked. She looked at him for a second and decided to do it. Eric almost got irritated, but then told himself you couldn't expect civilians to act like Marines and react quickly. He was going through the effects of an adrenaline dump. First it jacks you up, messes with your sense of hearing, your vision, and your time sense, and then it drops you. You get the shakes and you're exhausted.

He let her lead since he was the one with the rifle and he wanted to watch behind them. His next question was "Do you know how to shoot?"

She shrugged. "Pull the trigger?" she replied.

That meant "No" in Eric's world, so he slung the AR in a better position because he wasn't going to give it to her.

"Thank you. You saved me from... those guys," she said.

"It was the right thing to do," he tossed off, distracted by trying to look in all directions at once.

Daniela wanted to say something more. That "thank you" had sounded so lame, so inadequate for saving her from the promised horrors, but she didn't want to invite anything unintended. He wasn't listening much to her anyway.

"What did you say a second ago?" she asked instead. "It sounded like ass something."

He laughed a bit. "Unass the AO? Unass means to leave. You know, like you sit your ass down in a chair, so when you leave, you un-ass the chair. AO is Area of Operations. 'Unass the AO' means to get out of the area."

She turned and smiled and looked him up and down. She saw close cropped dirty-blond hair, green eyes probably made greener by the camouflage uniform he wore, about six feet tall. He was broad-shouldered and seemed to be built, judging by the generous biceps and forearms. He could use a shave and a shower but he'd clean up nicely, she judged. Very nicely.

"Are you in the military?"

"I did four years in the Marine Corps, a couple years back." They walked a few more steps. "My name is Eric Marten."

"I am Daniela Angelina Ruiz Vasquez. You may call me Dani. I'm 21. I go to San Jac," she replied. San Jac was Houston slang for San Jacinto, a campus of Houston Community College.

He looked like he believed that, in her estimation. She was exaggerating her age by three years, but she did read her sister's college books and even helped her with her homework. She wasn't just some dumb kid.

"Are you heading some place or just getting away from the city?" he asked.

"I'm getting away. There's nothing —" Dani stopped speaking. Tears formed in her eyes but she forced that emotion down. She looked away for a moment and cleared her throat. "There's nothing back there for me." Her voice was husky with emotion.

"I underst —" There was a sudden burst of gunfire, pistol, more than one, bullets sailing by them, coming from behind. That was exactly what he had been afraid of. He spun around, dropping to the pavement as he did so, and bringing his rifle up.

Yet another thug had popped up from somewhere and was banging shots off at them in true gangbanger style — two pistols held sideways, firing as fast as he could. One was rotated clockwise, the other counterclockwise. He had no possibility of actually aiming a shot. If he'd had an ounce of skill he could have taken one competently-aimed shot and had a good chance of hitting Eric, even at this distance.

But with the amount of lead he was slinging in their general direction, there was also a good chance he would hit one of them just by sheer dumb luck, and virtually any wound in this current world would be a death sentence. He had to be taken down quickly. Eric flipped the safety off, lined the sights up, and squeezed off a single round. For a Marine, all of whom qualify with rifles at five hundred yards, it was a pathetically easy shot at less than one hundred. The guy went down on his ass, then on his back. Eric put another shot into his crotch, which was pretty much center of mass from his current viewpoint. He kept his rifle on target as he stood, but his eyes were scanning all around again.

Damn, I hate living like a rabbit, he thought. *Always looking out, afraid something is going to pop up from any direction and kill you.*

He moved behind a car for cover and spared a second to look at his own body, making sure he wasn't hit and just didn't realize it yet. Looked good. He turned to Dani, who had had the good sense to crouch behind the same car and was peering wide-eyed at him through the frame of the bike, which she was still holding upright. It might have been funny in other circumstances.

"Are you hit?" he asked. "Stand up! See if you're bleeding."

She frowned at his barked order but realized she'd have to stand up at some point, so she gave him a dirty look and then stood. He looked her up and down, no blood.

"Turn around" he commanded.

"No! I'm fine! I'm not hit!" She crossed her arms defiantly. Eric's temper flared. He was trying to help her and she was being a bitch! He called her several bad names in his mind, and partly out of frustration, partly based on a plan, he set his rifle down on the hood and unslung the AR. He flicked the safety off and burned off the whole magazine as fast as he could pull the trigger, 30 rounds, in the general direction of the SUV where the thugs had been.

The plan part was that anyone in the area would be less inclined to venture into a gunfight, whereas they might be interested in checking out a few shots here and there. The frustration part was that it released stress to make loud noises like that, and the added benefit was that Dani was back in a crouch, hands over her ears to block the muzzle blasts and eyes squeezed tightly shut.

Too bad she was to my left instead of my right, he thought. *Then I could have rained some hot brass on her. Her ass would jump up if she got hot brass down her cleavage!* He immediately thought that was mean and was glad it didn't happen that way. *These last few days have really, really, really, REALLY sucked for everyone. Her included, not just me. I shouldn't be an asshole to her.*

He reached a hand out and said Dani's name softly. She couldn't hear him, and if he said her name louder, she'd get mad at him for yelling at her, so he just waited. After a few more seconds of no shooting, she tentatively opened one eye, then both. She looked at his hand, figured it for a peace offering, and took it.

Chapter 4

"We need to move out." Eric unhinged the AR upper, pulled the bolt carrier group, and pitched it off into the distance. The rifle was useless without it, and he just dropped it on the pavement where they stood. Normally, he'd treat a rifle with more care, but in this case he was deliberately sabotaging it anyway.

They walked on in silence for a few minutes, Eric keeping a close eye on their back trail.

"Like I said, I'm heading north. I have some property and a house up around Tyler."

Dani speared him with her eyes and a single raised eyebrow and asked "And a wife?"

"No... no, she... she passed away about two years ago. Cancer."

"Oh! I'm sorry. I guess that was stupid of me to ask." Now she could add guilt into her personal little Wheel of Emotion, spinning around in her head. She just wanted to curl up under the blankets in a nice warm, soft, safe bed somewhere right now. And cry, and then wake up and have everything back to normal.

"No, it's... kind of a thing now, isn't it? I know you lost people. I'm sorry."

Dani didn't reply, but it looked like she dropped her head a little. Maybe she was choking back tears.

What did I just do? Eric asked himself. *Did I just invite this girl to my place? I met her like two minutes ago! And this isn't like meeting a girl in a club and inviting her to your place. That's different. This world is way different. But it's not like I can't ever be with another girl. It's been close to two years. She's certainly hot! Beautiful girl with a smokin' hot body! About 5 feet 2 inches tall, maybe 105 pounds, tight little body, she works out, long dark hair. Okay, okay, calm down, think rationally, and think with your big head and not the little one!*

***

Did he just invite me to come live with him? Dani thought. *That's crazy. He wouldn't do that, would he? We just met! But he did just save my life. And he is handsome, and big, and strong, I'm sure. He owns a house and land. He has a plan. He's good with a gun. That was maybe not a good thing last week, but may be a very important thing from now on!*

They both stewed silently in their thoughts for a little bit while they picked their way through the cars and debris. During this time he had the chance to check her out in more detail than he had been able to previously, and he enjoyed checking her out. She was still hot. His original assessment had been correct. Her features were delicate, with full lips, an upturned little nose, and big almond-shaped amber-colored eyes that were enhanced with a little eyeliner. Her long hair was black as midnight, parted in the middle and falling down to the sides almost to her waist. She was tiny but had muscles that rippled in her arms. She moved with a grace that he would have called a dancer's, except for her arms. That made him think *gymnast*. Or perhaps martial arts.

They went a mile or so and saw a sign for an Academy Sports and Outdoors right off the highway. "Perfect, exactly what I wanted," Eric said. He smiled at Dani and asked "Want to go shopping?"

She laughed and replied, "I always want to go shopping!"

Someone had already smashed the doors in, so they were saved that amount of work. He went in quickly but as quietly as he could, to the left, got his back against a wall, got low behind something, and then scanned and listened for a minute. *People are impatient. Usually a minute is all it will take for them to decide the noise they heard is nothing and start talking or moving around again. Okay, so if he was alone, good. If not, he'd give a lurker something to think about.*

"Team 2, team 3, move out" he barked out in his command voice, then shuffled his boots on the floor a couple of times, not loudly but providing some sound effects of men moving. More scanning and listening and still nothing, so he eased back to the front entrance and waved Dani in.

Working in the dim light that came in the front glass, they found a nice mountain bike with a frame that fit her, hiking boots, socks, a backpack, and some clothing that was more outdoor-type than what she had now. As she was swapping her meager possessions from her school textbook backpack to the new one, she paused, holding her phone.

"Dead weight," Eric commented. "It's never going to work again."

She continued to stare at the phone for a few seconds, thinking of what it had cost, what it had meant to her, the photos of friends and family that were on it. The memories. It was a part of her. It had been within arm's reach, night and day, for years. She wiped a smudge off of the dead, dark screen and then gently set it down with a sigh and tears in her eyes.

Somewhere along the way, Eric noticed the pistol in her back pocket. He knew right away where she had gotten it and while he wasn't happy to have an untrained person with a gun, he liked that she wasn't afraid of them.

"Can I see your pistol?" he asked, figuring if he called it "her" pistol that would acknowledge her ownership.

She put down the top she was examining, turned her body so that the pistol was as far away from him as possible, and looked at him. Basically, her body language said that he would have to go through her to get the pistol.

He held up a hand. "I don't want to take it away from you. I just want to make sure it's loaded and safe to operate. I'll give it back to you in thirty seconds. And, later on, we need to train you how to use it."

She brightened. "You'll teach me? I want to learn! I want to learn to shoot and to fight." She drew the pistol out and extended it to him, muzzle pointed straight at his stomach. At least she had her finger away from the trigger.

Eric stepped around to the side to get out of the line of fire and took the pistol. It was a Glock 19, which he thought was excellent since that was what he was also carrying. He dropped the magazine and locked the slide back, ejecting a round into the stack of clothing they were standing over. After a quick function test and a look to make sure the barrel wasn't obstructed, he replaced the full magazine but didn't chamber a round. He believed in trying to not give people the opportunity to screw up.

He handed the pistol back to her. She put it back in her pocket and then asked "What about that one?" pointing at the ejected round. He looked her in the eye for a minute and her gaze was unflinching. She kept her finger pointed at the round, too. He had to laugh.

"Damn, you don't miss a thing, do you?"

Her only response was to raise one eyebrow, eyes still locked on his. "Okay," he said. "We'll do training. We'll try to get a practice session in this afternoon. If you absolutely have to use your pistol before then, all you have to do is rack the slide.

"First, the four basic rules for safe firearm handling: Treat all firearms as if they were loaded. Never point a firearm at anything you are not willing to destroy. Keep your finger off the trigger until your sights are on target. That's called 'trigger discipline'. And four, be sure of your target and what is beyond it. Repeat that back to me." She did, virtually verbatim.

He did a quick training session right then on racking the slide and let her dry-fire it a couple of times to get a feel for the trigger, and she was happy. At the end he handed her the one round and told her to put it in her pocket for later.

Eric checked for ammunition in Sporting Goods but it had disappeared off of the shelves. He considered trying to crack their warehouse stash, but wanted to get out of the area. He had lots of .308 at home, if he could make it there. He did find a pack of foam hearing protectors that they could use for shooting practice. There were no Glock holsters for Dani so the back pocket would have to do for now.

While he was gone, Dani knelt to say a prayer and just burst into tears. Sobs wracked her frame for a minute until she got them under control, pressing a T-shirt to her face to muffle the sound so Eric wouldn't hear. Once she was through, she said a prayer of thanks for her rescue and, as always, for her family. When she stood she had renewed strength and courage. She straightened her back, squared her shoulders, and a fierce light of determination came into her eyes.

I will survive. I. WILL. SURVIVE! Nothing is going to stop me. No one is going to victimize me ever again. I am strong. I can do this. I will *do this!*

When Eric came back he could tell that her eyeliner was smeared but figured that was normal. The girl had been through what was probably the most stressful day in her life. The most stressful week. She was allowed to cry about it, but she seemed all right now. If she had been melting down into a basket case, curled up in a fetal position on the floor, now that would have been a problem.

"Do you want a hat? Gonna be out in the sun for days," he asked.

She smiled. These items may not have been the jewelry and fashionable clothing she wanted, but she was smart enough to realize that she'd never be in high sch — *college!* — again, and never competing with the rich girls again. "Sure!" she gushed.

The way to a woman's heart, Eric mused, *is to let her raid an abandoned Academy.*

He found a hat he liked, one with a bigger brim than the boonie hat that he was wearing, and tossed the boonie on the display. Dani selected a cute rancher-style cowboy hat from the display.

They were packed up and heading towards the door when it darkened and someone came through it.

Chapter 5

Eric eased his kickstand down and stood the bike on it, then brought his rifle up. As quietly as he tried to move, he wasn't silent.

"Who's there?" called out the man at the door. His eyes hadn't adjusted to the dark interior of the store yet.

Eric pointed at Dani, so she nodded and replied "We're just passing through. We're trying to get out of the city." As she spoke, Eric was moving into a better position to cover the door, moving stealthily on the carpeted section of floor in the clothing department.

"Who is 'we'?" asked the doorway figure. Eric figured Dani was enough of a smartass to avoid the question and he was right.

"Why do you want to know?" she shot back. He had a good view of the figure now — older guy, heavy, no rifle, so maybe he was okay, but it might be good to keep him off guard. He grabbed an empty hanger and tossed it like a Frisbee off to his right, since Dani was on his left. The figure had been facing the sound of Dani's voice, but when the hanger smacked into something, he spun his head around that way.

Then Eric asked "Yeah, why?" and the guy looked towards yet a third direction.

He held up his hands. "We're friendly. I have a pistol on my hip but we're not here to arrest you or anything." He clearly didn't like being flanked by, as far as he knew, at least three people.

"Who is 'we'?" Dani called out. Eric almost laughed. *Smartass, all right!*

"We're, well, concerned citizens, you might say. We've had some trash come up out of Houston and had some trouble. As a matter of fact, there was a pretty good little gun battle just down the road about an hour ago. You don't know anything about that, do you?"

Eric had a gut feeling that this guy was okay. Or if he wasn't, then he had guys at all the exits and they had little chance to shoot their way out. *Que sera sera.* He slung his rifle, moved towards the man, and introduced himself.

"Eric Marten. I served four years in the Marine Corps." It didn't hurt to let him know that they were good guys. They shook hands.

"Pete Wilson," the man said. "Thank you for your service."

"Thank you. In answer to your question, yes, those four gangbangers attempted to rape this young lady." He held out his hand, palm up, and Dani played the role he hoped she would, by stepping forward and taking his hand in hers. He drew her to stand close to him. He hoped the gesture clearly indicated a couple of things — one, that he had a woman and wasn't looking to violate any of theirs, and two, that they were just a nice young couple who wouldn't harm a flea. Hopefully it would play well for the locals, whatever the facts were.

"Well, then another 'thank you' for taking care of them!" Pete beamed. "Normally we wouldn't want someone in here… taking things, but I'm sure we can view it as a fair trade."

"We appreciate that, and we'll get back on the road now." He and Dani got their bikes as Pete walked to the outer door and spoke to some people outside. When they emerged from the store, there were a dozen people outside, all armed, but two that Eric classified as shooters. They were a gray-haired gentleman and a stout mid-thirties woman, both with rifles. They also had tactical vests on that bulged with extra magazines. The rest of the people had pistols and were pushing shopping carts. Eric almost smiled at the thought: *two guards for security, protecting a working party. Been there, done that, many times.*

Pete confirmed it with his parting comment. "We have a big shopping list. We're going to get everything we need before refugees pick this place clean. Good luck and God bless."

***

They picked their way between the cars and debris for a few miles to Conroe. "I have to admit I don't know much about this place," he said during a water break. "Without a GPS I don't know where anything is. How about you?"

Dani shook her head. "I haven't been anywhere. Sometimes we'd go to Galveston."

"I'm looking for a place to spend the night. I don't want to travel in the dark. Too much trash in the way. We'd get hurt. So we need someplace secure to hole up. I'm thinking an office building since there's nothing anyone wants in there."

Dani nodded her head and looked at him. "That's pretty smart. Houses may have dead people, or a neighborhood watch like them, back there at the Academy. Stores with useful items are being raided. An office building —" she shrugged "— nothing interesting to steal, and nobody died at work, so they're empty."

They headed off of the Interstate to a multistory building and found that the doors were actually unlocked. They wheeled the bikes into the fire stairs and Dani stayed with the bikes while Eric scouted. He was back in a couple of minutes, having found what he wanted.

"The bad news is we have to get the bikes up to the third floor." He watched Dani to see how she would take it. Was she a spoiled little princess or would she accept the new reality and go with it?

She looked at him for a couple of seconds and, when he hadn't moved, said "Well, go, or get out of the way." Eric smiled, pleased that she was a trooper.

Once on the third floor, he led the way into a conference room. It had windows to the outside, but none into the hallway. He motioned Dani over to the windows. "Sniping," he began. "If you're shooting from a building like this, you want to break the window out first. If you shoot through it, the bullet may deflect and go off-target. But you don't want your window to be the one and only broken window, so you might have to go around and break out some others on different floors and down the hall.

"Also, you don't want to hang out the window, don't want to stick the barrel out. That way, anyone in a 180 degree arc can see you. Instead, you want to step back from the window. It narrows your field of view, but your rifle is hidden, and the noise and flash of the shot will be muffled inside of the building."

Dani nodded. Nothing he said was rocket science, and she could have figured it out if she'd thought about it, but she hadn't.

"Problem is, the higher up you are, the harder it is to shoot down at a target near the building. Long range, no problem. Close range, you can't see them. So what you do is you set up on top of a table or desk." He heaved one of the chairs up onto the conference table. "Hop up there and sit down. Now if you look down, you can see closer to the building than you would if you were sitting in one of these chairs on the floor. And you still have the long range visibility. Also, you would probably put a desk or table in front of you to rest the rifle on.

"That's it. I just thought this was a good opportunity to show you something." He held out a hand to assist her in getting down from the table. She took it and jumped down lightly.

"I want to shoot my Glock 19 Gen 5," she said. "The noise and flash of the shot will be muffled inside of the building." She was smiling as she said it.

Oh, that little — She boxed me in there, he thought. *And I never told her what the pistol was, so she must have read it off of the slide.* That exact designation is rollmarked on the left of the slide. It had taken her a moment with the first word, though. It looked like "LOCK" until she realized that it was inside a big "G." He smiled back at her, partly amused, partly proud of her, partly in grudging admiration of her using his own words against him.

Down the hall was a cube farm, a mass of cubicles. Eric figured that 9mm bullets wouldn't travel through too many cube walls before running out of gas.

"Okay, these cubes look like a good backstop for you. That would be rule number... ?"

She glanced up and off to the side momentarily, before replying "Rule number four, be sure of your target and everything behind it."

He gave her a quick instruction on holding the pistol and lining up the sights and equipped them both with the foam hearing protectors he had acquired earlier.

She picked a memo tacked to a cube wall and slowly fired her full magazine, with advice from Eric between shots. She rapidly grew better as she became accustomed to what was an entirely new experience for her. She'd never fired a pistol or rifle before. On the good side, she had no bad habits to unlearn. At the end of the session, she was smiling from ear to ear. She turned the pistol in her hand and gazed at it for a minute. The line from the movie *Scarface* came into her mind: "Say hello to my little friend." She thought about how if she had had — no, no, she stuffed that memory back down into its box and slammed the lid.

When she had paused, Eric almost stepped in and showed her how to eject the magazine, but then realized she wasn't searching for the release, she was thinking. She drew in a breath, let it out quickly, and then turned. "Can I get a reload?" While he reached for one, she ejected the empty magazine into her left hand and swapped it for the full that he handed to her. She released the slide to chamber a round and slide the pistol back into her back pocket. She was already handling the pistol as if she had done it for years.

He had three magazines full, and gave her two. Better to have two people shooting at a threat than one. He wouldn't use his pistol until his rifle was empty anyway. As he handed the other two magazines to her, he murmured "Good luck slipping these into those tight jeans." She raised her eyebrows and gave him a mild version of The Look, which meant, in the body language of women everywhere: *Warning! You're screwing up.*

Okay, enough flirting with the pretty girl, Eric thought. "Two things we need to do," he said. "One is eat, but first I'd like to secure this location more." They found two fire stairs and tied paracord from the fire door handles to the closest office door handles. That would delay anyone from coming through the doors onto their floor. Step two was to set up the conference room. It didn't have a lock on the door, so they pulled a coffee buffet table in front of it. Lastly, Eric brought out the hatchet from his pack and chopped through the sheetrock to open a door from the conference room into the next-door office. The office had a locking door but also had a window into the hallway. The plan was that they could sleep unobserved in the conference room but had the office as a retreat if needed.

When they finished, Dani surveyed their handiwork, hands on hips, making mental notes, and nodded.

She was still a little hyped from the battle earlier, and really wasn't ready to sleep yet, so she started telling him about her background. "My parents came to the United States from Columbia," she started. "They were fleeing from the drug violence. The narcotics traffickers were in a war with the Colombian government. Also there are Marxist revolutionaries that operate on their own sometimes, and work with the narcos sometimes. There were bombings and shootings all of the time. They bombed airplanes and killed everyone on board just to take out one man. They attacked the Palace of Justice and killed half of the Supreme Court judges. Imagine that here in the U.S.

"My parents were allowed to immigrate here. My father is a — was a doctor. A medical doctor. In Columbia, but not here. To become a doctor in the U.S., he had to take exams, which he passed easily. But then he had to go through a residency program, and he could not find a program that would accept him. It is very difficult for a person who is a doctor in another country to come to the U.S. and get into a residency program. So he sold used cars. That was the best that he could find.

"My brother was born in Columbia. My parents wanted him to go to college but could not afford it. He joined the Marine Corps, like you. There was some program that would allow him to go to college afterwards. He was in California the last I knew." She drew a couple of deep breaths and let them out slowly. She was trying not to cry. "Then my sister was born here, and me, and my little brother." Then the tears did start, thinking of her little brother, who she either loved fiercely or wanted to kill, depending on the moment. She remembered her last view of him, wrapped completely in a blanket, dead, with her parents crying over him, her doctor father powerless to save him. Then she lost it. She jumped up and went out of the conference room through the hole in the wall and walked the halls for a few minutes.

Having regained her composure, she returned. Eric looked at her questioningly and she waved like it was nothing. "Sorry. I'm okay now."

"Dani, you're been through a highly traumatic time. Some very bad events. If you need to cry, then let it out. It's natural. Don't bottle that stuff up inside you. It'll eat your guts out."

"Thank you," she replied, but she was staring at the floor when she said it.

"I guess I have an advantage over most people," he stated. "Everyone I loved is dead already, was dead before Hexen hit. My Mother passed when I was twelve. My Father died about two and a half years ago. Died at work. At his desk, if you can think of a worse place to die. And my wife died a little bit more than two years ago."

"I'm sorry," Dani murmured, rolling her chair closer and putting her hand on his forearm. She mentally kicked herself for commenting that "nobody died at work" earlier. *Nice way to remind him of his loss!*

"I joined the Marine Corps when I was 17. Finished high school early and I wanted to have some adventures. I didn't want to go to college then. I'd been sitting in classrooms for years. I was ready to *do* something. And I thought I was a badass, so the Marine Corps was the only choice for me. I deployed to Afghanistan and that was mainly boring. I was artillery and not on the front lines. I mean, we got shot at some, had to avoid IEDs, but I wasn't going hand-to-hand combat with the enemy."

"Anyway, I'd been in three years and married a girl I had dated in high school. Finished out my last year of enlistment and then went into a training program to learn computer networking. Got a job, you know, normal stuff. Then my Father died and the next month my wife was diagnosed with cancer. She didn't last but a few months." His voice had gotten husky and he coughed and looked away for a minute.

"I drank. Drank way too much and considered suicide. I think the property is what saved me. My Dad had bought some land when I was five or six. Forty-eight acres. Not big. Mainly trees with a big meadow in the middle and a little pond. That was our spot. We used to go there and make memories. We'd camp out in a tent and fish and target shoot. When I got older we'd hunt deer and feral hogs and rabbits. So that's where I went to heal.

"I had some money from my inheritance. My Father had done all right and made some good investments, plus his house was paid off. I wasn't rich, like independently wealthy, but I had more than enough money to build a little house on the property and enlarge the pond. I've been there about a year. And then all of this hits."

He sighed and then started to tell Dani about his journey.

Chapter 6

"I hadn't paid too much attention to the reports coming out of China from the BBC. I thought it was just another bird flu or another wildly overhyped Coronavirus. We had a little get-together planned, me and a Marine buddy and his wife. I got to their place just when the panic started."

Eric paused for a long moment. "They didn't make it."

"I'm sorry. You don't have to talk about it," Dani apologized.

Eric blew out a breath slowly. "Anyway, this is all his stuff, his rifle, his uniform I'm wearing. And I figured I also needed a bike. I found one around the neighborhood but it was a road bike. You know, one of those lightweight things with skinny tires. I wanted a mountain bike, something rugged, because I figured the road conditions would suck and I wanted something that could go cross-country.

"So I rode the one I found five or six miles to a Wal-Mart." He hesitated again, wondering if he should tell her the whole story, before he forged ahead.

***

Maneuvering through the stopped cars was not too bad. Most had just died in their lane, and there were sidewalks in places, and parking lots to route around the worst of the jams. The biggest problem was that Eric hadn't been on a bike in many years, and his muscles protested at this unusual workout. And the parts of him that came into contact with the seat became very tender.

His main concern was the people, however. There were a couple hundred that he saw in the journey. They ran the gamut, both in their looks and in their demeanor. Based on first impressions, there was a cross section of society, from rich to poor, all colors and nationalities. A few were guarding their stores with shotguns and rifles. Some were camping out with tents and small grills. Most were traveling, carrying packs and walking to some destination, although there was no clear consensus on what direction to go. More than half of them had some form of mask on that covered their nose and mouth. These ran the gamut from surgical masks to industrial painter's respirators to bandannas.

Eric found the Wal-Mart, and saw that someone had already smashed the doors open. He figured that would be the case, but he had brought a pry bar and hammer anyway. *And there was nobody guarding it*, he thought with wry amusement. *Yeah, no store manager is going to break out his shotgun to stand in the heat and guard Wal-Mart.*

He dismounted the bike, unslung his rifle, and started for the door. Some people loitering in the shade decided to vacate the area when he did that.

Inside, the store didn't really look as trashed as he thought it would be. With all electronics dead, there was no incentive to steal a big flat screen. He headed straight for the bikes and was relieved to find that there were several still on the racks. He had thought that he might have to assemble one in the back warehouse or something. After selecting a nice one with shock absorbers, he adjusted the seat and got things at least close to where he wanted them.

Air in the tires, brakes are adjusted correctly, thank you, anonymous Wal-Mart guy, for doing a good job, he thought.

A nearby display also held an adjustable cargo rack that would go over the rear tire and, hopefully, accommodate his pack. There were some other small packs that attached to the frame, and water bottles, and kits of tools and patches and air pumps, and even cans of compressed air to refill a patched tire. Eric grabbed all of it, one or a few of everything, and strapped it onto the bike.

He rode the bike a couple of rows down to the Hardware section to grab some tools to attach the cargo rack. That little job completed, he headed for the exit and made a mistake. He was taking things for granted and not being cautious enough. He should have peered around the corner first.

When he saw the three guys, he stopped out of caution. The thought that crossed his mind was that they would give him a "S'up" accompanied by a head bob, and keep going. He was armed, but his weapons were holstered or slung in carry positions and not threatening in any way.

They didn't react like that.

The three were young, late teens/early twenties, full of vim and vigor and multiplayer First Person Shooter fantasies. They were all armed with their dream weapons, and they all started swinging them towards Eric.

The guy on Eric's left had an AR pistol, which is an iffy weapon. If it has a brace, which is really an abbreviated shoulder stock, and an effective linear compensator, which will direct the muzzle blast forward and away from the shooter, then it makes a fair approximation of a short-barreled rifle. If not, it's a lousy pistol. It's three times as heavy as a normal pistol and big and clumsy. The mechanism is the same as an AR rifle but it has an extremely short barrel and a buffer tube that sticks out in the back. More importantly in this gunfight, the muzzle flash and blast from the short barrel are incredible. Even with hearing protection, an AR pistol can be painfully loud to shoot — and none of these three had hearing protection.

The AR pistol guy was right handed, so his muzzle naturally pointed to the left, putting his buddies in the path of the worst of the muzzle blast. And he was an idiot, since he had the safety off and his finger on the trigger. As soon as he saw Eric, he panicked and pulled the trigger. The thunderous blast from the seven inch barrel, attenuated by nothing more than a little A2-style flash hider, hurt everyone more than the bullet. The bullet went off somewhere and buried itself harmlessly in a wall. The blast slammed into everyone like a flash-bang grenade. The three punks all flinched, closed their eyes, and covered their ears. Eric, standing the furthest away, recovered first.

He let go of the bike and swung his rifle up into his shoulder. Adrenaline was pumping through his bloodstream now, and his vision narrowed to a spot. It was like he was looking through a tube, all peripheral vision gone, but intense focus on the threat. His sights were aligned without him realizing he had done it. His trigger finger went forward and snapped the safety off, then back to engage the trigger. Nice squeeze, a little push from recoil, then put round number two on target One. Target Two, the one in the middle, had an immense Desert Eagle pistol that he was swinging in Eric's direction. Sights were aligned, fire, bring it back down from recoil — and he didn't see anything. Target Two had disappeared. He tipped the rifle down further, and saw Target Two down, on the floor. Target Three became a flash as he ducked down a side aisle.

Immediately, he spun around and stuck an AK rifle out and started hammering out rounds. They were totally unaimed, he just had his arms stretched out as far as they would go and still allow him to pull the trigger. Eric moved to the right to get out of any possible random spray of bullets, estimated how long the guy's arms were, and started shooting through the display racks. He put two rounds where he thought the guy's body should be, moved six inches left and fired, again moved six inches left and fired, then went back to the right, a foot past his first shots and put one more in. Just before the last shot he heard a crash and clatter, and then screaming.

There was a loud, full-lung scream, then a couple of loud gasps, then another scream, not as loud as the first, flowed by a bout of wet coughs, and subsiding into a series of low "Oh, God, oh God" moans.

Eric scanned back to the first two, but there was no threat remaining there. He started to move up to finish the wounded guy, but stopped himself. He wasn't there to "close with and destroy the enemy by fire and maneuver," as Marines are fond of saying, so he saw no need to waste ammo making sure they were dead now. They were certainly all dead, even the guy screaming, he just hadn't finished bleeding out yet. Even if a doctor came running in the door right now, the guy was going to die.

Eric stepped back to get some concealment behind the corner, forcing himself to breathe and to scan 360 degrees for other threats. He grabbed the bike and moved back and away from the scene of the gunfight. There were two exits, so he headed for the far one, zig zagging through the aisles. He figured that anyone in the building would do one of three things. One would be to run, to get away from the gunfire. Two would be to hide, and three would be to go to the aid of the screaming guy. His mind was racing, but one of the things that came up was *reload*. He was in the clothing section and the displays were close together, giving him a little nest to hide in momentarily while he swapped magazines for a full one and put the partial one away.

As he did that his mind kept throwing things at him and he kept batting them down: *Cameras — they're fried, they don't work. Cops — doubtful, nobody can call them. Trial — self-defense, Jesus, look at the artillery they had, and they fired first. Witnesses — don't see any, but they're probably transients and I certainly am. Are there more of them? — no telling but doubtful, didn't seem disciplined enough to plan something that complicated. Fingerprints — yes, his fingerprints and DNA may be on the shell casings, and the military certainly had his prints and DNA, but how are they going to match it with no computers? Of course, everything above doesn't count for shit if I don't get out the door and down the street.*

The other exit was smashed open, too. Apparently someone had weighed the effort to walk down there versus the effort to smash this plate glass, and opted for the smash. Eric paused in the foyer, looking out for any threat. No SWAT teams, no blue lights, no cops crouched behind their cars, yelling through a bullhorn for him to come out with his hands up. No "Call of Duty" assholes with impractical firearms waiting for him, either, that he could see. Nobody seemed alarmed. *Maybe the gunshots were muffled by the building. No one outside heard anything?*

Eric stepped out the door and scanned all around, rifle pointed down but ready for action. No one seemed to notice him, so he slung the rifle, carried the bike out over the glass shards, and cruised through the parking lot. He wanted to make speed but he didn't want to race along into something bad, like an ambush. Plus, he had to get the bike in the right gear and he didn't want to pay attention to that right now. He was spinning his pedals a lot for not that much forward motion. Still, no one ran out the door, screaming bloody murder and pointing at him.

Yet, anyway.

Chapter 7

He got his bearings and headed towards the house. By the time he got there, he was sore, he had figured out the gears, and he was hungry. He didn't think that much about killing three guys.

Not that he was accustomed to that sort of thing. Not up close and personal, anyway. His job in the Marine Corps had been as an artilleryman. He and Bruce had been in a crew that served an artillery gun. Their unit had rained high explosive shells down on the opposing forces and killed them, but it seemed so far removed from them. They fired rounds when and where ordered, just like in training. The man directing the artillery fire told them they hit the enemy. Sometimes it even got a little more detailed, with a team going to the impact zone and counting body parts to estimate how many had been killed, and that might filter back to them. "Good job. That fire mission killed 12 enemy combatants." But it didn't feel real at all. Eric wasn't even the one actually firing the gun, and multiple guns fired each strike, so no one could say the fatal rounds came from this or that gun. It wasn't even like a video game. They never saw the enemy, never saw the impact of their shells. All of the feedback was word of mouth.

This was different. This was actually placing your sights on a man and pressing the trigger, seeing them go down in a limp sprawl, or hearing them scream in agony. But the purpose of the Marine Corps, any military for that matter, is to kill the enemy and destroy their stuff, so it wasn't a foreign concept to him. Besides, they had started it. And Eric was pretty numb by that point. It had been a rough few days. There were much more important things to worry about. The scene replayed in his mind some, but there wasn't a crushing emotional weight that affected him about it. Mainly, he wondered if there was any remote chance of prosecution. What if all of the power magically came back on tomorrow?

***

"Anyway," he continued in his story, "I met some of the people in the neighborhood. People just started to come out of their houses, like when a storm has passed and the sun is breaking through the clouds. Some wore masks at first, but I think most people had the same attitude as me, that they were at the point they didn't care if they were going to live or die.

"There were some guys that wanted to come with me, and I figured I'd have a better chance with some extra firepower versus being alone. That didn't actually work out too well."

***

There were three guys that joined Eric, all with bikes, but one had a leaky tire. A few miles up State Highway 99, the Grand Parkway, they figured they had to do something about it. There was a Wal-Mart coming up, so they took the exit. Eric volunteered to stay with their bikes while the other three went inside.

Not two minutes went by before Eric heard something, multiple somethings, maybe gunshots. Then the sound came louder. *Pistol shots, then rifle*, he figured, and started running for the doors. They were a hundred yards away and he had gone maybe a third of the way when a guy burst through the doors, or where the doors had once been. And this guy had a pistol in his hand.

Eric skidded to a halt, brought his rifle up, and yelled "Freeze!" The guy never broke stride, just swung his pistol up and capped off a few rounds in Eric's general direction. Eric fired once quickly and missed as he dropped to one knee to present a smaller target. He took in a breath, let half out as he tracked the target, and squeezed off another shot. The guy went down with a little grunt, face first, and bounced a little, the pistol skittering away from his lifeless hand.

Looking at him over his sights for a moment, Eric had the thought that he might have just fucked up. *What if this guy was running away from a gunfight? Not involved in it in any way? So he runs out and here I am, pointing a rifle at him. What would my response be in his place? Surrender to some random stranger? Fight back? This guy may have been totally innocent.* Then: *I have to put that on hold right now and make sure my guys are all right.*

He walked up to the still figure, keeping his eyes and rifle on him but not ignoring the doors. Blood was flowing out, likely gravity-induced since there was no spurting or flow under pressure. He kicked the pistol away further so he wouldn't have to bend down and be off-balance near the body, then walked to it and picked it up. Then he headed for the doors, tossing the pistol into the line of shopping carts by the entrance, making it difficult for anyone to get to it.

He slowed going into the store, moving rapidly but hyper alert, head and rifle swinging all about, safety off and finger outside the trigger guard. He headed for the bikes and sporting goods, which were side-by-side. He almost shot one big woman who was trying to hide behind a display that was far too small for the task. He had the sights on her and his finger on the trigger before he classified her as a non-threat. In a different situation, he would have laughed at her comically-wide eyes and dropped jaw, but not today.

As he got closer he heard someone calling for help. He slowed and used his hearing to vector in on the aisle the pleas were coming from. It was in Sporting Goods, and he skirted around to come at it from the least-direct angle. If anyone was waiting in ambush for him, he would come up behind them. Unless they were smart enough to have a rearguard, that is.

He peered around the corner and saw a body down in a pool of blood a few aisles down. It was no one he recognized. The body was at the end of the aisle where the person was asking for help. He eased around the corner for a glance and saw Nelson curled in a fetal position and bleeding, with Mike cradling him, calling for help in a voice choked with tears. Further down the aisle, Bill lay sprawled and limp.

He spun around and scanned for danger, since looking at Mike wouldn't alert him to any attack. "Mike, are there any more bad guys around?" he called out. He was amped up and it came out all in one long string, like it was all one big word: Mike-are-there-any-more-bad-guys-around?

Mike coughed and cleared his throat, then got out "I shot at one and the other one took off."

"The runner — black shirt, blue baseball cap on backwards? Had a pistol?"

"Yep! Did you get him?"

"He's down. How about Bill? Is he dead?"

"I... don't think there's anything we can do for him."

Eric dug into his first aid kit and pulled out a couple of QuikClot packets. He tossed them to Mike. "Tear those open. Put them on the — wait, is there an exit wound? Turn him over and look."

There were some deep groans from Nelson and a soft voice from Mike, then "No, no exit wound."

"Okay, tear open those packets and put them on the wound and apply pressure. I'll be back."

He walked over to the opposite side of the store and grabbed several packets of gauze and a bottle of the strongest Motrin he saw. On the way back, he stepped out the door to make sure the bikes and packs were still there. *Maybe the presence of a recently-shot corpse is a deterrent, he thought.*

He ran through his medical training: *Start the breathing, stop the bleeding, treat for shock — need a blanket or sleeping bag — and protect the wound. Probably won't get that far.* Sporting Goods had sleeping bags and Mylar space blankets, so he took one of each.

Back in Sporting Goods, he checked Bill and wished he hadn't. He'd taken a close-range shot to the face. Looking up, he saw tears running down Mike's face, falling on Nelson's shirt. He knelt, facing Mike, and squeezed his shoulder. "Take a deep breath. Now take another. I need you to be strong. Get outside and get those bikes in here. You did good, all right?"

Mike nodded and went to carry out his assignment. Eric pulled the QuikClot away from the wound and quickly put it back. Nelson's teeth were clenched and his eyes closed but he was conscious. "How bad is it?" he asked.

"It's not good." Eric thought again about his medical training. One of the things they were supposed to do is to give the patient hope; act like any wound is survivable no matter how severe. Of course, that was with the benefit of Corpsmen, medevac helicopters, and state of the art surgical wards within easy flight time. The quantity of those three things they had available was zero, zero, and zero.

"It doesn't matter. Everyone else is dead, anyway." Nelson started to cry. Eric felt helpless. He could assist, but nothing he could do would save this young man's life. Absolutely nothing. He'd never felt so helpless since his wife's cancer. He covered him with a Mylar blanket and kept pressure on the wound, and it seemed that the bleeding was slowing. Unfortunately, he had lost a lot already. Eric was kneeling in a pool of it, and there was nothing he could do about the internal bleeding.

"Here, take these," he said, handing Nelson four Motrin and a bottle of water, then applying pressure again. He didn't know what the right dosage was, probably no more than two, but there was really no downside to an overdose.

Mike got the bikes inside and positioned around their aisle. Eric swapped places with him again, asking "What happened?"

"They just opened fire. I was getting the tire stuff and Dave and Nelson here went to sporting goods. I didn't hear anyone say anything. It was just boom, boom, boom. I looked around the aisle and saw that one guy shooting, and I shot at him. The other guy ran and I shot at him. Oh, God, oh my God, what are we going to do?"

"Doesn't sound to me like there's anything else you could have done."

"Lord, I wish there had been."

Eric made a few trips back and forth, gathering some cushions to get Nelson off the floor and some water and chips from the grocery, and a blanket to cover Dave. Since he was in the area, he also shopped for some new clothes for himself — socks, underwear, and T-shirts to refresh his stock, since he'd brought two changes of clothes and was on his fourth day.

He got the clothes partly because he needed them, but more for the need to function normally. Everyone was dying all around him and he could either go to pieces or he could function. As long as he could, he was going to function. When he got the chance, he was going to have more than a few beers, but in this world, he'd have to have some sober and heavily armed Marines standing watch when he did it.

Back in Sporting Goods, Nelson was asleep or knocked out and he seemed to have stopped bleeding, externally, anyway, and Mike was sitting on the floor at his side. Eric took soap and a brush to his pants where Nelson's blood had soaked them and hung them up to dry while he planned their next moves.

Coldly, realistically, Nelson was going to die, probably within the next few hours. He wasn't going to abandon him. He'd keep him dosed with Motrin and unconscious until the end. This was not a movie, so there were not going to be any gallant last words from the brave young soldier. No "tell my Mother I love her." She was dead. And his Father. And his girlfriend. There is nothing romantic about a young man slowly bleeding to death on a battlefield.

Anyway, they'd be here for the night, so he'd better make arrangements. Mike was a wreck, but at least he wasn't in the fetal position sucking his thumb or rolling around on the floor, screaming. He could carry out orders. He took another walk around and found what he wanted. A little work with a pallet jack and it was acceptable. He came back rolling the pallet jack with an empty pallet.

"Mike, I need you, Nelson and I need you, to focus. We're going to spend the night here, so we need to fort up. I have created a space in the warehouse. We're going to get Nelson in there, then we're going to stock up on food and whatever, and then we're going to stand guard, okay?" He spoke a little slowly and deliberately because he got the feeling that Mike was slipping away on him.

They loaded Nelson on the pallet and eased him into the fort that Eric had created. He had gone back to a corner and shuffled pallets of goods around to form a hollow square that backed up to the cinder block wall on two sides. Once Nelson was as comfortable as they could make him, with cushions and pillow and blanket, they laid in groceries and rolled in the bikes and then plugged the gap with another pallet full of boxes.

Eric made a quick pass through the bike section and hardware, to get chain lube and tire inflators and a few tools. He dropped some pallets of boxes in front of the nearest doors. It wasn't a complete block, but it would slow down an intruder and make them make some noise getting in. The military has what they call PM, Preventative Maintenance, which means frequent checks on vehicles and equipment to lube and adjust and clean them, and he performed PM on the bikes. He also took the opportunity to remove all of the reflectors from the bikes. There were ten altogether on his bike alone. No need to worry about cars seeing you at night any more, but it might be very good to be stealthy on this trip.

***

He ate chips. Did pushups. Napped.

The day passed slowly. Mike kept close watch on Nelson but there was nothing he could really do, short of loading him up with Motrin when he stirred.

The sun went down and they ate and set a watch schedule.

Eric had found a kitchen timer that was mechanical, so it still worked, up to one hour. He set two-hour watches and took the first one. It was boring, as most watches are. Nelson stayed asleep and alive, and nothing stirred that he heard back in their little fort. He was sleeping after two watches, so it was at least six hours past sunset, when there was the blast of a gunshot. He rolled over to bail out of his bunk and crashed into a pallet. He rolled back the other way and came up with his rifle ready to go. He scanned the area, fast to pick up an obvious enemy, then slower for a more detailed view.

Nothing.

Suddenly he realized that Mike was gone.

He held his breath and listened hard.

Still nothing.

"MIKE!" he shouted.

Still nothing.

He knew what happened.

He bent down to check Nelson and felt no pulse, wrists and neck, no pulse.

If he was right, he didn't need to be quiet anymore, so he pumped up the pallet jack and rolled it out to open the fort. *Mike just climbed over the top of the boxes so as to not awaken me.*

Mike was not far away, but as distant as he could get from a living man. *He felt responsible, Eric* thought. *The only reason we came in here was because of his flat tire. Then Bill was murdered, Nelson was wounded, and he killed a man. He never said "I shot him," he always said "I shot at him." And now Nelson has died. Mike thought every bit of that was his fault. Add that to the grief of losing whatever loved ones died from Hexen...*

He was glad it was dark and he didn't have to look at Mike. A .45 round to the temple does not do nice things to a human skull. He was in a sitting position, leaning up against a wall. Eric gripped his feet and dragged him away from the wall enough that he was flat on his back, and covered him with a blanket. Back in the fort, he covered Nelson's face and waited for dawn. He thought *I am NEVER going to go in a fucking Wal-Mart again!*

Chapter 8

Eric had soup and coffee heated on a butane stove long before sunrise. He needed the caffeine to get going this morning. He had gotten a nap the previous afternoon, but not much sleep last night. He didn't want to count the hours because that just made it more painful. He had heated two cans of beef and potato soup and eaten it with a fork so he could pick out the beef and potatoes and not fill up on the actual soup. After that he just waited until it got light enough to see.

He pounded the pavement hard today. He started off heavy, with a pack filled with bottles of water and energy bars. He stopped every hour by his kitchen timer and drank two bottles of water and ate two bars and kept going.

The traffic jam was the same. All of the roads were packed with dead cars. The EMP or whatever it was had killed all of the electronics in the cars and shut them down cold. But there were no wrecks, since all of the cars had been stopped anyway. There were simply too many cars on the road, and the occasional breakdown, flat tire, car fire, or drivers dying from Hexen while at the wheel, had brought the traffic to a complete standstill.

At that point, the people got out, decided what they could carry, and walked off. Maybe they camped out that night, slept in their cars, but eventually they figured the machines were dead and they moved on.

He kept going.

The stench was the same. People died. Some moved into nearly subdivisions, too burdened with children or age or other impediments to travel any distance on foot. A lot of them walked until the pain in their heads grew unbearable, and then they found a place to lie down and die.

That was what the survivors would always remember — the cars and the bodies. And the flies. They were everywhere.

The cars, at least, were more limited to the roads, especially the elevated sections, and wherever there were concrete barriers keeping them on the road. Where the roads were at surface level, the cars had spread out. Trucks and SUVs and the bolder drivers of regular cars had taken to the grass, the dirt, whatever was on the side of the highways, sped forward as far as they could, and then tried to jam their way back into the traffic when they came to a bridge or other obstruction. Some of those drivers had died in hails of gunfire from those they were trying to circumvent.

The bodies were worse, since they were the remains of what had once been living, breathing humans. And they were everywhere. *Everywhere.* The one redeeming factor was that the pain brought on by Hexen grew in intensity, so that the victim had time to seek a place to die. Very few just dropped dead suddenly as they were walking. They moved off, out of the path of foot traffic. And they littered the landscape. Tents had sprouted by the sides of the Parkway like mushrooms, inhabited by the dead. Many more lay under tarps or blankets or shirts, covered by themselves or by companions or by the compassionate, until the coverings or the compassion ran out in the face of the millions of dead. The most difficult part of this was the little tents and blankets, the ones with the unicorns or cartoon characters. Eric didn't spend time looking at them, not wanting to see a tiny pair of legs sticking out from under one.

He pushed himself onwards.

The swarms of flies were the same. In the daylight, the bodies were covered with flies, a feast for the maggots and the turkey buzzards. At night, the buzzards roosted and the maggots were joined by the coyotes, feral hogs, rats, and other scavengers that would creep out to eat their fill. Ownerless domestic dogs and cats would soon join that list, if they hadn't already.

The stench was truly ungodly. If anything ever deserved that term, it was this. A human's sphincter muscles let go when they die, voiding their bowels. That smell of excrement, however, was the rosiest smell in the world compared to the tons — literally, *tons* — of rotting flesh. Most people have smelled chicken scraps that have been too long in the trash, but that amounts to probably an ounce. Others have smelled dumpsters behind restaurants, which may be — what? — 10 pounds of rotting meat? One hundred? Multiply that smell by tens of thousands and that is the putrid miasma that drifted around the Grand Parkway. It felt — not just smelled, but *felt*, like a cloud of oil, like a heavy, wet fog that was moist with putrefaction. Clouds of flies drifted with it.

He kept going.

Still on the Grand Parkway, he made it to State Highway 249 and that was all he had for the day. He saw a couple of new car dealerships and headed for one. Rather than try to smash the plate glass doors in front, he rode around the back to see what employee doors were available. One was standing open at the side of the shop and a guy was backing out, pulling something heavy. *Probably a mechanic getting his tools. Or stealing some.* Eric turned the handlebars in a tight circle and went to the other dealership. He *really* didn't want any conflict tonight. He breached a door with his hammer and pry bar, then found a chain to loop through the handle and bolted it through the leg of a workbench.

He breached the parts department door, which actually took more effort than the exterior door, and explored the area. It was bigger than he needed but pretty secure. He raided a snack machine and filled water bottles from the dispenser in the break room and holed up in the parts department. He jammed his pry bar in the bottom of the door as a doorstop and pulled a display rack in front of it.

Should have gotten some cushions somewhere, he thought, but he wasn't moving much anywhere else tonight. He shed his equipment, almost fell asleep eating beef jerky, and turned in for the night. He slept late the next morning, since the parts department didn't have any windows that would let in sunlight to wake him up.

Then after lunch he had spotted some guys fighting with someone inside an SUV and made a couple of decisions that would affect everything about the remainder of his life.

Chapter 9

How many people would have done that? Dani thought. *He risked his life to save mine. And he didn't know me, didn't even see me until it was all over and I got out. It could have been anybody, and that didn't even matter to him. Would I have done that? True, he did shoot first but there were three of them. Four, actually. He could have been killed.* She thought about thanking him again but didn't want to get too effusive about it and encourage him to want repayment with her body. Sex was definitely a possibility but she wanted it to be more on her terms, and definitely not as a payment. And if nothing else, not when both of them needed a bath.

Partly to derail any thoughts along that line and partly because she wanted to know, she started asking questions. "What happens next? At your place? Is there food?"

"There are ranches and farms all over the area. I figure the same percentage of people died up there as died in the cities, so that means that a lot of those places are going to be abandoned. That means there are whole herds of cattle that are going to eventually starve to death or fall prey to coyotes. The people in the cities need to eat, so I think the simple solution is to get some ranchers and farmers to teach people from the cities how to grow food."

"So if you take over abandoned farms and ranches, do you think you'll be allowed to keep them? After things get back to normal?" Dani had an idea forming, depending on his answer.

"Sure, I don't see why not. You're going to have to have people producing food. If you have a farmer that dies, then you need someone to step in and keep the farm going. Now you have someone that used to be a mailman, or a sales clerk, or an IT guy, or whatever, now he's a farmer. You don't need any of those other professions. You need him as a farmer, so of course there will be a method to become the owner of that property by virtue of having worked that farm. Like squatter's rights. If you live there and work and maintain the place, then you should be granted ownership."

"How long do you think it's going to take to get things back to normal?"

"At some point we'll have electricity and Internet and cell phones and all that again. But that point may be years, many years off. Like twenty, thirty, forty years."

Dani's mouth dropped open and her eyes were wide.

Eric held up a hand. "That's for the whole works. Now if you're just talking about electricity, I'm hoping that solar panels can be repaired easily. I have solar now, so I may be able to get power back on at my place fairly quickly. Hopefully. On a small scale, we can generate electricity with wind and water, too. The big scale is where the problems come in.

"Power plants require huge transformers. Immense. They weigh hundreds of tons apiece. If the ones we have in place now can't be repaired, then we have a big problem. Most of them are manufactured overseas, and if the whole world was affected by the EMP, then those other countries are going to first have to get back on their feet. Only then can they start making new transformers for us. With full resources it takes a year and a half or two years to make a transformer. Then you have to ship it here, so you have to have ships that work, and dock facilities like cranes, and trains to get it into position. Even if we build them here, that only cuts out the ships and docks. You still have to have the functioning facilities and workforce to build them. It's kind of a Catch-22. You have to have electricity to make components to make electricity. But we obviously did it once, so we can do it again."

"But that means that we'll be *old* before it's like it was!" Dani was aghast.

"It's not something that's going to be fixed next year. I mean, I hope I'm wrong. I really hope this is just some localized anomaly. Highly unlikely, but…"

He trailed off, which was fine, because he'd kind of blown Dani's mind. She sat there, thoughts swirling around like crazy. She was actually glad when he changed the subject and mentioned food. She was famished.

"Look, let's eat and get some sleep. This close to the city and with the Interstate right out there, I think we need to run watches. You know, have one of us awake at all times."

He fired off the little one-burner camp stove and started to boil some noodles. Maybe that was their mistake, showing a light that someone spotted. Or maybe someone had watched them go into the building and wanted the cute young girl. Or they had inadvertently invaded someone's territory. Or maybe people were just going bat-shit crazy. Maybe a mild version of the flu killed off enough brain cells to bend something in the brain that should be kept straight.

***

Eric just sat in a chair, feet on the table, and tilted back as far as he could. Service in the Marine Corps had trained him to sleep anywhere, in any position. That service had also trained him to lay his rifle and extra magazines within easy reach.

Dani figured out she could flip two chairs over, top to top, and lay on the cushioned backs which were now horizontal. Taking her cue from Eric, she also laid her pistol and magazines nearby. She hadn't known if he was going to expect sex in return for saving her earlier, but he didn't even hint at it. He gained a few Brownie points in her estimation.

They were going two hours on watch, two off, kept on track by the kitchen timer. They wouldn't get a full night of sleep but they could turn in early tomorrow, once they were away from the city. Dani used her time to walk the halls and practice with her pistol and an empty magazine, dropping the mag, inserting the mag, over and over. She wasn't really awake enough to think about anything, just worked on getting the muscle memory down. And she couldn't see what she was doing so it was good practice. There's nothing wrong with looking down briefly during a mag change but even better if you can confidently do it without looking. That way you can keep your eyes on the target or scanning for targets or moving to cover.

Hours later, while on watch again, she had to go to the bathroom. She wended her way through the office and down the hall. Of course, with no lights or windows, the bathroom was dark as pitch. She put a hand on the wall and carefully made her way around the room to the stalls, flicking a lighter here and there. As soon as she sat down, she heard voices, multiple ones, right on the other side of the wall, it seemed. Shit! Shit! SHIT! SHIT! She no longer had to pee. She got out of the bathroom in record time. It was the shortest bathroom visit in history by a woman, ever. She peered out the bathroom door, which was near the stairs. Whoever they were, they were *right there* on the other side of the door, and they were trying to open it!

Chapter 10

The intruders could pull the door only a little bit due to the paracord, but then they started forcing a crowbar or something into the gap. That would open the door a little more, and then all they needed was to cut the cord and they were in.

Dani bounded out of the bathroom and sprinted down the hall as fast as she could go. She didn't run like a girl, either. There was nothing ladylike in her sprint, just a severe need to get to her goal.

Eric had slept for what seemed like seconds when Dani started shaking him as hard as she could. "What? What? What?" he croaked in a dry voice, grabbing for his rifle.

"I went to the bathroom. There's somebody trying to come through that fire door!" she blurted out, and pointed down the hall. As Eric started out of the chair, they heard the door crash back into the closed position. Someone was in the hall now.

"Get down behind that table leg. Take my Glock, too," Eric said, sliding the weapon across the table. She put her hand on it to stop the slide and stood there, wide-eyed and trembling. He hefted his rifle and an extra magazine and went through the hole in the wall into the office. A pang went through her heart and she wanted to ask him to not leave her here alone, but she knew he was likely doing the right thing, so she remained quiet.

***

Eric wanted to set up the classic L-shaped ambush. If someone tried to get into the conference room and he was in it, all of them could shoot at him, but if he could shoot down the hall, then only the two in front could shoot. All of the others would be blocked from shooting by their own men in front of them. The military called it enfilade fire. And if Dani would shoot at them, then they'd have bullets coming in from two directions.

He unlocked the office door, eased it open, and peered out from floor level. People expect an opponent to be standing or sitting. Get above or below that zone and they are slower to notice you. Eric was lying on the floor, pretending to be carpet.

They were checking every office but coming down the hall fast. He didn't know how many, six or eight, maybe more. The offices were generally unlocked so they were opening doors, checking inside with a glance behind the desk, then moving on. A locked office didn't delay them long; the lock was more a courtesy thing to keep co-workers out, not a determined individual who didn't care about subtlety.

He could open up on them from long range, relatively speaking, but then they would disperse throughout the floor and he'd have a room-to-room fight on his hands. He'd be almost sure to lose it. No, he wanted them bunched up at the conference room door. He didn't have long to wait.

They tried the door and found it was unlocked but blocked. That told them someone was inside. A couple started in on the door, pushing and prying with the crowbar, and another one drew a *katana,* a Japanese sword, of all things, and started hacking away at the sheetrock beside the door.

***

Dani crouched behind the table leg, waiting. She had both Glocks, plus one full magazine, and no time to load the empty she had been practicing with. She breathed a quick and silent prayer and crossed herself. *Be calm, chica* she told herself. *You know what they want to do to you. You know what you want to do to them.* A chill ran down her back that didn't signify fear, but an icy, cold fury.

***

Seriously, a katana*? Some idiot watched* Kill Bill *too many times*, Eric thought. He realized he hadn't told Dani to shoot, but she was smart, she'd open up when he did. He hoped. He eased out a little more into the hallway and slid his rifle along the carpet and up into his shoulder.

One of them saw the motion and opened fire with an AK, rapid shots booming one right after the other, lighting the scene with a strobe light of muzzle flashes. The bullets made loud, sharp sonic booms as they tore down the hall near Eric's head.

Eric responded in kind, pulling the trigger as fast as he could, sending shots straight into the muzzle flashes, which shut down the AK, but at the same time something slashed across his eyes and he had to close them. Even trying to force them open with all his willpower only opened them partway, and they were watering so badly he couldn't see at all. He wondered if he was on fire somehow. Usually, with a charge of adrenaline, a person feels no pain, even if severely wounded.

This was different. He wondered if he was blind. His first thought was to pull back, to shout for a Corpsman and let his fellow Marines continue to engage the enemy, but that was rapidly overruled by the grim thought: *No Corpsman. No Marines. Only me.*

***

Dani heard the booming of Eric's rifle to her left, plus another loud one and a couple of lesser ones in front of her. She figured they were bunched up behind and beside the door, so she opened up, rapid shots, swinging right and firing more, sweeping the area. She quickly emptied her pistol, fifteen rounds, opened her hand and let it fall to the table, then grabbed up Eric's pistol. As she did so, someone figured out where her shots were coming from, and bullets started coming through the wall at her, some gouging tracks in the thick tabletop and sending up sprays of splinters. She ducked under the table and figured out that she still had a good shot from under it, so she started blazing away through the wall again.

***

Eric could hear a cacophony of multiple weapons firing, including what he hoped was Dani's Glock. He continued to fire, using muscle memory for elevation and the office wall as a delimiter. *Shoot to the left of the wall and you won't shoot into the conference room* he thought. He blasted away, shooting into the center, drift right and fire, drift left and fire, lower elevation and fire, running through his whole 20 round magazine in seconds, before he scooted back to reload.

As he fumbled blindly for the extra magazine, found it, got it inserted, and sent the bolt home, the firing stopped. It had gone from multiple weapons firing madly to half that, to almost zero, a couple of last shots, and then suddenly nothing. No firing, anyway. There were moans from the hallway and someone starting saying "Mom, Mom" over and over in an almost normal tone of voice.

With the barrel pointed at the door as best he could tell, he took a second to touch his forehead. It wasn't on fire but felt gritty, and he had washed his face before going to sleep. He assumed that was glass from the office window to the hallway, and was afraid to touch his eyes, wary of grinding the glass into his eyeballs and scratching them.

"Dani, are you okay?" he called out. "Can you bring me a bottle of water?"

"I'm okay," she replied, but it sounded funny, even to her, almost like she was underwater. The words came out with a pause between each syllable, and she realized she was taking shallow breaths like she was panting. She reloaded and grabbed a bottle of water, then she was through the hole in the wall, pressing the bottle into his hand and moving on. She peered out the office door, a quick peek out and then snapped back, like she had seen Eric do when she was in the SUV.

In addition to dark, the hall was misty with drywall dust and strewn with bodies and somewhere, someone was moving. She popped out again and fired a shot into the nearest body. Eric jumped when she did it and demanded "What's going on?"

"I'm busy," she replied tersely. She then proceeded to very deliberately shoot all of the bodies in the hallway to make sure they were dead. The moans stopped. The voice calling for Mom cut off abruptly. She eased down the hall towards an office where she had heard someone moving, and suddenly she was back in the gunfight.

A guy leaned out of the office with an AR and started blasting away where he had last seen Eric, where Dani had just been standing. The various muzzle flashes had half-blinded him so he compensated for aimed fire with a high volume of fire. Fortunately, Eric had moved away from that spot and Dani was now on the other side of the hall. His bullets missed her by four feet but the flash and blast was pretty horrendous. She automatically crouched and squinted, before realizing she had to fight back. She started firing back, punching hollow points into the chest of the shooter, aided by the glowing night sights on this pistol. He fell back against the door jamb and slid down it, trying to catch himself and swing his weapon on her at the same time. She stepped closer and shot him twice in the face.

Suddenly, a figure bolted from the same office, leaping over the body and tearing down the hall. Dani jumped back, surprised, accidentally triggering a wild shot. Then she lined up the sights and fired more carefully. The fleeing figure stumbled, ricocheted off of a wall, and kept running. She lined up again and her pistol didn't fire. She turned it sideways to look at it and saw the slide locked back. She bent and set it carefully down on the carpet, then took the AR from the guy she had shot out of the office.

The last guy was already out the fire door and tearing down

the stairs, but she brought the rifle up and squeezed the trigger anyway. Nothing happened. Dani made a guttural noise, almost a growl, and threw the rifle as hard as she could down the hall. She bent back down to the guy, ran her hand along his belt, and came up with a big knife from the sheath she found.

She went down the stairs as quickly as she could in the dark, slipping twice in the blood trail the guy was leaving. She had hit him good with her one shot, and when she came out the door on the first floor, she saw that he had fallen in the parking lot. He rolled over and looked back, saw his pursuer was a tiny girl without a gun, and almost laughed.

"BITCH!" he screamed. "Come on, BITCH! Come on, let's FINISH THIS!"

Chapter 11

She walked towards him, almost stamping her feet, knife in hand. He couldn't stand, but his arms were considerably longer than hers, and he could kill her if he got her close enough. He almost did. She jabbed the knife at him, but he avoided it and grabbed her ankle, pulling her off balance. She fell and hit hard right on her tailbone. He grabbed her leg and slid her closer. She tried to stab him in the chest but he was blocking it with the other arm, and he didn't even flinch when the blade sunk into his arm. He just grabbed a handful of her shirt and pulled her close enough to get his hands around her throat.

When he reached for her throat, he used both hands, which dropped his guard. His chest was now fully exposed. She went into a frenzy, stabbing him repeatedly in the chest as his hands closed on her throat and closed off her air supply. One or two of the stabs hit ribs and stopped, some skittered off of ribs and sunk in, and some hit home, sinking deep into his chest cavity. In the movies, he would have stiffened up and then immediately gone limp, dead with the first stab. The movies lie. Instead of dying, he pulled her closer, as if to deliberately drench her in his blood and sweat and body odor, unwashed for days now.

But he was fading rapidly as he bled out from her earlier gunshot and her current stabs. As strong as he was, he could have crushed her larynx with one squeeze if he had been at full strength. Now, his fingers were getting numb and he was losing control of them.

Frustrated with the apparent ineffectiveness of her stabs, she switched her target to his throat. She added her left hand to her grip on the knife and shoved the blade at his throat with all of her strength, up between the arms that still attempted to strangle her. It went in surprisingly easily until it encountered something more resistant and deviated in its path, but still plunging deeper, almost to the hilt. She twisted it a quarter turn to the left and then dragged it to the right, trying to open as big a wound as possible. It first sliced, then caught on something that wouldn't cut, and the serrations on the knife went tick tick tick tick, more a feeling than a sound, as they dragged across a tendon or whatever it was. The feeling sent shivers down Dani's spline, like fingernails on a chalkboard, but a chalkboard that was gushing warm, stale air and hot blood on her arms. She could feel her wet shirt sticking to her skin, and hot droplets on her face that turned cooler as a breeze wafted through. Still more blood pumped onto her shirt with the spurt-pause-spurt-pause of a heart doing its duty until at last the spurt became a dribble and the pause lengthened. She had tried to wrench the knife further to the right but had no more leverage, so she started back to the left. She didn't know what else to do.

He should be dead! Why won't he DIE?

As if that thought was the final straw, the hands lost all strength and dropped away from her throat and he fell back, just collapsed like a balloon deflating into a limp pile of material. His throat fell away from the knife and she kept it up and ready to stab again if he so much as twitched, but he didn't move. She pushed back from him with a hand on his chest that caused air and foamy blood to expel from the stab wounds, scaring her into thinking that he was going to arise and come after her again, like a movie monster that is defeated but gets back up just when the audience heaves a sigh of relief that it is finally dead.

Dani got her legs under her and scrambled back on hands and feet until she was some distance away before she stood, breathing hard. She spat a few times, not aware of any blood in her mouth but taking the precaution. She wanted to at least wipe the blood from her face but everything on her was soaked in blood, literally dripping blood.

She stayed there on hands and knees for a minute,

overwhelmed by everything that had just taken place. Then she remembered that Eric had been hurt, and jumped to her feet and ran upstairs.

***

Eric had flushed his eyes as best he could with the water. They were still tearing up but he had to find Dani. He groped around to get back to the conference room, then groped for his boots. He knew there was broken glass and who knew what other sharp objects on the floor, and he couldn't afford to slice his feet up and be unable to walk, even for a couple of days.

He was headed for the stairs when she pulled the door open and came through it. He brought his rifle up when the door started to open, moved it down and to the left when he saw a small figure that had to be Dani.

"Don't shoot!" she shouted, holding up her hands.

"Did any of them get away? Anyone going to be bringing back some more troops?" Eric wanted to know if they were going to be attacked again.

"No one got away." Dani, in a dead-calm voice.

"Okay, I got something in my eyes, both eyes. I hope it's just plaster dust but the window got shot out so it might be glass."

"Let's get you leaned back in a chair, and I saw a bottle of saline solution on a desk. Let me get that."

She flushed Eric's eyes with the saline, squeezing the bottle to get the stream to shoot out. Several rounds of that seemed to do the trick. He had plaster dust in his hair and on his face, but no glass, fortunately.

Dawn was starting to send light in through the windows. As Eric's vision got better and the light revealed what Dani looked like. Eric's jaw dropped open.

"Are you wounded? Is any of that blood yours?"

"No." She was a mess. A lot of bullets had gone through sheetrock into the conference room and dusted her with white powder, especially visible in her dark hair. But mainly, it was the blood. She looked like someone had thrown buckets of it on her. She had been locked in hand to hand combat with a man she was stabbing to death, and his blood was in her hair, on her face and hands, all the way up her arms, all over her shirt and pants. Prior to that she had walked among the bodies in the hallway and had gotten their blood on her lower pants legs and her white sneakers were turning tan as the blood dried.

The blood would have been more noticeable on her if it had been a smaller quantity, as odd as that sounds. A large splotch of blood would show up, for example, because it would contrast with her light blue shirt. In this case, the blood had soaked her shirt so much it simply looked like she was wearing a dark blue shirt.

"Are you okay?" he asked again.

She sighed. "I'm tired, and I'm shaking. I want to take a bath and a nap."

"We can arrange that, more or less. Why don't you get your stuff and I'll meet you in the lunchroom?" She nodded wearily and walked down the hall, stepping around the bodies.

***

Eric tied the door closed with paracord again. In the lunchroom down the hall, Dani had soap and shampoo ready by the sink. The water worked in the building, at least for now. There was a large water tank at the top of the building and gravity allowed the faucets to flow normally as long as it was full. Washing one's hair in a kitchen sink is rather clumsy, however. Eric brought his canteen cup and poured water over her hair that she couldn't have reached as she soaped it a couple of times. Satisfied, she shooed him out the door but kept the cup to pour water over her body to rinse the blood off.

He surveyed the scene of the gunfight in daylight for the first time. He didn't like looking at dead bodies but he wasn't going to vomit over it either. He'd skinned deer and hogs his whole life, and seen blood and gore. Besides, he respected deer more than the trash that lay dead on the floor.

The walls on both sides of the hall were riddled with bullet holes, bits of shredded flesh, and spattered blood. Eric figured that if the enemy had fired just ten shots on average, since he and Dani took some down before they fired a single shot, then that would be eighty rounds. He fired twenty, and Dani emptied three magazines plus one pistol had a round in the chamber, forty-six rounds, that made almost a hundred and fifty shots fired. Plus Dani's bullets went through multiple walls, so what amounted to only a few seconds of firing made the place look like a war zone.

The bodies were shredded. All of the dead had two bullet holes in them at minimum, since Dani had made sure of that, but more than likely none had only the minimum. The .308 bullets that Eric fired could go through two or three men's torsos if they didn't directly impact bone, and six of the men were in a tight group when he and Dani had opened fire. Even if half of their shots had missed, that was ten rifle rounds and fifteen 9mm going into six bodies, or over four shots per body.

The carpet was squishy with blood. It actually bubbled up when stepped on. And the smell... urine, feces, the vomit-like contents of stomachs and intestines ripped open, raw meat, the coppery odor of blood, a *lot* of blood, was pretty horrendous. He figured Dani didn't need to see and smell it all, so he moved their gear and bikes down the hall away from the scene, to a nice, big corner office. He hadn't chosen that office the previous day because it had a hallway window and was close to the other stairs. He had wanted some distance so no one could breach the stair door and be on them immediately. Now, in the daylight and with one gang eliminated, he hoped it would be safe enough.

His task now was to gather the weapons, ammo, and equipment from the bodies and select a rifle for Dani. *She did good*, he thought. *Damned good. When I was out, she continued the fight, eliminated the threat, then brought back medical assistance. What more could you ask for?*

The attackers had all brought a pistol, at least one knife, and a long gun. The long guns were a Remington 870 shotgun, two AKs, and the rest were ARs. He immediately rejected the shotgun as being too heavy for Dani. As for the AK versus AR debate, he favored the AK for its reliability and bigger round, but it seemed like everyone in the U.S. had at least five or six ARs, so parts, magazines, and ammo were easy to come by. He selected the best AR, one with a six-position stock that they could adjust for Dani's comfort, a mid-length gas system for reliability, and a better trigger than the others. He also gathered some additional Glock magazines and full equipment for Dani: a holster, pistol magazine pouch, knife, and AR magazine pouches. All of it was bloody, and he cleaned it as best he could.

While he loaded magazines with 9mm and 5.56mm, Eric thought about his own rifle. He was down to about two magazines and he wasn't even out of the metro area yet. On the other hand, things should be quieter away from the cities. Finally, he grabbed the next-best AR, deciding to keep it until they got out into the countryside and away from the gangs. He didn't need the extra weight, but they might need the extra security.

Chapter 12

Dani emerged from her bath, barefoot and with fresh clothes. She mumbled something about napping for an hour and curled up with her blanket on the floor behind the desk. While she slept, Eric busied himself with scavenging a supply of water, candy bars, crackers, and any other snacks he could find. He noticed that she had left all of her bloody clothes in the kitchen, and everything was bloody. Every single piece of clothing was bloody except maybe one sock. He realized he didn't know exactly what she'd done, but she'd returned holding a knife and covered in blood, so it didn't require someone on the order of Hercule Poirot to deduce that she'd stabbed one of those thugs to death. He walked back into the office and looked at her out of curiosity. She looked angelic, curled up in a blanket and sleeping peacefully.

It takes serious balls to stab someone to death, he thought. *Shooting someone is just a squeeze of the finger. You can do it at long distance. Stabbing someone, now that is a* whole *different situation. That is as up close and personal as you can get. That is getting intimate with them.* He was impressed. Possibly even a little intimidated.

As he ate breakfast and drank coffee he thought about things, mainly Dani. She wasn't melting down because her cell phone and Instagram account were gone. She had been pretty shocked by his statement about things not being back to normal for many years, but this morning she had saved both of their lives. Marines have a feeling of superiority over all of the other military services and then the slimy civilians are below even that. But Dani, now, she was a different story. His first impression of her was that she was hot and he'd love to have her as an enthusiastic partner in bed. Since then, she'd proven to be smart and quick to catch onto things. And earlier this morning, that was courage, plain and simple. She could have just crouched behind that table leg and maybe shot at a bad guy once they'd killed him and came after her. Of course, if she'd done that they would have either shot or overwhelmed her.

She hadn't done that. She'd opened up on them through the wall, pretty effectively, it seemed, even in the face of incoming fire. Then she'd shot the wounded to take them out of the equation before she went after the survivors. Wounded men may be able to shoot you in the back if you pass them up, so while that was not technically legal, it was exactly the right thing to do in the circumstances. And going after the last guy — he was going to have to ask her about that. It was great. He didn't want the guy to go bring in some more friends for another fight.

He estimated an hour, gave her some extra, and gently woke her up. As she sat and sleepily munched chocolate chip cookies for breakfast, she commented "I was just exhausted!"

"Adrenaline does that to you," he replied. "It burns up all of your energy and you just want to crash afterwards. But you did an outstanding job. You didn't just hide, you shot and you hit the enemy. And when I got that debris in my eyes, you hunted down the last of the enemy and eliminated them. That saved our lives, both of ours."

She stopped eating and looked at him intently with those big, amber eyes. "Really? Are you sure?"

"What do you mean, 'am I sure'? Of course I'm sure. You could have been killed, and you just marched down that hall and kicked their asses!"

She went silent and her eyes unfocussed as she replayed the events in her mind. "I just... it was the right thing to do. They threatened us, they must die. I didn't plan it or reason it out, I just... did it."

"And you did good. You are hereby promoted. Here's *your* rifle." Her eyes went to the AR that he held up, and she stood, starting to reach for it but stopping before she touched it, and put her hands back down. "Will you teach me?" she asked.

Eric silently awarded her more respect points for that.

They went through another session like they had with the Glock the day before. Since they actually had more ammo than he wanted to carry, he had her run three magazines, ninety rounds, through the weapon. The AR recoil is low, almost nonexistent, and she was rapidly able to put double taps into a row of Post-It notes at about thirty-five yards, which was as far as their impromptu indoor range would allow. Her eyes were shining and she had a big smile on her face the entire time.

"Oh, also, your Glock sights glowed in the dark," she mentioned. "I want that, too. And I think the trigger was easier to pull."

Damn, this girl doesn't miss a thing he thought. *The sights, sure, that's obvious, but noticing a lighter trigger pull in the middle of a gunfight — wow.* He didn't say a word, just smiled and handed her his pistol. She smiled and did a little double bounce, like an abbreviated jump for joy, and they swapped pistols. She examined it intently, and asked "So they just glow automatically? Did you do something to make the trigger easier?" His answers were yes to both, and he explained how he had swapped some trigger parts for aftermarket ones for a lighter trigger pull.

They got her all togged out in her new holster, pouches, and paraphernalia, and her new hiking boots from Academy, then it was time to hit the road. They walked the bikes down the stairs and were almost to the door when it abruptly swung open and a man started through. Seeing Dani, in the lead, he stopped and put up both hands, palm outwards. "Peace be with you," he said.

"And also with you," tumbled out of Dani's mouth automatically, the statement and response a part of Catholic mass. An onlooker would have found it to be a strange scene because Dani and Eric both had drawn pistols when the door opened, and the man looked as if he were dressed for a casual Friday, in khaki slacks and bright blue golf shirt, but with a pistol on his belt and a rifle slung over his shoulder. He backed out, saying something over his shoulder to one or more people behind him, and closed the door. Since he had come in from the lobby, Dani headed out the other door, which opened directly to the outside. As they rode off through the parking lot, they looked at each other and both burst into laughter.

"I hope his office is not on the third floor!"

Chapter 13

The traffic jam was worse on I-45 than it had been on SH-99, if that was possible. It was the major north-south corridor between Houston and Dallas and, realistically, was almost not up to the job of handling normal traffic conditions. It was also Dani's first full experience with the fields of the dead. During her entire trip through the metro area up to this point, she had been among buildings. Most of the people who left the highway to die somewhere had gone into a building alongside the route. They were not visible to someone on I-45 and the buildings muted the smell of their decomposing flesh.

Not so, as they began to leave the built-up areas behind and enter the countryside. Here, as along the Grand Parkway, there were untold tens of thousands of bodies, covered or not, rotting away in the sun. Eric could see bones showing in a number of them where scavengers had been at work, but there weren't enough scavengers in existence to clean up this mess. They ate their fill and more without making any real dent in the supply.

Dani turned positively green as the horrendous smell wafted over them. She looked wide-eyed at Eric, horrified, as he hurried to equip her with a bandanna.

"Put some perfume or something in there where your mouth and nose are going to be," he instructed. She gagged a couple of times before she got it on but kept her chocolate chip breakfast down. She could have looked comical with a cowboy hat and bandanna mask, like a little Wild West bank robber, but Eric didn't laugh at her.

Now that she could do something other than crouch away from the wind and cover her mouth, she gazed around in amazement. Looking at Eric, still wide-eyed, she stammered "They're... they're... *bodies!* They're dead!"

She had dismounted her bike to get to her perfume. Now

she put her hands up to the sides of her head and staggered back until she bumped into the fender of a car. Tears started to soak her bandanna and Eric stepped forward to comfort her, but she took off her hat and thrust it in his direction, which stopped him. She sank to her knees and prayed while he held her hat. He waved some flies off of her but other than that he stood back to give her some private time. Nominally, his parents had been Methodist, but he had rarely seen the inside of a church. He did realize that it was very important to some people, though, so his policy was that they could do whatever they wanted as long as it didn't impact him. He broke out some water bottles and snacks since they were stopped anyway.

When Dani was finished, she turned her nose up at the food. "How can you eat with... all this around us?"

"You need to at least drink some water so you don't dehydrate." He held out a water bottle to her. She looked like she was going to refuse, then took it.

"How far before we... get past this?"

"I want to hit Huntsville by the end of the day. This side, south side of town, we'll cut off on highway 19. That will run us out into the woods pretty quickly. Now the bad thing about 19 is that it runs more-or-less parallel to I-45, and some people could have used it as an alternate route to go north. You can bypass Dallas on 19, where 45 goes right through it."

"But you also have to wonder where all of these people were heading. If they're running away from Houston because there's Hexen there, then they're not going to go to Dallas because there's Hexen there, too. And the people on the south side of Dallas may have headed south on 45 to get out of town. I don't know if they met somewhere in the middle or what. How about you? Where were you going when you headed north on 45?"

She shrugged, looking down. "Away. There were —" tears came to her eyes again, and she sniffled and turned away.

"Ah, damn, I'm sorry! I didn't mean to bring up bad memories. That was stupid." She walked slowly around a couple of cars and was under control by the time she completed the circle.

"Let's get the fuck out of here," she said in a hoarse voice, waving off a fly.

He maintained his usual schedule of one hour travel/ten minutes rest, despite Dani's protests. She thought that the fields of the dead were only here, and that they could simply travel faster and get past them. She just couldn't believe that this was the landscape that existed for untold miles and miles. And, truth be told, that existed alongside every highway in the entire world. Neither did she want to be among the dead for any longer than necessary.

"Let's gooooo! I am NOT going to spend the night out here, with —" she gestured at the dead and a chill went down her spine that visibly shook her body.

He relented, and they gave up on the breaks, stopping only to pull water and snacks from the packs. Dani refused to eat any lunch except more candy bars. When Eric opened a can of tuna, she spun around and walked off a ways, out of range of sight and smell. He finished it in a couple of bites, flung the can away, and called her back, to get back on the road again.

Moving through the traffic jam and debris on a bike was ten percent riding, forty percent dragging or lifting the bike over something, and fifty percent walking. Most of the time it wasn't worth mounting the bike and pedaling because you would just have to dismount to get over or around some other obstacle almost immediately. And it went on and on like that forever. Fortunately, most of the people had moved on, and they didn't have to avoid many pedestrians. The few they saw mainly gave them as wide a berth as possible.

Part of that was Eric. He took the lead and gave anyone they encountered a greeting and a hard stare. The greeting was something like a brisk "good morning, sir. We're just passing through," and the look said "and if you try to stop me I will blow your fucking head off in a New York second." He knew how to give that look. He had spent years perfecting it.

***

Since she had asked to be trained, he spent most of the day giving her tips and advice, hoping to keep her mind off of the fields of the dead, but also finding her an eager pupil.

"The philosophy of fighting," he started. "One of the things we say in the Marine Corps is to be polite. Be professional. But have a plan to kill everyone you meet. Our parents and teachers spend years telling us not to hit our classmates, maybe punishing us for doing so. That builds up a trained resistance that we have to overcome. A fight involves violence. If you are in a fight, you have to go for it with maximum speed and violence and sheer brutality. Destroy the enemy by inflicting the maximum amount of violence upon them in the shortest amount of time. There are no rules. No fair fights, no referees, no judges, no three-minute rounds, no standing eight counts. Welcome to the jungle, you know? No sympathy. You can't worry about causing pain to someone. They aren't worried about causing you pain, so you are a fool if you are concerned about them.

"If you find yourself in a fair fight, then you have planned poorly. If you expect to be in a fair fight, then you are a fool. That means you fight to win, and anything you do is fair. Anything at all. Bring a shotgun to a fistfight. Hit them when they aren't looking. Get five friends and all of you kick the shit out of one guy. Run over him with a truck. It doesn't matter. The only thing that matters, the only thing at all, is winning. Never stop. Never hesitate. Never surrender.

"One final note — once the fight starts, never evaluate your opponent while they are standing up. Before the fight, evaluate your opponent, yes, learn as much as you can about them. During the fight, no. Never hit an opponent and then look to see how he reacted. You hit them, you hit them hard, and you hit them multiple times, as quickly as possible. Never hit someone once when you can hit them eight or ten times.

When they fall down, you kick them. When it looks like they are going to stay down, now you can evaluate them. Now you can decide if you need to step on their face a bit or kick their ribs into their lungs or whatever.

"And you have to be able to bring this violence and brutality when you're cold. If someone hits you in the face, you get pissed off and you want to hit them back. That's hot, your blood is up, you're mad, you want revenge. But you have to be able to start the violence if necessary, from a cold state. That's when they haven't hit you yet, you're not pissed off, you're just minding your own business and you see something that says you have to take action and bring some pain down on some assholes."

"Like when three gangstas are trying to rape a girl?" Dani replied.

Eric turned and looked at her to see if she was okay. Did she mean something or should he take that at face value? "I wasn't actually bringing that up, but yes, when three gangstas are trying to rape a beautiful young lady. It's a good example." He could tell she smiled, even buried underneath a hat, bandanna, and sunglasses.

"Did I ever thank you for that?" she asked. "If not —"

"You did, but no thanks necessary. It was the right thing to do. Besides, you saved my life back there at the office building. Thank you for that."

Dani was pleased that he hadn't made an asshole comment along the lines of "you can thank me as soon as we find a nice soft bed."

South of Huntsville is Sam Houston National Forest and Huntsville State Park. Eric wasn't sure where one stopped and the other one started but they did cover a huge area on both sides of I-45. Almost to Huntsville, there is a huge statue of Sam Houston, sixty-seven feet tall on a ten foot granite base, billed as the "World's Tallest Statue of an American Hero." It is made of concrete but is white. Eric didn't know if the concrete was dyed or if it was painted. Either way, it is an obvious landmark and a number of people had apparently made plans to meet there or thought it was a good stopping point.

A little community of tents and signs had cropped up there. By this time, people seemed to have figured out that if they were still alive, they were immune to Hexen, and they didn't have to stay away from other people. The tents were mainly back in the trees a bit to take advantage of the shade, and ran the gamut from high-tech, high-dollar tents to old tarps and blankets tied to trees with shoelaces. The signs showed the same variety, from elaborate, painted poster boards to sheets with spray painted text to a white shirt with ballpoint pen notes. Many of the tents had names spray painted on the sides.

Eric wasn't interested in the signs. He was worried about people. People can kill you; scenery can't.

"Dani, I don't like this situation," he told her as they approached. "I don't want anyone trying to stop or delay us. No one, for any reason. Things are too wild right now. Be on a hair trigger. If we need to shoot someone, don't hesitate."

He gave a hard look to anyone that was anywhere close to them. A few people approached them to beg for food but he had encountered that before and kept a couple of small cans of tuna in a jacket pocket that he could toss to them before they got too close. That took care of those people, no threat.

The real threat was coming up.

Chapter 14

Eric was walking down the left side of the northbound lanes, which meant that he had two lanes full of abandoned cars between him and the little tent city. He didn't know if it was best to have some cover between him and them, or if it would be better to be more in the open to see someone coming, but he had to choose one or the other. Things were fine until a big woman holding a baby stepped in front of him. With a closer look, Eric saw that she was more of a girl, late teens or early twenties, probably sixty pounds overweight, dirty blond hair with purple streaks, nose ring, some guy's name crudely tattooed on her wrist and some other ink on her neck and shoulder. She was at the end of an SUV and Eric was passing the SUV, so he was blocked unless he backed up. "Sir, my baby needs food," the woman stated.

"Ma'am, you might have seen that I already gave all of my extra food out to those other people. Please stay out of my way," he replied. He tried to steer the bike around her and she sidestepped to remain in front of him. His temper started to rise.

***

Dani had seen the big girl block Eric and she went on high alert as she put her AR rifle to her shoulder in the low ready position he had taught her. She was a car length behind Eric, so she was beside the next car behind the SUV. She snapped the safety off and looked around her. That's when she saw the man slipping around the back of the SUV, eyes focused on Eric's back. He had a pistol in his hand, and he didn't see her. He was moving quickly and Dani didn't even have time to shout a warning. She swung the muzzle up and blasted away, four shots to the guy's back at a range of about ten feet. He jumped and fell against the SUV, leaving splashes of blood on the tailgate before sliding to the pavement in a heap and curling up. He looked like he was out of the fight.

Dani went looking for other targets.

***

When the shots went off behind him Eric let go of the bike, snatched his Glock from its holster, and crouched. He was turning and swinging his pistol towards the gunfire when he caught movement out of the corner of his eye and thought "GUN!" The big girl was drawing a big stainless steel revolver from the blanket that swaddled her baby, and she was dropping the blanket so she could get a two-handed grip on the revolver. Obviously there was no baby. Time seemed to go into slow motion for Eric as he raced to reverse his turn to meet this new threat. He swung back towards her and put a double-tap into her chest — two shots, and then fired a single shot into her face, trying for a spot between her eyes. It wasn't a tough shot since she was only about three feet away from him. Any one of the three shots would have been fatal, and her knees folded and she fell on her back with a meaty thump.

***

Dani saw another guy who had been following the first guy. He ducked down, turned, and ran, trying to stay as low as possible. She raised up over the hood, intending to shoot him, but another guy behind that one opened up on her. Bullets smashed into the windshield and made sharp cracks as they sped by or ticking noises as they went through the sheet metal of the car. She ducked down behind it and ran to the back, out of the line of fire.

***

Eric turned back towards a new flurry of shots and saw someone shooting in Dani's direction, or where he expected Dani would be. He shot at the guy through the SUV windows and over the trunk of the car beside it, hoping the glass wouldn't deflect the bullets. There was no "one shot and the bad guy flops to the ground," no double taps or controlled pairs, nothing neat at all about it. After the first shot the glass fractured but most stayed in place and interfered with his view, so he just dumped a half dozen rounds at the guy and something worked, because the guy seemed to go down out of his sight. He was glad he had sunglasses on, feeling glass fragments hitting his face. Then he heard a louder boom and a crack as a bullet sped by at the front of the SUV. *Somebody has a big rifle out there!* He ducked and bobbed, trying to get eyes on that shooter without offering his head up as a stationary target, while a stream of smaller caliber bullets were coming through the SUV windows at him.

That's two shooters at least, maybe three.

***

Dani brought her rifle around the back end of the car and saw no one between the two lanes of cars, so she moved on to the outer car, the one closest to the right shoulder. Peeking around that one she saw one guy down, three guys with rifles, and one running away. One was shooting in Eric's direction so he was the priority.

She put the sights on him and opened up. He twisted around immediately with the first shot but she had planned on three shots and she put all three into him. Then the odd man out, a guy that was older and dressed in nicer clothing than the scumbags that had attacked them, shot the other guy with a rifle, who had been trying to reload.

Odd Man Out saw Dani with her rifle pointed in his general direction and held his rifle up over his head with both hands, then with just his left as he showed an empty right hand.

She figured that for a sign of surrender and tracked the running man. He was about to get into the woods when she shot him in the back, a spine shot that shut his legs down immediately. He fell and skidded in the pine needles and started screaming.

***

The gunfire, so loud and furious, stopped abruptly with a deafening silence.

"Dani, are there any active shooters?" Eric yelled. He was scanning frantically for threats and had swapped his pistol for his rifle. "Look all around you."

Dani kept her rifle more or less on Odd Man Out and looked back over her shoulder. "I don't see any more," she yelled back. "There's one guy with a gun, rifle, but I think he's friendly. He's holding his rifle up over his head."

"Don't shoot!" the man was yelling. "I'm friendly! I'm on your side!" He kept repeating those three phrases.

Eric knew the woman was down, for a certainty. If she ever got back up, he'd shoot himself. He moved towards the one who had tried to sneak up on him. That one was lying on his side, almost in a fetal position. He kicked him in the face, a heavy blow that turned him over on his back, rag-doll limp and vacant eyed. He kicked the man's pistol away and eased around the SUV, checking the bodies for any sign of aggression.

The one he had shot with his pistol suddenly sat up and pressed a wad of his shirt against his bicep, trying to stop a wound from bleeding. He was visibly trembling and saying "Oh, shit! Oh, shit!" over and over. Eric carefully lined up a shot and sent a .308 bullet into the guy's chest. It went all the way through, kicking out a spray of blood on the other side and causing a small explosion of dirt when it hit the ground. The guy fell back and his legs kicked some and went still.

Eric eased further around the SUV until he could see and talk to Odd Man Out. He didn't specifically point his rifle at him but the muzzle was in his general direction.

"Is that all of them? How many were there?" he yelled at the man.

"Seven. They're all down, and good riddance!"

Eric looked again and replied "I count six."

The man smiled. "That's because I saved your behind. You didn't see the other one at the front of that SUV near the woman. Can I put my arm down now? This thing is heavy."

"Yeah, put your rifle down in the grass there. I think you're friendly but let's talk some more first."

Eric stepped out from the SUV and walked closer to the man in a circular route, checking out the guy at the front of the SUV. He was face down with a hole in his back at the center of mass, exactly where it should be, and leaking blood.

Dani picked up the pistol that Eric had kicked away from the one guy and walked over to the three bodies lying in the grass. The one that had been shooting at Eric was on his back and when Dani stood over him he raised one hand in the palm out "stop" position and begged her "Please don't, please don't."

She looked at him for a moment, holding her rifle by the handguard with her left hand, extended her right with the pistol, and shot him through his hand and into his face. He started thrashing around and she shot him again to make him stop. Odd Man Out put his hands on his hips and watched Dani walk over to the other two and shoot them in the head or face, however they lay. Then he watched her walk up to the woodline where the spine-shot man still screamed. She walked around to look him in the face and he begged her for help.

"Please! Please! Get me a doctor! I wasn't with them! They made me! They made me do things with them!" he babbled. "I'm the victim here! I got shot for nothin'! I didn't do nothin'! You have to get me medical aid! You have to! I know my rights! You can't just shoot me!"

Dani smiled and the guy paused his rapid-fire blather momentarily, thinking that he had won her over. "I'm right, aren't I?" he asked.

"I have rights, too" she replied. "Like not getting attacked by bastards like you." She shot him in the face. As she walked back past him she casually extended her arm and shot him again in the back without breaking stride.

***

Odd Man Out turned to Eric and said "Is that your girlfriend? Son, don't ever get on her bad side, Lord Almighty!"

"I think she believes in doing a thorough job." He did turn that word over in his mind. *Girlfriend? No, not exactly. I'm interested. I mean, of course I'm interested! But I have a huge amount of respect for that girl, too, so I'm actually interested in her for more than just sex. And she just saved my life. Again.*

"Well, she's making damned sure of it. Lord! But I can't say they didn't have it coming to them. This group, these seven punks, have been shaking down people, robbing people, making life miserable for everyone in this tent city here and folks passing by. I have this rifle, but it's only a five shot and there's no way I can take on seven to one odds. I figured sooner or later someone meaner than them would come along, 'meaner' not being an insult to you and your girlfriend, you understand. So I was ready when y'all started taking them down. I thought I'd help."

"Thank you, Sir. We do appreciate the assistance." He bent down to pick up the man's big Marlin lever-action rifle and handed it to him. "What is this, a .45-70?"

"Yes, sir. It has a pretty good kick on both ends."

***

Dani walked around the two bodies at the front of the SUV, looking closely at everything as she circled. She checked her targets and what was behind them, and shot the man in the head and the woman in the chest. She took a moment to sling her rifle to free up her left hand, moved closer, and checked out the wadded-up blanket that supposedly held a baby, finding only blanket. Lastly, she walked back to the first man, the one that had tried to sneak up behind Eric, and shot him. The bullet went up through his throat and exited the top of his skull since she was standing at his feet. She tossed the pistol off into the grass.

***

There were some cheers from some of the tent city people that were coming back and were glad that the bad guys were down. Still, it would only take one sympathizer with a pistol to ruin their day.

"Let's get back on the road. Thanks again, Sir." Eric nodded to Odd Man Out.

"Thank you, and you, young lady." Odd Man Out watched them go and thought that they were pretty cold-blooded, shooting wounded men like that, especially the girl. But then he remembered times that he had shot a wounded deer when his first shot wasn't immediately fatal, and figured that maybe they were doing the wounded a favor by putting them out of their misery. Maybe not the guy that was shot in the arm. He might have lived, but then, who was it that said something like "Don't do your enemies a minor injury"? In other words, they can recover from a minor injury and will get you back, so hit them hard if at all. Nietzsche? Sun Tzu? No, no, had to be Machiavelli. Maybe they had the right idea, but it looked like the girl enjoyed it a bit too much. And the wounded weren't deer, either. The wounded were men.

He resolved to say a prayer for the girl's soul that night. The man, too, but especially the girl. Especially the girl. He couldn't complain, though; he'd been waiting for someone mean to help him take down that gang. He'd gotten it, all right. In the future he'd have to be more careful what he wished for.

Chapter 15

Not far down the road, Eric called a halt. "Dani, are you okay?" he asked.

"Yeah." She drew that single word out in a way that meant "yes" but also "why do you ask?"

"Let me see your eyes."

She took off her sunglasses and looked him in the eye. One eyebrow arched up. *Well?*

"I mean, I can understand — that was pretty traumatic. And last night, I mean, shit, we've had two gunfights in, what, nine or ten hours? Are you really all right?"

She looked down for a few seconds, not more than ten, swept her eyes back to his, and said "I think it's sweet that you're concerned about me, but this is actually good for me. No, maybe that's not right. I am good with it. I haven't really had a chance to process it all, but this is the first time that I can take charge of things. All my life, my family and I have been pushed around. Not by the government or anything nebulous like that, but by people. People just like those back there. Murderers, rapists, and thieves. My older brother beaten up and robbed, people threatening us, we see a crime committed and can't report it for fear the men who did it will come and hurt us. We can't have nice things because someone will just steal them." A fire came into her eyes and her jaw muscles tightened. "Well, those days are over! I am not putting up with it anymore! I will kill a thousand people like them just like I would a cockroach, no sympathy, no regrets, no remorse!"

Eric smiled and Dani's blood pressure started to rise, thinking that he was mocking her, but then he said "I like you more and more, the better I get to know you. I trust you more in a fight than anyone else I know." He clapped her on her bicep and started walking again.

Dani pondered that last comment. She figured that was a seriously huge compliment. He'd been in the Marine Corps, he'd been in a war, and he trusted *her* in a fight more than anyone? Wow!

***

The exit for SH-19 was only another mile and a half down the road. Dani and Eric took it and then headed almost immediately into a subdivision. They needed water, and it would be easier to find bottles of it in a kitchen than to find a natural source off in the woods somewhere and purify it. There would be plenty of that later.

They went in a few streets, then turned in and left the bikes at the curb about halfway down the block. Eric scanned three hundred sixty degrees, as always now.

"No signs of recent habitation," he said in a voice loud enough for Dani to hear but no louder. "No windows open, no tents. But I feel like someone is probably watching us." He pulled the flat wrecking bar from his gear and walked up to the nearest house, Dani following.

Abruptly, the front door flew open and a big man stood there, not tall but big around. Eric wasn't noticing his physique, focusing instead on the shotgun in the guy's hands.

"Hey, we're friendly," he said, putting his hands up slightly, empty except for the bar in his left. He stepped back and to the right, away from Dani, getting off the man's property and trying to get her out of the line of fire. "We're good guys. We were just looking for some water. We're traveling and need some water." He kept backing up and away from Dani. She also had her hands raised and was backing up.

"Stay still!" the man demanded. His shotgun pointed at Eric but he cut his eyes towards Dani. "Not you. You come here. You need to stay a while. Spend the night." He leered at her. "Come on in here and I'll be your sugar daddy. Looks like you need a real man." He guffawed at his own wit. It was pretty stupid, considering his physique compared to Eric's.

Eric tried again: "We're backing up. We're retreating. We're not threat —"

"SHUT UP! You go ahead and get the hell out of here! The girl comes inside!" the man yelled.

"You're kidnapping her? Is that right? With the intent to rape her?" Eric tried again to bring the man to reality.

"You see any cops around here?" the man yelled. "Get on out of here!"

Eric glanced at Dani and she was looking at him, half in surprise and half in a *why don't you do something* look. He gave her a tiny shrug. *Shit, there's nothing I can do right at the moment.* She clenched her jaw and turned back towards the guy in the doorway. By the time she was facing him again she was smiling, even though her stomach turned at the sight of him. He had obviously been bearded, balding, fat, and sloppy before the end of the world, he hadn't improved since. No, you could add smelly to that, since he didn't have a working shower any more, not that it had gotten frequent use when it had worked.

She drew herself up to her full height and squared her shoulders so her breasts thrust forward as much as possible. She didn't have much height or a huge bust, but she did the best she could.

"You're right," she said. "Maybe it would be good to be with a real man." She started walking forward slowly, that hip-swaying walk where girls act like they're on a tightrope, one foot placed directly in front of the other. She started to unbutton her shirt as she walked, continuing to talk about how much she wanted it. The man giggled. Eric watched for an opening but the guy still had the shotgun leveled at him. All he had to do was squeeze the trigger. By the time Dani sashayed close enough to him for him to point the shotgun up at the sky to get it out of her way, she was between him and Eric.

The man stepped back inside the house as Dani

approached, and as she stepped inside the doorway she dramatically pulled her shirt open with both hands. That placed her right hand within inches of her pistol. If she had reached down there earlier, anyone, even the least savvy civilian, would have immediately thought she was going for a pistol. Doing it now, it was just part of another action, the man was totally distracted, and his weapon was out of play.

Dani pulled her Glock, thrust it towards the man's chest and pulled the trigger as fast as she could, as many times as she could, BAMBAMBAMBAMBAMBAM. The would-be kidnapper screamed and jumped and danced and tried to get away, dropping the shotgun. He turned and started to run, but his leg hit a recliner chair and he took a header over it and landed on his back on the floor. Dani stalked around the chair to get a better aiming point. When the man saw her loom up over him he gave a little squeal and tried to scoot away by digging his hands and heels into the carpet and pushing. Dani took a two-handed stance and started pumping more bullets into his body, BAMBAMBAMBAMBAM. Eric was inside the house for this flurry of shots. He lowered his rifle when he saw he was not needed. Then the yelling began and he eased back out the door.

Dani was shouting in Spanish at the top of her lungs. Eric's Spanish was not great but he did pick out "no" and "fucking police," so he assumed her first sentence was "NO, I don't see any fucking police around." After that, she pretty much demonstrated an in-depth knowledge of curse words and there was a repeated thumping sound.

She's kicking him, he realized. *Straight in the balls, I'm sure.* Then there was another shot and the bullet came out through the side of the house. Eric stepped around the truck in the driveway to put the engine block between him and Dani. He hoped that was her last round. He never even entertained the thought of reminding her to keep her finger off the trigger unless she had a target in sight and was ready to shoot. Not right now. Not only no, but Hell, no.

Things quieted down after a minute and there was a pause while Dani got her clothing back in order before she came storming out of the house. She tried to slam the door but it was a cheap lightweight thing that didn't gain enough momentum to slam. She stomped by Eric and shot him a dirty look.

"WHY DO ALL YOU MEN THINK WE'RE JUST PIECES OF MEAT?" she yelled as she went by. He turned a palm up in a *it wasn't me* gesture and opened his mouth to reply before he realized what he was doing and stopped himself. *My God, man*, he jokingly chided himself. *You don't argue with a furious Latina! That would be like trying to baptize a cat. And she's armed. Oh, HELL, no!*

He kept quiet and stayed still and small and unobtrusive until he thought Dani was gone. After a minute he went back inside the house with the shot-to-rags, thoroughly dead would-be kidnapper/rapist on the floor.

"That didn't work out too well for you, now did it?" he said under his breath.

He wasn't interested in looking at a dead body, though. He went through the house and collected useful items, specifically bottled water, coffee, cans of food, lighters, and two nice treats. The one that delighted Eric was the .308 ammunition, almost a hundred rounds. He muttered "Thank you, dead guy!" when he found it, and immediately topped off his almost-empty third magazine. He also found some 9mm to replace Dani's load.

The other treat was a nice knife. The knife was a custom, not a mass-produced product from one of the big companies, but handmade, one at a time, by a skilled knifesmith. It had a four inch drop point, which made it an excellent all-around utility knife, and beautiful Micarta handles with a red-and-gold swirling pattern. He stuck it in a cargo pocket to give to Dani later.

The question was, where was Dani? He hadn't seen her since she stomped off.

Chapter 16

The neighborhood still didn't have any signs of life. Cussing only a little under his breath, Eric walked down to the end of the street until it dead-ended, then came back. A Dachshund came out of some bushes and made a beeline for him, wagging his tail, and sidling up to him to be petted. Eric scratched his back, thinking that the dog had to have been fed and watered, so there were people alive nearby. He stood and commanded the dog "Go home". The dog obediently wheeled around and trotted down the street, looking back over its shoulder to see what Eric was doing.

He followed, and a block later heard women laughing, then spotted an open garage. Dani and an older woman were sitting inside on folding chairs, out of the sun and near the opening to catch the breeze. This was the end of winter, when the mornings are cool but the afternoons are hot. People — when they had had electricity — had to turn on the heater in the morning and the air conditioning in the afternoon.

Dani and the woman smiled and raised their wine glasses in greeting. *Thank God* he thought. *Alcohol and feminine companionship cure many ills. They cause a lot, too, but I guess that's when men are involved.*

"Hi, I'm Susan," the woman said, standing and offering her hand. As he introduced himself Eric noted that she had a big revolver in a hip holster and an AR rifle on a box nearby. He pointed them out, saying "So, a Colt .45 and a rifle, the military would classify you as a 'Lady, Texas, standard, issue one each', and assign you a National Stock Number".

She laughed and said the rifle was her son's, who worked offshore. "I just hope he can get off that rig," she sighed. Eric figured the odds of that were low to none but didn't say anything. Anyone surviving Hexen on an oil platform fifty or a hundred miles or more out at sea, with no electronics, no functioning helicopters or boats, was royally screwed. There were survival pods but they were never designed or intended to be rowed or sailed to shore. On the other hand, some platforms were within sight of shore.

He accepted a warm beer from her, which was the only way he was going to get it for a long time. Susan was obviously delighted to have visitors, especially those with news from outside the local area, and didn't seem the least bit fazed that Dani had gunned down one of her neighbors. Eric wanted to bring that up right at the start, rather than get comfortable and then have a group of local militia come to arrest them.

"Did Dani mention that some guy down the street tried to kidnap her?" he asked.

"She did! And believe me, we're better off without that sorry excuse for a human being," she replied. "I know that's terrible for me to say, but it's God's honest truth." Switching gears quickly, she offered "You have to spend the night. Dani said you were looking for a place to camp out. Stay here. I have a room and the couch available. Maybe you can stay for a couple of days!"

"Thank you," Eric said, then glanced at Dani. She smiled at him and nodded. "We accept." Susan beamed, and swept Dani along with her to go do whatever was necessary to make the house habitable by guests. Eric retrieved the bikes and supplies, accompanied by the Dachshund.

That evening was uneventful. He met a few people from the neighborhood that came by, and heard that arrangements were being made for a cookout the following night. Some men had shot a huge feral hog in the State Park, which actually bordered the subdivision. Susan insisted they stay for it. Eric was eager to get back on the road and tried to refuse, but she insisted and noted all of the food that was going to be available, which included homemade bread, which he loved, since he had so rarely gotten it. Dani also got into the act, so it was only a matter of time before he relented. He told himself it was the food, though. Several days of canned food for all three meals had made the idea of fresh chops and bacon and pie sound like Heaven.

He had a few beers and worked at Susan's grill to heat water for baths. He toyed with the idea of making a pass at Dani but rejected the idea pretty quickly. He didn't know how well that would work out here, in Susan's house. On the one hand, she apparently thought they were a lovely couple, but then she assigned Dani to the guest room and him to the couch. Besides, Dani was no little fuck toy. She was a smart, tough little trooper, and he respected her. He was definitely going to make a pass, just not here and now in these circumstances.

He bathed last, chatted for a short while, stretched out on the couch, and fell asleep. Susan and Dani stayed up, talking and drinking wine until late, and they were both moving a little slowly the next morning. That didn't stop them from suggesting he go to the nearby student apartments and scavenge for alcoholic beverages "for the cookout". He loaded up with his pistol and extra mags, hammer, crowbar, and a wheelbarrow and started walking. His new buddy, Pepper the Dachshund, accompanied him.

***

He was getting pretty good at jimmying doors, and was thankful to find that most of the apartments were empty, as in no dead bodies. The ones that did, he knew instantly by the smell, and just closed the door and moved on. There were plenty of apartments and he filled the wheelbarrow quickly. He dropped the load off at Susan's and went back for two more before midmorning. She and Dani were looking more chipper by then but Pepper was pooped. She flopped down on a cushion and snored.

They were just chatting when there was the mechanical roar of an unmuffled V8 engine. Eric put his water bottle down on the nearest surface and ran out the door to listen, figured out it was the house directly behind Susan's, and ran back into the house. He dodged around the girls, ran out the back, and hopped the fence. He found three guys in the garage, one in the driver's seat of the shell of a 1970 Plymouth 'Cuda up on jack stands. He blipped the accelerator and the 440 cubic inch engine bellowed through open headers and torqued the whole car noticeably over to the passenger side. He let the engine wind down to an idle, a lumpy rump rump rump sound that indicated a high performance camshaft, then shut it down. He came out of the car and high-fived the other two men, huge grins on everyone's faces.

Eric had a huge grin on his face, too, as did the spectators that were running up, including Dani. She skidded to a stop, putting her hand on Eric's chest to brake, and he gathered her into his arms and they hugged briefly. Then the crowd broke into applause, and the 'Cuda owner bowed. He held a hand up and said "Please hold your questions for now. I'll explain". He pointed at a dozen car batteries on the garage floor. "Car batteries work, most of them. I don't think there's anything wrong with them. The problem is the electronics. All your circuit boards, relays, LEDs, computers, fuses, they're all dead. This old thing here is mainly mechanical, like the fuel pump. We're going to have to pull the old school equipment out."

Eric gazed at the 'Cuda and it was the most beautiful thing he had seen in a while. Actually, it looked like hell, with the body in gray primer, no windshield, and the fenders off, but it was a symbol of rebirth to him. He stepped forward to get a closer look and ask the owner more specific questions, never realizing that he and Dani had put their arms around each other after they had applauded.

Chapter 17

That evening, the entire neighborhood was buoyed by the thunderous roar of the 'Cuda. Obviously the owner had to fire it up and run it again as a kind of ceremony. Since it was such a big deal, the cookout centered around his house, which meant Susan's was directly in the middle, too. Plus, Eric had hauled three wheelbarrow loads of alcoholic beverages to her house, so it was only natural that the festivities occur there. Eric took a few boards out of the fence that separated the two properties so that people could pass more easily from one to the other, provided they ducked under the two by four crosspiece.

Certainly, the crowd was still shell shocked and in mourning with the Hexen deaths, and there were some fits of crying when someone had a bit too much to drink. But Eric saw that the neighborhood — what was left of it — was pulling together. Leaders were emerging, not by vote at this point, but by being leaders. They had rescued some kids and people were stepping up to foster them. Committees were being formed, lists were being made, and duties assigned. Eric was no fan of bureaucracy, but he thought that the human race would survive.

Eric looked around and saw what he would expect to see after a plague — damned few kids and damned few elders, for a start. Probably damned few who had been sick or ailing or recovering from an injury. There was no cure or medical treatment for Hexen, but those with a lifetime of good health care had probably fared better than those who lacked it. Basically, the survivors were the strong, but sometimes the strong were not those you'd expect.

"So you were in the Marines," one of the emerging leaders started. "We could use a military man here. We'd be glad for you to stay here." He looked around for support and got more than a few nods and yesses.

"Well, I appreciate that, but I have a place I want to get back to. And, to tell you the truth, I don't know if any of you are going to be able to stay here very long." That didn't go over very well. There was a chorus of "Why not?" and "What makes you say that?" questions.

"I understand that the grocery stores have three days' worth of food. Now, even if the population was reduced by ninety percent, which is what your rough count indicated, that's a thirty-day supply of food. So what are you going to do in 30 days?" That brought a tide of comments and discussion, and a couple of people even turned and walked off, either refusing to hear the truth or going to make their own plans away from the group.

The man sat, thinking, for a moment, then asked "Okay, so what do we do?"

"Go back to the land. Herd cattle. Farm. Fish. Hunt."

"No, no, no!" cried one woman. "The government will send us disaster aid! Just like a hurricane! Send in FEMA and the National Guard!"

"There are two problems with that. When a hurricane hits, there's one disaster area. Okay, say it goes through Florida and then goes into the Gulf and hits Texas. Two disaster areas. But that's all. Just two. What we have now is that the *entire United States* is a disaster area. *Everywhere.* So now where do they send FEMA and the National Guard? By the way, that would be the FEMA and the National Guard that has just lost ninety percent of its members. You don't have the whole FEMA workforce to go to two disaster areas — you have ten percent of FEMA to cover the *entire* United States.

"Second problem: How in the *Hell* is FEMA going to truck in 18-wheelers full of supplies when the 18-wheelers don't run and the highways are jammed, totally filled, with dead cars?"

"They'll do *something*!" the woman almost shouted, then turned and flounced off.

Eric snorted in disgust and looked left and right at the

people sitting and standing around the patio table. "That woman, people like that, will get you killed. She would have you sit here and starve to death, waiting for help."

"So, you say move out to the county, find a farm or a ranch where someone died from Hexen, and take it over?" asked a man.

"That's exactly what I am saying. How else are you going to eat? Everything in that grocery store comes from fishing, farming, or ranching, and you're not going to do any of those things around here. You can't. It's all concrete and buildings. You don't even have enough yard to plant a decent garden."

"You really think we're on our own? The government isn't going to assist us?" came a question from the group.

"No." Eric answered. "How can it? They don't have the people. This electrical outage, that's just icing on the cake. Even if the government had the people, it doesn't have the ability to do anything. Think about it. Even if they have some trucks that do run, they can't get down the roads because there are literally tens of millions of dead cars jamming the roads bumper to bumper.

"Look at it on a small scale. Suppose you run your own business. You have an 18-wheeler and four men that work for you. Every day, you load this truck and drive to downtown Houston and unload the truck. Easy, right? Now, boom, the truck won't run, the roads are jammed, and you lost all four of your guys. But you still have to get that truckload of stuff downtown! How are you going to do it?" He scanned the crowd and pointed at one. "You, tell us your plan." The man's mouth dropped open and stayed that way. "How about you?" Eric pointed at another. The man shook his head and looked down. Eric turned in his seat and looked at an older woman with a drink in her hand. "Ma'am?"

"We're fucked," she replied immediately, which brought a small ripple of laughter.

"Wait, wait. You're jumping to conclusions here," declared one man. "I'll agree that all of the country was affected by Hexen, but not the electricity. How can you say that?"

"True. I don't know how widespread this electrical outage is, but if it is EMP, then it's a massive area, half the U.S., if not all of it. So the short answer is: I don't think the government is going to *be capable* of coming to your rescue, and I wouldn't risk my life on the hope that it will. I'd rather die on my feet, trying to survive, than on my ass, sitting and waiting for someone to come help me." Eric waved a hand dismissively.

"Wait, what did you say? EMP?"

"Yes, Electro Magnetic Pulse. EMP is caused by a nuclear device deton —"

"A nuclear device? A BOMB?"

"Yeah, a bomb."

"Who? China? Terrorists?"

"I have no idea," Eric replied. "But not a bomb that hits a city. And since Dani and I would have noticed if Houston was nuked, then it had to be a high-altitude explosion, too high to blow up a city. So a device is detonated at a high altitude and it kills unshielded electronics in a wide area. If it's not EMP, then I don't know, but the power grid going down, which could have been done by a hacker, for example, is not going to kill cars and flashlights and cell phones."

"On the one hand, EMP shouldn't be that effective. On the other, no one has really done any large-scale tests of EMP, so maybe this is one of those situations where the reality is different from the theory. Maybe it worked way better than they thought it would. Or maybe there was some new type of EMP."

He thought about it for a moment, and continued "But I don't know of any electrical device that's alive. Anybody? Is any electrical device working?"

"Nothing."

"Not a damned thing."

"No." A couple of people waved dead cell phones that they

were still carrying.

"Well, I don't know what's happening. But we're hitting the road tomorrow, heading home."

"Where are you going?"

He didn't want to get too specific on that answer, so he replied, "I have a place in East Texas, around Tyler. It's 48 acres, not a farm but there are farms and ranches all around it. If my neighbors didn't make it through Hexen, then I need to get back there before their cows all die. I admit I don't know much about ranching but I guess I'll learn."

Eric had to fend off a couple more offers of joining the local militia, even one to head it up, but that was the extent of his worries. As far as Dani was concerned, the main problem was a certain early-thirties blonde named Tanya.

First, the blonde had snubbed her when they were introduced, passing her eyes over Dani briefly, murmuring a "Hmm", and then turning her charm up to eleven when she was introduced to Eric. She had taken his hand and kept hold of it, stepping so close to him they almost touched, and staring deeply into his eyes. Eric had been charming to her, as he was to almost everyone, which Tanya had taken as him responding to her flirting. Tanya's Step #2 now was to mix with the crowd some, supposedly disappointing him when she left, so that he would be so glad to see her when she came back for Step #3. Or he would chase her when she initiated Step #2, which was even better.

He did not chase her. Instead, when the food was ready, he sought out Dani so they could fill their plates and eat together "unless you're tired of me," he commented.

"No," Dani replied, looking at him with a little suspicion. "You're not tired of me, are you?"

"Absolutely not!"

Dani was somewhat reassured by this, but the blonde (she wouldn't even think of her as "Tanya") intimidated her. She was so obviously one of the pretty, popular, and snobbish mean girls that had grown up but never grown out of her high school clique. And she was undeniably pretty, with long blonde hair, green eyes, an upturned nose, and a hot body, tall and thin, well endowed, with a tight ass from serious gym time. She was nicely dressed, with strappy high heels, tight jeans, and a top that showed a good bit of cleavage. The gold chain she wore was long enough to disappear down that cleavage and draw the eye to it.

She's probably closer in age to Eric than I am, Dani thought. *And she's certainly more similar. I'm just a poor kid from a bad part of town whose parents fled the drug violence in Columbia to immigrate to the United States.* That made her think of her deceased parents, and brothers and sister, and she almost sobbed.

After they ate their fill, Eric got pulled into a discussion of what the community should do going forward. A lot of his answers were off the top of his head. He hadn't really thought about it, but it made him realize some things about the new world they had been forced into.

***

Dani drifted into conversations with other women and girls, indulging in a little wine as the night wore on. Maybe more than a little. Somewhere along the way, Tanya decided it was time for Step #3, which should end up with Eric in her bed. Why not? It had worked like a charm plenty of times in the past.

She worked her way into the discussion that Eric was participating in, out on the patio, and started reeling in her fish. Dani stood in the kitchen, glaring daggers at Tanya, who had jumped at the opportunity to move into the just-vacated seat next to Eric. She pulled it closer to him as she sat down, brushing his thigh with her knee. As she talked to him, she leaned in closer and placed her hand on his leg. Dani was furious and also confused. She tried to step back mentally to analyze her emotions.

On the one hand, she was jealous. Highly jealous. She wanted to kill that *puta*. On the other hand, she had to ask herself if she had the right to be jealous. There was nothing between her and Eric, technically speaking. They had never promised anything to each other, had never even kissed or anything beyond some light flirting. They had made no commitments.

But I want him! she thought, realizing that was the first time she had actually admitted it, or maybe the first time she realized it. Just as an experiment, she looked around at all of the men and boys she could see here, and summed it up: *Not a one. There is no one here that I want to be with, but him. I am not even slightly interested or intrigued by anyone else.*

Susan sidled up to Dani about that time and commented in a low voice "You might want to mark your territory," as she inclined her head to indicate Tanya. Fortunately, Dani couldn't hear what Tanya was saying to Eric right then, or she'd have shot her on the spot. Tanya had been telling him how lonely she'd been since her most recent husband died, "lonely" apparently being a flexible term that didn't include the series of men who had occupied her bed for one or more nights. Susan had secretly nicknamed her "Take a number" Tanya.

Tanya stood, hand firmly on Eric's thigh, bending low to give him a good look down her manmade cleavage, and murmured "I have to go freshen up. Don't let anyone take my seat."

In truth, he saw her for the opportunistic, life-sucking gold digger that she was, and was totally disinterested. In other circumstances, he would have gone for it, say as a young Marine, intoxicated and horny for a one-night stand. Now it was a different world, a much more serious one, and he was older and wiser. He might not have specifically thought of Dani at that moment, but people were asking him questions and he didn't have much time to himself for reflection.

Tanya walked past the kitchen to the bathroom. Dani counted to sixty and then walked down the hall after her, fire in her eyes.

Chapter 18

Dani placed herself against the wall directly opposite the bathroom door, and when the door started to open, she launched herself off of the wall, using her arms to push off. Her hiking boot hit the door and shoved it, imparting the full force of her momentum. The wood slammed into Tanya's face with a satisfying thump, causing the blonde to grunt and curse. Round two was a repeat of the first, crashing into her opponent's head since she was bent over. Dani's opponent staggered back to get out of the way in case the door was going to swing again. Her legs hit the tub and she fell into it, smacking the back of her head on the tile wall.

Energized by her success, Dani swung the door open and grabbed the sink with both hands. Using it as leverage, she drove the heel of her boot as hard as she could into the gold digger's face, slamming her head into the tile with a deep boom that seemed to echo throughout the entire house. Tanya's body went limp and slumped over, if not unconscious, then very close, never having seen her attacker. Blood ran from her nose and it looked like it was cocked off to one side, but maybe that was just the flickering candlelight. She might have had a broken finger or two also, since she had had her hands in front of her face, rubbing her injuries from the earlier hits.

Satisfied, the young Latina spun around and walked back into the kitchen. Susan immediately handed her a platter of chunks of cheese with toothpicks. "Could you take these outside?" she asked innocently.

She took the platter, smiled at her, and mouthed "Thank you" on her way out the door. She was offering up snacks to a whole host of witnesses within seconds of the fight, and seemingly innocent, innocent, innocent a few minutes later when the alarm was raised. Two men ended up carrying Tanya to her house, with another couple of people to open doors and administer assistance. Someone asked for volunteers to help keep her awake, since that was what one was supposed to do with concussions.

***

Eric watched them carry her out with no reaction. He didn't have any medical advice that he could offer, and he just really didn't care that she had slipped and hurt herself. As a matter of fact, it saved him from having to fend off her advances. Dani was keeping a close eye on him and was happy that he didn't jump up and rush to Tanya's side. Now she had one more concern. She casually strolled over to Susan to refill her wine glass, took a deep drink for courage, and asked "Do you think I went too far?"

Susan smiled and replied "I think the worst that could happen is that she'll wake up the same bitch as before. Who knows? Maybe she'll turn into a better person."

***

Later on, Eric was ready to go to sleep but Dani, Susan, and three other females were in the living room drinking and talking a mile a minute. Since he was sleeping on the couch, and they were sitting on the couch, he had a dilemma. He stood there long enough for Dani to notice him and the conversation to go down to a dull roar. "I'll go sleep in the guest room, and remember we need to get on the road tomorrow morning." He could tell from the way Dani's chin tilted that she was getting her "don't tell me what to do" defiance cranked up, so he added "Have fun," with a smile and a wave and a quick exit.

He pulled the blanket and a pillow off of the bed and stretched out on the floor. He didn't want to complicate things with Dani right now by being in what was "her" bed. Physically, he wanted her, but he also wanted things to be right with them. He could have lain awake and contemplated the implications and nuances of that, but he had a few beers in him and he fell asleep quickly.

Later on he was awakened by a thump and a muted "Shit", as Dani staggered into the bedroom and bumped into the door. She sat on the bed in a semi-controlled fall and looked around the room, squinting, trying to see in the dark. Her eyes were partially adjusted to the dark since she had had only candle light to see by earlier, and she spotted something on the floor.

"Eric? Izzat you? Why ya on th' floor?" she slurred.

She is thoroughly drunk, he thought. "Just trying to sleep."

"Come up here. Inna bed. Wiff me." She tried to pat the bed beside her seductively a couple of times but her coordination was off and she slapped it hard, WHAP, WHAP.

Oh, no no no no no, drunk and horny, that's not going to be good for anyone, now or in the morning! "Okay, Dani, now that the party's broken up, I can go sleep on the couch." He stood up, grabbed the blanket and pillow, and was going to make another quick escape when he saw that she was flat on her back with her mouth open. Then she started snoring.

Oh, thank God! I dodged that bullet. What an excellent time for her to pass out!

He quietly went out to the living room and found one of the women, actually a teenager, sleeping on the couch. He chose the best piece of carpet he could find, in front of the TV and not in a pathway where he would be stepped on or tripped over, and went back to sleep.

Chapter 19

Eric was up early as usual, stoking a fire in the grill and making coffee. The teen on the couch got up, shyly said "Hi," and skittered out the door. Breakfast was pie and homemade bread with honey. Next was a walk down the street to the student apartments where he had gathered the alcohol the day before. This time he loaded the wheelbarrow up with bottles of water or other non-sugary beverages, ramen noodles, candy bars, and other snacks. He figured the best technique was to start out heavy, with extra packs of water and snack items, to consume at the breaks. The load would get lighter as the day wore on and their energy level dropped. When they were in the more built-up areas, they didn't have to carry as much, since they could easily scavenge from nearby buildings. Now they were going to be out in the woods more and would have to carry everything they needed.

When he got back he took water, coffee, bread, and pie in to Dani's room to get her rousted out of bed. During the night she had crawled under the sheet, including her head, and was still fully dressed. His efforts to wake her were met with moans and groans, especially when he pulled the sheet down enough for the sunlight to hit her eyelids. He finally got her to sit up enough to drink the water. She tried to slide back down into the bed after that but he stopped her.

"Ooooooh, why are you being so mean?" she mumbled.

He laughed. "I'm not being mean. I brought you breakfast in bed, Little Miss Grumpy. How many guys would do that for you?"

She opened her eyes for the first time that morning and looked at him, then took the pie. "Thank you. I feel like shit."

"Eat. You'll feel better when you get something in your tummy." He left her mechanically stuffing forkfuls of pie into her mouth to pack his last-minute items and strap everything on his bike. Since he had replenished his .308 ammunition supply, he left the AR rifle and magazines he had brought as backup. Taking a bottle of water, he went back by Dani's room to check on her. Actually the water was an excuse to make sure she was getting up.

She was combing her long, dark hair and took the water into the bathroom to brush her teeth and wash as much as she could.

They finished packing, said their good-byes to Susan, and made sure she had the "pickup intersection" written down. This was the location near Eric's house that he had sent to his entire phone list a few days ago, before the EMP had happened, and that he had given to the people in Bruce's neighborhood. He told them all that he would come through that intersection every Saturday. Obviously he wasn't going to make it this Saturday, but nobody trying to get to his place would have made good time, either.

Highway 19 was better than 45 had been as far as dead cars, but jammed was jammed. As soon as they got away from Huntsville, which was almost immediately, they were in the woods and back amongst the fields of the dead. Dani caught a whiff and bent down, holding onto the rear view mirror of a car and throwing up everything in her stomach. Eric rushed over and gathered her long hair in his hands so he could hold it up and out of the way. He got a little queasy from the smell and noise Dani was producing but he had a strong stomach and it passed.

When she appeared to be finished, he gave her a bottle of water and a wet bandanna for cleanup. "Oh, shit," she moaned. "That was stupid. I shouldn't have drunk so much."

"It's not a problem. We've had kind of a rough week. Once we get to my house I'm going to have more than a few beers." Dani closed her eyes and shuddered when he mentioned beer.

***

They didn't get far that day. First had been the late start, then Dani was moving slowly. At least they were making some progress. By midafternoon, Eric figured he needed to give Dani a break for the rest of the day. They took a turn off of Highway 19 into what looked like a small subdivision and Eric ranged out ahead, scouting. They could actually ride here, the first relatively open road they'd seen so far. They found an empty house, empty of both the living and the dead, and holed up for the night. The place only had one bed, so Eric offered it to Dani.

When he told her they were stopping for the night she had looked around to gauge the time of day and realized it was early. She looked guilty and asked, "Are you mad at me?"

"No. It's fine. You've been doing a great job. You deserved a little release back there. Tomorrow we need to dig in and get some mileage going. Tonight, let's get a good night's sleep."

After they ate she asked if he had nail clippers and went to work on her nails. She had started out with nice nails, neatly trimmed and buffed and perfectly painted. They were ragged now, the color chipped off, and two of them were broken down into the quick. She cut them all down to nothing, completely functional and nothing more. She held her hands out in front of her, displaying all ten fingers, and sighed.

Am I losing parts of me? she thought. *I loved my nails. I loved my phone. I loved my cute clothes and shoes. All gone now.* Guilt washed over her, guilt that she was placing the loss of possessions above the loss of her family. *I'm not. It's just — does this world have to take everything from me? Can't I keep anything? Who am I going to be?*

Her throat clenched up and tears flooded her eyes. She sniffled some and said "I'm going to sleep. Are we setting a watch?"

"No. I'm just going to block the doors. We both get a full night's sleep."

He threw the couch cushions on the living room floor. The

couch was too small for him. As he tried to go to sleep, scenes from their shootouts came unbidden into his mind. He analyzed his feelings and there was no guilt. Logically, he couldn't see that he did anything wrong. Tactically, he was good. Legally, he thought he was okay, whether a functioning legal system still existed or not. Militarily, well, he had been a trained, paid, professional killer in the Corps, hadn't he? He almost laughed at that. Damned few people, military or police or whatever, actually ever got into a gunfight. And he wasn't carrying out military operations, or chasing criminals, or robbing banks, or anything that should be dangerous. All he was doing was trying to get home. Why was that so freakin' difficult?

Frustrated, he got up and checked on everything, looked out the windows, went to the bathroom and got a drink of water. He looked in on Dani from the hallway. She was snoring quietly. *There's nothing disturbing* her *sleep*, he thought. He lay back down and thought of Dani, but not in a sexual way. Not entirely, anyway.

She was… something. He didn't have words. There wasn't a simple description for her. Obviously hot and smart, but beyond that. Tough? Yeah, definitely. He'd meant what he'd told her: he trusted her in a gunfight more than anyone he knew. Not that he had much experience with gunfights, but trust was the issue, not the number. There was a quote he'd read and he tried to pull it up from memory. It was ancient, from a Greek a couple thousand years or more ago, but it was spot on straight through all of history to now. He was sure he had the numbers wrong, but it went something like "Out of a hundred men in battle, ten shouldn't even be there. Seventy five are just targets. Fourteen are the fighters and will do all of the work. But maybe one will be a true warrior, and he will carry them all." Dany was a warrior. She didn't run or hide or scream or cry or freeze up. She just dropped into some kind of Terminator mode and kicked ass.

He liked to think that he did, too. Things just didn't rattle him. Take a car wreck for example. He had been the passenger in a car that a friend had been driving when they were in high school. There was an accident, and while his friend and another passenger were paralyzed with shock from the crash, he made sure they weren't hurt, checked on the health of the other driver, called the police, and waved at some oncoming traffic to slow down. Dani was the same way. If something happened, she took action.

He didn't think she enjoyed killing people. It was just a chore that sometimes had to be done. Shooting the wounded was merely doing a thorough job of it. It was just business, nothing personal, nothing enjoyable, but nothing to shrink from, either. That very lack of passion one way or the other made her coldly, ruthlessly efficient. She neither hesitated nor paused to savor the experience.

At the same time, she was still a young girl, an untrained civilian, other than what instruction he had provided on their journey. She had been ripped from her innocent little environment, stripped of everything she had and all that she was, and slammed into this new and dangerous world. No wonder people were walking around in shock or committing suicide or going wild. They had gone through the same thing and they couldn't handle it.

He was different. He'd already been stripped of his loved ones before Hexen. His life didn't revolve around social media. He'd always been more interested in the woods than the mall, and in actually talking to someone over email and text. The more he thought about it, the more he had to give her credit for keeping it together.

Unbidden, the term "wife material" floated up into his consciousness. His breath caught, thinking of his beautiful Ashley. He didn't want to think about either of those two subjects right now, so he started to make a mental list of things that he had to do once they got to his house. Of course, that involved Dani, too, and he wondered how to handle the sleeping arrangements. Offer her the guest room? Invite her into his bed?

Frustrated, he tried to blank his mind and then make a different mental list, one of things to do after the house was squared away, whatever that meant. What neighbors had survived? What equipment could be resurrected? What did they have to do to keep cows alive and get crops planted and harvested?

Eventually he dozed off and tossed and turned all night.

Chapter 20

Dani was awake first since she had gone to bed so early. She realized she had been a pain in the ass yesterday, so she decided to get some coffee brewing to start making amends. She opened the garage door manually to get some ventilation and gathered together some scraps of cardboard and wood from all of the junk that packed the garage. Eric had a little camp stove but if they had materials for a fire readily available here they could save the fuel. She found a gas can and poured a little on her scrap pile, then lit it off.

It WHOOSHED into flame and she jumped back. Some flaming droplets hit the floor and she realized that she still had the gas can in her other hand and IT WAS ON FIRE! *SHIT!* She flung it away from her — straight into a pile of cardboard boxes filled with junk that was apparently flammable. Naturally, the can landed upside down so that all of the gasoline could pour out into the rapidly-building conflagration.

OH SHIT! OH SHIT! OH SHIT!

She started for the door to the house, turned back to look at the fire, then ran into the house as fast as she could.

***

Eric had been stirring slowly. His muscles shrieked. Shrieked was the word he decided on, after thinking about it for a while. Screamed, yelled, roared, none of those were right. But shrieked, now that denoted the right, high-pitched intensity. He hadn't been on a bike in better than ten years, and the riding had stressed his muscles in an unusual way. Now, he was violating them every day, pretty much all day long. He started to wonder if he was going to be the one lagging. Dani just seemed to bound along tirelessly, like that pink battery bunny.

Dig in and push through the pain, just like Basic he thought. *Pain is weakness leaving the body and all of that motivational crap.* He almost laughed when he remembered a drawing he had seen that pertained both to his boot camp memories and his present agony on the bike:

Marine Basic Training is easy. It's just like riding a bike. Except the bike is on fire. And you're on fire. And everything is on fire. Because you're in Hell.

He was not going to be delayed by the rain that was drizzling down but he wasn't looking forward to slogging through it, either. However, he came awake and upright quickly when Dani came charging through the door and skidded to a stop.

"FIRE! FIRE! IT'S ON FIRE!" she yelled, pointing at the garage. Eric ran through the kitchen in his bare feet and looked into the garage.

He came walking back and said "Get your stuff packed," matter-of-factly, moving to get his socks and boots on.

"But we need to put it out! Call the —" She stopped as she thought about what she was saying.

"Pack, and get out. That's all we can do."

***

Dani looked around the house, thinking *Aw, damn, I never meant to burn down someone's house!* Dejected, she went back to the bedroom to throw the few items that were out back into her pack. A rumble of thunder alerted her to get her poncho out, too.

On the road, she looked back frequently at the rising column of smoke. Every time, she sent out a mental "I'm sorry."

The good thing about the rain was that it suppressed the flies and the stench of the dead. Other than that, it was fairly miserable. Their lower legs were wet and the ponchos were hot and uncomfortable. It either rained on them and got them wet, or they wore the ponchos which made them sweat so they were wet. At their first break, they took shelter underneath the cargo trailer of an 18-wheeler.

"Are you mad at me?" Dani asked, looking down.

"No, not at all. Why would I be mad at you? I just need to teach you how to start a fire. I mean, a small one. A controllable one." She was still looking down, so he put a finger under her chin and pushed up until her eyes met his. "Really. It's okay. You could burn whole subdivisions down to the ground and it wouldn't affect anybody. It's fine."

She shrugged and looked down again. "And I was hungover yesterday. I slowed us down."

"Sure, but you got up and got on the road. You gutted it out. You're a trooper." She peered up at him through the locks of her hair that were obeying the law of gravity and hanging down. "Cheer up, Miss Grumpy, we're making progress. Speaking of which, let's get back on the road."

***

The rain continued to fall in a slow, sloppy drizzle that was occasionally supplemented with a heavier shower, and they frequently had to don their sunglasses because the sun came blasting through breaks in the clouds, just never over them. That was typical Texas rain. If you were driving, your windshield wipers were on full blast because it was raining so hard, but you had to have sunglasses on because it was so bright just over to the side or in front.

Midmorning they came up on the outskirts of Trinity, a town of a couple thousand or thereabouts, known for having been the site of one of John Wesley Hardin's gunfights. Eric hoped it wouldn't be the site of any more gunfights while they were there.

As they got closer they spotted some type of box that towered over the traffic jam.

"What the hell is that?" Eric queried, squinting. He hadn't brought binoculars or any optics, having had to pare weight where he could. Ounces equal pounds and pounds equal pain. "Either someone had that strapped to the roof of their vehicle, or it's a sentry box. Couldn't be a sniper's nest unless they are the stupidest sniper in the world. If it's a sentry box, they've already seen us. I'm sure they have binoculars, so we'd look more suspicious cutting away than just going right up the middle."

They moved forward more cautiously until they could see that it was a wooden box big enough for a man or two, basically a deer blind that had been placed on the roof of an SUV. The roof was slanted to spill rain off and there were big windows, really just openings where the plywood walls were short enough to not reach the roof, on three sides. And it was occupied.

They also saw some new structures off to the side of the highway, on both sides. Gallows. There were three on each side, double gallows big enough for two people each. They weren't elaborate things with stairs and trapdoors, they were just two simple posts set upright, about eight feet tall, with a crossbar at the top and some other boards at forty-five degree angles for bracing. That meant that the people who were hanged here died of strangulation, not by having their necks broken as is the case with a long drop-style gallows. Their shoes were in the grass near the gallows, where their convulsing bodies, starved of oxygen, had kicked them off.

The gallows had signs accompanying them: "No Looters," "No Trespassing," and more menacingly, "Are You Next?"

The first gallows were full, two bodies each. The next set had one on the west side and two on the east. Dani stopped and stared at that pair, then looked at Eric. "Gangbangers," she said. "Look at the face tattoos." She turned back to them and spat in their direction.

They kept moving and reached an area where the vehicles had been cleared off of the road, starting at the sentry tower and going away from town, to offer a cleared area in front of the sentry. The cars hadn't been moved far, just pushed off into a nearby parking lot and shoved together as close as possible. The burned out husk of one truck remained on the shoulder in the cleared zone, victim of an engine fire that had burned until it ran out of things to burn and taken out all of the tires.

As they approached the cleared area, Eric told Dani to hang back a couple of rows with the bikes. He walked slowly into the zone a few feet, hands up and empty. He had noted two men to each side of the one in the box. It went without saying that all were armed, and none looked happy to be out in the rain.

Chapter 21

"Morning," Eric called to them across the hundred feet of cleared road. "I know guard duty in the rain sucks. Been there, done that."

"Morning, young feller," a skinny gray-bearded man replied. "If you've been on guard duty, you must be ex-military."

"Well, you know us arrogant Marines. We don't say 'former' or 'ex'." As he spoke, Eric slowly lowered his hands to push up his poncho and sleeve to reveal the Marine Corps emblem tattooed to his forearm. He couldn't quite make out what was embroidered on Gray-Beard's ball cap. Gray-Beard had a poncho on, too, and it covered most of the cap, but it was black with gold and red and the emblem of some service in the middle.

"Hah!" Gray-Beard laughed. "I was in the Army six years before I learned that 'fucking Marine' was two words." Then he turned serious again. "Who's that with you?" He nodded back beyond Eric.

"I've got a young lady with me. We're going to my place in East Texas. We just want to pass through. We don't need anything, don't want to stop, just passing through."

"How about you bring her up here."

Eric walked back to Dani and together they pushed their bikes into the cleared area until Gray-Beard stopped them. No one was aiming a weapon at them but Eric was uneasy. There was no cover available so they were basically defenseless.

"Young lady, what's your name?" Gray-Beard asked.

She drew herself up, looked the man in the eye, and replied "Daniela Angelina Ruiz Vasquez."

"That's a beautiful name."

"Thank you."

"Are you related to this man?" he nodded at Eric.

"No. We've been traveling together for a few days, ever since he saved my life. He killed four gangstas that were going to rape me." Eric thought she said that with some pride, but he wasn't sure.

"Really?" He looked at Eric with a heightened degree of respect. "That's God's honest work. Lord knows we've had enough trouble from that type." He looked back at Dani. "Are you going with him because you want to? You're not going against your will, are you?"

"No, I want to go. If he was kidnapping me, I don't think he'd give me guns and teach me to shoot, do you?" She smiled and tilted her head to the side a little. Eric was definitely getting the impression that Dani was proud that someone would do those things for her. She was bragging!

Gray-Beard smiled back. "Okay, one final question. How old are you?"

"I'm 21."

"All right, that's all I have. I'm going to pass you through town with no escort. That means I'm trusting you. Follow me and I'll give you a pass." He turned to speak to the man in the sentry box. "Fred, get out of there and come down for some coffee. Chris, take a shift upstairs."

As Dani and Eric moved up they saw that immediately behind the sentry box was another, much smaller clearing, only four cars moved away. This clearing held a large tent that was obviously the command post for this checkpoint. Before they could enter, there was a cry, then a meaty thud. Fred had slipped getting down from the sentry box, skidded off of the wet metal roof of the SUV, and slammed into the pavement below. It knocked the wind out of him, but when he got his breath, the pain from his broken leg made him yell. "God —" he started, then stopped, not wanting to take the Lord's name in vain. He clenched his teeth, breathing in and out rapidly between them, then cried "SHIT!"

Everyone in earshot ran to the scene, including Eric and Dani. Chris was the first, since Fred had fallen right at his feet.

He bent and tried to roll Fred's pants leg up to look at the injury. "STOP! Stop! Don't do that!" Fred gasped.

"Hold everything. I have scissors," Eric commanded. He had a first aid pouch on his belt and he had a pair of medical scissors out in a flash. He bent and gently cut away Fred's pants leg up past the wound, which turned out to be a compound fracture, with the bone protruding through the skin, bleeding profusely. Eric pulled a gauze bandage from his kit and placed it over the wound, applying pressure. He turned to Gray-Beard.

"Do you have any medical people?" he asked.

Gray-Beard was looking goggle-eyed at the injured man and was unresponsive.

Eric looked at a teenaged boy, probably no more than twelve years old, and asked "Are you a runner? Can you go get a doctor, nurse, vet, some type of medical personnel."

"Yes, Sir!" The boy ran to a bike parked nearby, whipped a plastic bag off of the seat, and pedaled madly away.

Eric looked at another teenaged boy. "You, come here and apply pressure to this wound." He showed him how to do so, with enough pressure to stop the bleeding but not so much as to hurt the patient.

Eric turned to look at the other man, searching his memory for his name for a second until he came up with it. "Chris, I need some rope or something to strap one leg to the other and a piece of plywood or something to go under his legs."

"You got it!" Chris was back almost immediately. He had some rope and there was a piece of plywood nearby from the construction of the sentry box. Eric tied Fred's legs together, slid the plywood under both legs, and then tied the plywood to his legs as best he could, since it was bigger than he would have liked.

"Chris, you are going to take that shoulder. I will take this one. You —" his head swiveled like a tank turret and fixed Gray-Beard with his gaze"— will take his legs but use your hands on that plywood, not on his legs. Dani, hold the tent flap open for us."

Everyone jumped at Eric's orders, and they got Fred into the tent and onto a camp cot, not the best thing for an injured man but better than lying on the wet pavement in the rain. Eric saw a blanket nearby and covered him, except for the injury, to treat him for shock.

"That's about all I can do," he told Gray-Beard.

"I... I just froze up," Gray-Beard murmured. "I didn't know what to do. I never had medical training like you did."

"It's fine." In truth, Eric wanted to bitch-slap him for being incompetent. "You were going to give us a pass."

"And is there a Catholic church in town?" interjected Dani. As it turned out, there was one on their route, not even a one block deviation required.

***

Once out of earshot of the checkpoint, Dani turned to Eric with a big smile and said "That was amazing! You just stepped in there and took charge! 'You — do this! You — do that!' and they were all like 'Yes, SIR'! And they were all things that needed to be done. Not arbitrary or anything. Like in school when they — I mean back in high school — when they just tell you to do something and there's no reason for it."

He laughed. "That was just the crusty old Marine NCO in me coming out. Automatic response to a situation."

"Encee — something? What did you say?"

"NCO. Non-Commissioned Officer. It means a corporal or sergeant. Then 'staff NCO" means a staff sergeant, gunnery sergeant, a higher rank sergeant."

"You must have been a great NCO. Those other guys were just standing around watching that one bleed." As they continued, she thought *Is there a bad side to this guy? Everything is just so perf*— Then a horrible thought struck her that made her jaw drop. *Is he gay? Is that why he hasn't tried to get into my pants?*

She was so shocked by the thought that she turned to stare at him, as if that would tell her his sexual orientation. Fortunately he was a little ahead of her and didn't see her stare. Frantically, Dani began running through all of their interactions, everything he had said and done, looking for some indication of his sexuality. *That was a flirt, and that, and that other time, but just a little. And he did hold my hand at Academy but that was just for show. He could be gay and still have done all of those. Oh, but he was married. Then why hasn't he hit on me? Maybe he was married and figured out he was really gay. That's happened before.*

Maybe he just doesn't like me.
Shit!

Chapter 22

Her mind was still running hot when they came to the church. There was a covered walkway that would keep rain off of Eric as he waited outside with their stuff. He had declined earlier to go in, but Dani tried again. "Are you sure you don't want to go in? It's okay, we don't do anything weird."

"Somebody's got to stay with the bikes and gear. No way I'm leaving this stuff out here unguarded."

Dani accepted the logic of that, and left her weapons with Eric.

With time to kill, he checked over everything, just making sure all was in good shape. He found the red-handled knife for Dani that he had packed away and thought tonight might be a good time to give it to her. She seemed to need some cheering up after burning the house down.

Eric didn't know if there was a mass going on or what, since it was Monday, but a few people wandered in and out of the church, and eventually Dani came out. She was smiling and seemed more at peace. He was surprised when she walked straight up to him and hugged him. He responded but was hampered by his battle gear. He didn't want to crush her against magazine pouches and other paraphernalia and hurt her.

She laid her head on his shoulders for a few moments, hugging his neck, and then raised up. She was so close their noses were almost touching, breathing each other's air, and Eric's male hormones went from zero to full throttle in about 0.42 seconds. His hand on the small of her back slipped a few inches closer to her ass, and he moved his lips towards hers, going for the kiss. He could almost taste the kiss already, pressing his lips against her soft, full lips, their tongues playing with each other, hugging her closely to him, running his fingers through her long, dark hair.

She let his lips get within millimeters before she loosened her hug and stepped back. Her eyes were shining. "I prayed for my family and for your friends in Katy that you were staying with," she said. "And I prayed for us. For safety on our trip."

"That's a good thing," he managed to say, when he wanted to say "What the hell was that? You just got me all hot and bothered and then you back off?" He could just imagine kissing her, wet and passionate, having her naked, taut, smoking hot body pressed against his in a nice, soft bed, with his hand on her cute little ass while he — *STOP, Stop, stop, it might happen but it's not happening right now, so calm down. You're just getting yourself all worked up for nothing. And if this raging hard-on doesn't calm down in a minute or two I'm going to have to rearrange things down there because it's uncomfortable.*

***

Dani turned away from him to get on her bike and smiled widely, ear to ear. *Not gay! Not gay! Not gay!* She almost jumped for joy but that would be too obvious. *I'm sorry to tease him like that, but I had to know. I'll make it up to him later. With interest. Definitely with interest.* She started to think about the two of them together in bed, locked in a passionate embrace, a deep French kiss, his strong arms like steel bands around her, while his rock-hard — *calm down, chica, calm down, you haven't had a decent bath in days. You probably smell like a goat. He doesn't want that, not for your first time together. When we get to his place. That should be the right time.*

Aroused but trying to cool down, they hit the road. Dani was smiling from ear to ear and happy. Eric was grumpy and frustrated.

There was another checkpoint on the way out of town, same setup with the deer blind on top of a convenient SUV, and a few gallows with a couple of bodies swinging in the breeze and dripping rain. Apparently the heaviest scumbag traffic was on the other side of town.

The traffic jam was better along this stretch of highway. Not clear, but better. Texas State Highway 19 is two lanes plus generous paved shoulders, with nice, wide grassy areas beyond that in most places. Traffic could more easily flow around any obstruction like the inevitable broken-down vehicle. Also, as they got further away from Houston, the traffic had other choices, other routes. The cars were spread out more so the going was easier.

"Tell me something," Dani said when they could be reasonably certain of riding side by side. "Teach me some Marine stuff."

"First off, forget everything that Hollywood — no, wait — *remember* everything that Hollywood does, and know that it's wrong. You can't stab someone and they fall over dead, for example. Even if a major artery is severed, they may have twenty or thirty seconds to fight back, and they can kill you in that time. Gunshots, same thing, so you are doing the right thing when you shoot the wounded. You can't really shoot to wound someone. If you hit them in the leg, there's an artery there and they may bleed to death. You can't shoot them in the shoulder or arm without the risk of crippling that arm for life and maybe killing them. Hit someone with a hammer, they may turn around and kick your ass, so you have to hit hard and often until they're down. Also, you knock someone out, they may go into a coma or die of concussion, or have headaches and not be able to walk for months or something like that. Gas tanks don't blow up if you shoot them. They just leak. It may take a couple of minutes to strangle or drown someone, not ten seconds."

"If you have a choice between a pistol and a rifle, a rifle is considerably more powerful. This rifle I'm carrying is a .308. The Europeans call it a 7.62 by 51 millimeter. It is three times as powerful as a .44 Magnum. It is more powerful at five hundred yards — that's over a quarter mile — than a .44 Magnum is at one inch. At a good bit more than half a mile, it's more powerful than a nine millimeter at one inch. The rifle you're carrying is a .223, or 5.56 by 45 millimeter. It's, oh, at least twice as powerful as a nine millimeter."

He talked more about guns after that and they roughed out a list of things that Dani would need to know, like familiarization with different types of firearms, some Krav Maga hand to hand fighting techniques, and field expedient explosives and incendiaries.

***

They made it to the south side of Crockett, the longest stretch they had made on the trip. Right at the intersection of 19 and State Highway Loop 304 they found a nice brick office building. They checked the doors and ended up jimmying a side door without too much difficulty.

"This used to be Angelina Community College, Miss Daniela Angelina" Eric commented.

Dani smiled at him. "Good job, remembering my name!" Then she thought *Oh crap, what if he's all hot and bothered from earlier and wants to bed me tonight? I need to put him off.*

Chapter 23

They took a quick tour of the facility and selected a room to bunk in, one of the offices. Dani went to the women's restroom and then commented "We need to find a drug store or grocery store tomorrow."

"What do you need?" he asked.

"Women things. Monthly things." That always made guys stop asking questions.

"Oh, God. Not a Wal-Mart. I had to shoot my way out of the last two Wal-Marts I was in. Well, out of one and into the other, but still."

***

They ate what canned goods they had, and Eric figured that they had to scrounge for food tomorrow anyway. He made a mental note to try to find a place out in the country to hole up in next time so that he could try to shoot a hog at dusk. They couldn't preserve the food, but they could get one good meal out of it anyway.

"Hey, I have a present for you," he told Dani, pulling out the knife. "This is a custom, handmade thing. It's a great length for an all-around utility knife."

She was surprised that he had a gift for her, and she loved the gift itself. She looked at the red-and-gold swirling pattern of the grips and said "This is beautiful! This is bad-ass. It fits my hand perfectly!" She carefully put the knife down and hugged him. *Oops! Don't get things cranked up*, she thought. She kissed him on the cheek and separated quickly. "I'm sure you can teach me how to use this."

"Sure" he replied, thinking that she was the only one in the room that had killed someone with a knife. "There are two ways to kill someone with a knife, and four ways you can grip a knife. The two ways to kill are severance of the spinal column, which takes a heavy blade like a machete or a sword, and blood loss. You have to make them bleed so much that they pass out and then bleed to death."

"Now, how do you make someone bleed to death? The most efficient way is to cut their throat, specifically the arteries in the neck area. These arteries supply blood to the brain, so if you cut that off they'll go down very quickly, a matter of seconds. The problem is, if you're fighting someone, they are going to protect themselves, so you may have to just start hacking."

"Someone fighting you is probably going to have their arms out, right? So go for those arms. Slash their wrists. If you cut the tendons, they'll lose control of their fingers and won't be able to fight you. Same thing if they try to kick you. The eyes are a great target, or cut their forehead and blood will flow down into their eyes and blind them. Any part of their body that they place near you, stab or slash it. Just chop them down like an oak tree. When we get to my house I can show you some charts that tell where the arteries are."

He went on to show her the fencer, reverse fencer, hammer, and icepick grips and the pros and cons of each.

After that they chatted a little and then lay down to sleep, near each other but more than arm's length away. They had secured the outside doors and then the office door, and felt safer overall being further away from the big city.

"What do you think happened?" Dani asked. Eric didn't answer for a few moments, gathering his thoughts. She almost figured he was asleep when he answered.

"Let's start with what we know. Just the facts, ma'am. Avian flu starts in China, mainly, or elsewhere in Asia. Some cases have been in the Middle East. It seems to crop up periodically, infect a few dozen or a few hundred people, kill over half of them, something like sixty percent, and then disappear. Problem is, it mutates, so every time it comes back, it's different. Even if they were to develop a vaccine one year, that doesn't mean that vaccine is going to work the next year. The flu may have mutated such that it is not affected by the vaccine.

"The other important thing to know is that the disease is almost always transmitted from animal to human. There are only rare instances of human to human infection. That's facts, or as near as I know. I'm not an expert. I think it's obvious that Hexen mutated so that it spread easily from human to human, and it is also more deadly. It seems the fatality rate or whatever you call it is more like eighty-five or ninety percent. Or maybe less. I don't know. It may only be the sixty percent and the other missing people just fled. It certainly spread more easily. There's no disputing that. I think the only question is whether it mutated by itself or was engineered."

"Engineered? You mean like the government tried to weaponize it?"

"Yeah. Just think, if you could vaccinate all of your people and then release a flu and kill everyone else… well, you've just won a world war. The world is yours for the taking."

"Shit. Is that what happened? We're going to be invaded?" Dani sat up and looked in Eric's direction, but neither could see the other in the dark.

"I have no idea. I hope that the entire world is in the same condition as the U.S. That may be bad to say, wishing people dead, but if we're hit this badly, I hope every other country is hit just as hard."

"We won't even know until the Chinese tanks come over the horizon, will we?"

"Dani, don't waste time worrying about it. We can't do anything about it even if we knew that they were coming. Which I doubt they are. I think this is natural. Remember, all of the reports about the flu started in China. Their people were dying first."

They lay there in silence for a minute before Eric started up again. "The second thing is the EMP. Starting with facts again: we found out in the early '60's that EMP existed. We were testing nuclear weapons in the Pacific Ocean, high altitude explosions, and they blew out electronic equipment in Hawaii, nine hundred miles away. Now, beyond that, I am not aware of any large-scale EMP testing, but again, I'm not an expert. There may have been some highly classified tests. I do remember reading that two devices could shut down all of the electronics in the U.S. A lot of what I've read about EMP said that it's fairly easy to shield equipment from the effects but you have to realize that these were written by people who had zero knowledge of what the military was doing. You have to think that they've had almost sixty years to come up with an EMP weapon that was more effective than the 1960's version."

"Also, we have to consider that the EMP was natural. Solar flares can do the same thing. Sometime in the 19th century, I don't remember when, there was a period of intense solar flare activity and it blew out the telegraph lines. But I have to think that it would be too coincidental that the sun hit us at the same time that Hexen hit us."

"You're saying that someone did slam us with an EMP bomb?"

"It's possible that China or Russia hit us with an EMP because they thought we were responsible for an attack on them using Hexen. Or maybe we used an EMP on them and it was a lot more powerful than we thought, and knocked out everyone's electronics. We just don't have enough information. Hexen either came about naturally or it was engineered. If it was engineered, then it could have been an attack or it escaped from the lab. Same thing for the EMP, pretty much. Could have been natural. Could have been an attack. Could have been something that got out of hand."

"Thanks for clearing up everything," Dani commented dryly, and Eric laughed.

She mulled things over for a minute and then spoke up. "It doesn't really matter at this point if we know what happened or not. What matters is that we have to take measures to survive. Food and clean water is obviously going to be top priority. And food means raising cows, chickens, pigs, and whatever and farming crops. And hunting and fishing."

"Sanitation is very important to prevent disease. Defense is a top priority or you could lose everything else," Eric threw in some suggestions. "Everyone is going to have to be trained and have weapons close at hand if they need to rush in to defend the community."

They were both tired and the conversation wound down pretty quickly after that. Eric fell asleep first. If Dani was on her period, nothing was going to happen during the rest of the trip at least, so he tried to just turn off any thoughts in that direction.

Dani lay awake longer. She thought about Eric and the weird relationship they had been thrown into. It was so wild, so completely off the charts that she could have never imagined it. They would have never met had the world not ended. He would have visited his friends and then gone back to his place and lived his life. She would have completed high school and college and created her life. Less than two weeks ago she had been a high school student, getting good grades but also concerned with clothes and nail polish and boys. Now she was carrying a rifle and pistol and knives and magazines full of ammunition, all day long, and sleeping with them all within reach. She *owned* the rifle and pistol and knives and magazines. They belonged to her. She was a warrior. That was a weird realization to get her mind around.

And she had killed men. *Killed men.* She rolled that thought around in her mind for a bit, like swirling wine around to get a good whiff and a good taste. That was fairly earth-moving. She. Had. Killed. Men. They deserved it, of that she had no doubt. They were rapists and murderers and thieves. She was not bothered by killing them, just kind of amazed that she had actually done it. It had been necessary and she had risen to the task, not shying away from her duty.

Her duty? Yes, it was, now that she thought about it. It

should be everyone's duty to fight evil whenever and wherever they found it. She had been confronted with the situations and she had handled them. She felt a glow of pride in herself.

How many men had she killed? The ones in the hallway were unknown. She had fired thirty one rounds through a wall into what she estimated was the mass of them, but Eric was also shooting into them. Who knew who had killed a particular one? She could say she had delivered the final shot to at least one wounded man. Certainly the one that had popped out of the office in front of her. Certainly the one she had killed with the knife. She had been bathed in his blood. Certainly the three at the Sam Houston statue. Certainly the would-be kidnapper that she had filled with lead in a rage. And she had yelled at poor Eric after that, for something he had no part of, other than being male. She had apologized later, but she'd make that up to him, too. So she had undoubtedly killed seven men by herself and had shot at five others who ended up dead by either her or Eric's hand. She was good with that.

As far as everything else, she was rising to the challenge, with, admittedly, some stumbles along the way. She had drunk too much at the cookout and been badly hungover the next day. She had started the fire that burned down the house. She resolved to do better. On the good side, she hadn't fallen into a fetal position because her phone and pretty much everything else had stopped working. Her entire family had died and she had not become catatonic. She didn't complain all day long because they were wet from the rain. She was being strong. She was trying very hard to be brave.

What would the future bring? On the one hand, she wanted to ask Eric about his plans. The earlier conversation about food and clean water and sanitation had been in general terms. She had some more specific ideas for them. So far everything had been focused on just getting to his place. That should only take another couple of days. What happened after that? On the other hand, she didn't want him to think about it too much, and decide that he had better options for a partner (girlfriend?

wife?) than her. Once again, she must do better so that she was the best option.

She knew of one thing that would help, once they got to his place and she had a nice bath. And he took a bath, too, of course. And shaved. She smiled and saved that thought for later.

Having thought that through, she allowed herself to fall asleep, imagining Eric spooning her, snuggled tightly against her, one heavy arm thrown over her protectively.

Chapter 24

It rained through most of the night and was still raining the next morning. They started off in dry clothing that was soon wet and made their way around Loop 304. They spotted a Wal-Mart and stopped and stared at it.

Dani felt bad about deceiving Eric, but if she didn't need feminine products now, she was going to in another two weeks.

"Let's go a quarter-mile and see what else is available. We'll come back if we don't see anything," Eric grumbled. About a quarter mile later, he almost jumped with joy when he saw a grocery store sign. There was a large foyer where the grocery carts were stored. Dani worked her way back behind them and they moved the bikes in between baskets to hide them. She would stay for now while he scouted.

With no lights and an overcast sky, it was dark inside. Eric stopped frequently and listened. He made a circuit of the store and it seemed they were alone. Of course, the store had been stripped. It was mainly empty shelves, glass containers that had broken when people were frantically pulling things off shelves, and the stench of rotting meat and fish from those departments. Flies accompanied the stench, as they seemed to do everywhere now.

Eric came back and got Dani out of her hideout. Then went in with him in the lead, her behind, watching their backs. At the appropriate aisle, there were still some boxes on the shelves, but Dani had to fire off a lighter to see. She wasn't happy with the results, so they grabbed the bikes and pushed them into the warehouse space and went through the same drill. It was more difficult to find what they wanted, but more fruitful. Most people seemed to think of a store as only the retail space up front. They never even considered the larger warehouse that was right behind retail. Some had, and there were significant stocks missing, but Dani found what she wanted, and Eric even found some more canned meat, cheese, pasta, and crackers.

They had filled water bottles from the break room water dispenser at the college, so they were really starting off heavy. The route was Loop 304 to SH-21 to Alto. The highway was fairly clear. Most of the traffic issues had been caused when the electricity died and speeding cars and trucks suddenly had no lights and the power steering and brakes became non-power. People had gone into ditches and trees but at least those were out of the roadway. The ones that had stopped in the lanes of traffic were spread out enough that Dani and Eric could ride around them, zigging over into the oncoming lane and then zagging back when they came up on a stopped vehicle in that lane.

The weather was the real problem with travel. It started raining much harder than previously. The ponchos and hats protected their upper bodies and heads but the ponchos flew up if the wind blew or if they made some speed, and the tires kicked up sprays of water that soaked their legs. The raindrops were actually bouncing up off of their shoulders and hitting them in the face, then dripping down to wet their shirts. They turned off on an FM, which is a Farm-to-Market road, and went down it for a while before they saw a house. An older woman was sitting in a carport, smoking and drinking bourbon.

As they rode closer, Eric told Dani to stop and have her rifle ready, then he went to the foot of the woman's driveway. He waved at her and called, "Good afternoon."

"What's good about it?" came the gravel-voiced reply.

"We're all alive and it's a beautiful day if you're a duck," he replied, holding out a hand, palm up, to catch some of the raindrops that were falling.

The woman snorted. "I'm almost out of food and insulin. I'm diabetic, so *I* don't have much longer to live."

"We might be able to help you on the food. Can we talk?"

"Come on up. I got nothing to steal and you're not gonna rape me when you got that cute little thing with you."

Eric dismounted his bike and walked it up the woman's short driveway and waved Dani in when he saw she didn't have any weapons. Her name was Lori.

After a little get-acquainted talk, Eric got down to business. "We have some food with us, but I'd really like to shoot a hog or a cow or something and get some fresh meat. We just want a couple of meals and then you can have the rest. What we need is a place to stay tonight and dry out our clothes. Everything we have is wet to some degree. We can sleep on the floor or whatever."

Lori nodded and started to say "I can do that —" when Dani interrupted: "What about the diabetes? Do you use insulin? Is there any place around here we can get insulin?"

"Yeah, there's a man that lives down that way about a mile and a half," Lori indicated the direction with her head. "I couldn't make it there and back myself." She moved her cane back and forth to call attention to it. It was an impressive affair, with a square plate at the bottom with a rubber foot protruding from each corner. "He's a diabetic, too. I doubt he survived. Hell, I was surprised he was alive every time I saw him!" She chuckled at her joke and then descended into a rheumy cough.

They got a better description of where the man lived, hung their clothing from yesterday up to dry in Lori's house, and got on the road. "The sooner we leave, the sooner we can get back." Dani rode her bike but Eric pushed a wheelbarrow.

The man's house was easy to find, and they knocked and called his name for a while before Eric went at the door with his pry bar. He donned a bandanna first since he knew the smell would probably hit him as soon as he popped the back door, and it did. He went around the house, breaking windows that were painted shut and opening the front door, too, letting the breeze blow through the house to air it out. They didn't wait too long, since they had to stand in the rain and they were already wet. After a few minutes, Eric looked at Dani, she nodded, and they went in.

The man was in the bedroom and Eric went by the bed trying not to look at the body. He hit the bathroom and found the insulin under the sink. He checked the medicine cabinet and raked the dozen prescription bottles into his pack. He didn't bother to read the labels since he wouldn't know what he was reading anyway. He wasn't interested in anything else in the house so he intended to head for the kitchen, where Dani was foraging. She was going for the usual: canned meat, crackers, candy bars, and any other portable, non-refrigerated foods. What stopped him was a random glance into the open bedroom closet. There was a rifle leaning in the corner of the closet, which would have been completely unremarkable except for the big can at the end of the barrel. Eric stopped abruptly as soon as he saw it, snatched it up, and fled the bedroom, closing the door behind him.

He checked on Dani and helped her finish in the kitchen, then they went out the back. Outside, he held out the rifle to take a better look at it. It was a Ruger American Predator in 6.5mm Creedmoor, a bolt action with a twenty-two inch, heavier tapered contour barrel and a Leupold scope. The really interesting thing was the suppressor screwed onto the end of the barrel. Eric's rifle had the threads but not the suppressor, but he was willing to bet this suppressor would work on his.

A suppressor is a can with baffles that reduces the sound of the rifle shot. Also known as a silencer, it doesn't really silence. It will only bring the blast of a high-powered rifle down a notch or two, and it does nothing to stop the sonic boom that a bullet makes. For all that it does not do, a suppressor does make it more pleasant to shoot by cutting down the muzzle blast and reduces the distance at which a shot may be heard. They are legal to own in some jurisdictions, after going through a lengthy licensing process with the federal government. Eric wasn't worried about the feds at this point.

"Did you find a new toy?" Dani asked, teasingly, boys and

their toys and all of that.

"I have one like this. I think this one is yours." He handed it to her. "I'm going to go back in and look for ammo." Now Dani was interested in the rifle, and she was looking through the scope at things in the distance when Eric came back out of the house with four boxes of ammo in hand.

"It's heavy," she said.

"Yeah, I guess with the scope and can it's nine or ten pounds. I'll strap it to my handlebars, but you have to carry the ammo." He walked to the back fence and gazed at a cow that looked at him suspiciously. Slowly, so as not to spook it, he eased his rifle out from under his poncho and into position, aimed, and fired a shot between the cow's eyes. It fell over on its side, killed instantly. Then Eric got to work with his knife. He had never butchered a cow before, and was not quite sure what cut was where. The closest he knew was that if you rode a cow like a horse, then you would be sitting on the ribs. Between the ribs and the rump was the loin, which was where the T-bone, filet mignon, porterhouse, and all of the good cuts were located. He didn't know anything more specific, so he just hacked away and loaded up the wheelbarrow with a generous quantity of beef. He felt bad about killing a whole cow just for three people, but he really needed some meat that hadn't spent months in a can.

Lori cried and hugged them both when Dani presented her with the insulin.

Eric dragged her grill under the carport, cleaned the ashes out, and managed to get a fire going. She had a wood burning fireplace, so there was some dry firewood in the house. He placed wet firewood near the fire so it would dry out, and started heating pots of water for baths. It looked like the rest of the day might not be so bad.

Lori bathed first, at their insistence, then Dani, then Eric. As he came out of the house afterwards, he saw the girls in the carport, Dani in a chair holding a mirror in front of her and Lori behind her holding another mirror. Dark hair lay on the concrete. A lot of dark hair. Dani turned to face him directly and asked "What do you think?"

"I liked it long," he said, realizing even as he said it that it was the wrong thing to say. The look on Lori's face that said *Don't screw this up* gave him a hint, too. "But, you know," he continued with only a slight pause, "I think I really like it like this."

He made a "turn around" motion with a finger and Dani stood and pivoted. Her hair was six or eight inches shorter and now only brushed her shoulders. In the front, it had been all the same length and just fell to the sides and down her back. Now the hair framed her face better and was less likely to blow into her face and obstruct her vision. The cut was much better suited to their current situation, easier to maintain and less likely to tangle. "Nice! I do like it better this way." That earned him a smile from Dani. He looked at Lori. "And good job cutting her hair."

Dani sat back down and stared into the mirror. *Not a loss,* she thought. *My family, yes, of course that is a loss I will never get over. But the clothes, the phone, the nails, the hair — no. It's an adaptation. All of those things were for that other world. They don't belong here in this one. In* my *world. I will make it mine!*

A plan was forming in her mind. She didn't want to voice it yet. She needed to get to Eric's place and see the situation, and she needed to see how their relationship would go. So far, he seemed like a great guy. He put her comfort over his, he wasn't forcing himself on her, and he respected her. He was smart and confident and well-versed in the ways of war. As long as he didn't get drunk and beat her… but that would only happen once.

This is an opportunity for the survivors. For me. For us. With ninety percent of the people gone, that means ninety percent of everything is just sitting there, waiting to be taken, or taken over. Taken over by people who know how to fight, if needed. People who are kind and helpful to their own, and brutal to their opponents. People who will shoot the enemy wounded in the head but feed and protect an orphaned child. We won't merely survive, we will take over!

She jumped when Lori said her name. "Are you all right, girl? You were breathing pretty hard and looking into the mirror like you were going to bite it."

"No, just a lot of things to think about."

Lori cut her eyes towards Eric, feeding the fire in the grill with fresh wood, and back at Dani, who nodded and replied "Partly." She had a faraway look in her eyes and it had nothing to do with romance.

***

The grill was big enough that Eric could have a fire going on one end and drag red-hot coals down to the other end to cook with. He had done some better carving of the meat in the kitchen and now had something that resembled filet mignon steaks.

As the steaks started to cook, the local dogs began to gather, drawn by the smell. Dogs had been present throughout their entire journey, frequently barking at them, but never offering any real threat. They had never felt like they had any food to spare, so none had adopted them, although some had walked along with them for a while. Eric knew that dogs would probably be a threat in the future as they reverted to the wild, and rabies would become more of a danger. He threw some of the more fatty pieces on the grill for the dogs and a pot of green beans for the side dish.

He had thought about getting a dog when he moved into the house on the land and just hadn't gotten around to it yet. Now he wished he had, but he could probably have his pick of any dog he wanted without much effort now. Mentally he started assembling a pack. Maybe a smaller house dog, but nothing too small, no rat-dogs. Or maybe not, go with all big dogs, Dobermans, German Shepherds, like that. A couple of females and four or five big males.

They went inside to eat since otherwise they'd have been mobbed by dogs begging for scraps, but Eric came out afterwards, opened the grill, and tossed nice fresh pieces to the pack. Afterwards he sat down and the dogs crowded around him for rubs and scratches, and he threw some sticks for them to retrieve. When he went in for the night he figured they'd either stick around or they wouldn't, and follow them back to his place or he'd find some others. That should be easy. He wouldn't be at all surprised if dogs outnumbered humans, now.

When Eric wanted to go to bed, the girls were still talking, so Dani insisted he take the bed and she'd sleep on the couch. Once he got the door closed, Lori asked in a quiet voice "Y'all aren't sleeping together?"

"Soon," Dani replied. "We ought to be at his place tomorrow."

"Don't let that one get away. That's a *really* good man."

Chapter 25

They started out the next morning after a steak breakfast. Some of the dogs were still around and followed them for a while, but eventually all of them peeled off to investigate something in the woods and never followed, or never caught up if they did.

In Alto they turned onto Interstate 69 North, seeing some people but no one threatening, and now that they were this close to his house, Eric had no inclination to stop to chat. The geography had been getting more interesting. In Houston and for many miles north, the land is flat, pool table flat. The view from a high floor in a Houston-area office building will show a horizon that is low and level in every direction. The only thing sticking up from all of that flatness is manmade. Out of Crockett the land had been going more and more to low rolling hills. Now that they were further north, the hills were getting higher. They had to run through the gears to get up some of them, but could coast down the reverse slope. Fortunately, the cars along here were few. Alto was apparently not a big destination for people fleeing Dallas-Fort Worth, and too far from Houston for any refugees to flood.

Eric, in the lead, crested one hill and got down on the brakes. At the bottom of the hill were three guys working on a truck. It was an older model truck, with no computers or electronics, and it would almost start. It probably only needed some small part to be replaced or rewired and it would be good to go.

Unfortunately, the brakes on Eric's bike made a high-pitched squeal that the three guys heard. Fortunately, they didn't pull guns and open fire, just stood up from bending over the hood and looked.

Eric waved at the men in a friendly manner and turned to Dani and said "Bounding overwatch. Let me get to the top of the next hill, count to sixty, and then just ride past those guys. If we get split up, go back about a mile and find a position where you can watch the road. I'll come back but it may take some time."

Bounding overwatch is a technique that the military uses to advance over potentially hostile territory. Teams A and B start at the same place. Team A will take up a defensive position behind cover, ready their weapons, and then scan for the enemy. Team B will then move forward quickly to a defensive position. Then they will scan for the enemy while Team A advances past Team B to a new defensive position further forward. They continue to leapfrog forward as needed. Dani had been taught the technique by Eric and they had practiced it briefly as they traveled, so she just nodded, took up a position in the trees and brush on the side of the road, and readied her rifle.

While she did that, Eric dismounted and walked his bike down the hill towards the men. "Hey, sounds like y'all almost have that thing started!" he grinned widely, wanting to seem as friendly as possible while watching them closely. He was on foot because he didn't want to try to dodge bullets on a bike. He could move and seek cover much better on foot.

"Mornin'," said the oldest of the three. He was an old-style farmer/rancher type, skinny but made of nothing but sinewy, corded muscle, probably seventy years old but able to outwork any teenage football star. He had glasses and was in overalls and a straw cowboy hat. One of the others was skinny but it looked like meth-skinny, no front teeth and a perpetually amazed look. The last guy was a big, beefy farm boy type who nodded and said "Sir" by way of greeting. Just on first look, Eric trusted the farmers but not the meth-head. He kept his eye on him. Meth-head would steal from his mother for a hit.

"I was in Vietnam," the old man said, "and I reckon your friend is aiming a rifle at us right now."

Eric was almost up to the men and he slowed his walk and looked the man in the eye. "Yes, Sir, that's correct. I apologize, but these are uncertain times. And I'm going to be up on that hill with my rifle when she comes by you. I do thank you for your service."

The old man didn't look a bit happy but he turned to his companions and made a "move" gesture with both hands. "Step off to the side of the road while these folks get by," he commanded. "Give 'em room."

Eric got past the men and felt confident enough to mount the bike and ride up the next hill. At the top he got into position and saw Dani come speeding down the road a few moments later. As she blew past the men, standing on the pedals to get more speed, the meth-head got a look at her ass and just had to make a cat-call. He drew in a breath and started "Whoo — ." He didn't finish. The old man spun around with surprising agility and slammed a roundhouse punch into his belly. Meth-head fell to his knees, trying to draw breath into a body that wasn't taking any in right now.

"YOU GOD DAMN IDIOT!" the old man screamed. "That man is aiming a God damn rifle at us right now and you want to God damn scream at his woman? You God damn idiot!" He drove a punch into meth-head's jaw and started to kick him in the ribs, and then in the kidneys when the man curled up into the fetal position. They weren't little dominance kicks for show, either. The old man was putting his weight behind them. Not that he weighed much, but his big work boots did. Eric had to laugh, but at the same time he hoped the old veteran wasn't going to have flashbacks. Apparently he had had rifles aimed at him before and had not enjoyed the experience.

***

They arrived at the house without really seeing anyone else, and found the gate locked, just as he had left it. So far, so good. Eric had purposely cleared a winding driveway that snaked around oak trees with branches that met overhead, forming a green tunnel. The original driveway was more straightforward, but he was letting that one grow over in favor of a more scenic route. Dani was a city girl and had never seen anything so beautiful. She'd never even seen that many trees all at once, before this trip. She stopped a couple of times to just gaze at the beauty. Eric also enjoyed the beauty but he was eager, damned anxious as a matter of fact, to get home after this long journey.

"Why don't you hang out here for a half hour or so?" He suggested. "I want to check the place out." He left his bike, unslung his rifle, and moved off into the woods. He stayed in the woods but moved around the house, no closer than he had to be to get a good look. He circled the place enough to see all of the sides but it looked unmolested, so he moved in closer to confirm. All was in order, so he went back down the driveway with no attempt at stealth.

He came around a curve and saw the bikes, but no Dani.

Chapter 26

A spike of fear shot through him and he whipped his rifle up into a low ready position — buttstock in his shoulder, but muzzle down so he could scan without the rifle in the way. Other than that he remained still, only his eyes scanning the area.

Maybe she's going to the bathroom. No signs of a strugg
—

"Bang." She didn't scream it, just said it in a normal conversational tone of voice and volume.

He spun around towards the sound like he'd been jabbed with a hot poker, the rifle almost coming up to his sightline, then recognized the voice and realized what she'd done. He snatched the rifle up to point at the sky. "Shit! Shit." He let out the breath he was holding, and then felt a chill that caused him to shiver. He took in and expelled a deep breath and tried to glare at her.

Dani was crouched behind a tree, laughing uproariously. He had to laugh along with her. He couldn't even act mad at her.

"Alright, SEAL *chica*, let's get to the house." She stood and walked by him, towards her bike, with a big smile still on her face. He smacked her lightly on the butt when she went by and she jumped, but kept going. If anything, she smiled even more.

I might have a little surprise for you tonight, she thought.

As they rounded the last curve and came into sight of the house, Dani stopped again. It was beautiful! Like a fantasy house nestled in the woods. It was a dusky blue-gray with a black roof, with white trim around the windows and doors. There were huge windows on one side, and the other side in view appeared to be entirely composed of windows. Beyond it, through the trees, she could see a pond. There was a color-matching garage/shop off to the side. She thought she was in Paradise. She didn't know places like this existed.

"I imagine the solar panels were knocked out. That means the food in the fridge and freezer are spoiled, so the first thing to do is to get them out the door and open all of the windows." He unlocked the door and left it open, then rushed around opening windows. Dani stopped just inside the doorway to take it all in.

Eric had taken an existing floorplan and modified it to suit his needs. It was originally a twelve hundred square foot, three bedroom design, with two small bedrooms downstairs and a large upstairs master. The living room, dining room, and kitchen were all one big room, with a fireplace in one corner. The master bedroom was at the top of the stairs, with a balcony that overlooked the downstairs. This gave the living and dining rooms a ceiling that soared to eighteen feet at the peak, and made the area feel huge.

Dani had lived in a house that was smaller, and that was with two parents and three siblings. It had been dark and cramped. This place was huge and airy and flooded with light from the windows. Her eyes teared up at the thought of living here.

Eric was back but didn't notice. "Can you help? We need to get the fridge and freezer out of here." She did notice a bit of rotten meat smell in the air but there was good airflow through the house. They rolled the offending units out the front door, made a temporary ramp with plywood and 2x4s, and rolled them onto another sheet of plywood.

"The best we can do at this point is to get them into the woods over there," Eric said regretfully. "God dammit, I never wanted to be a redneck with broken appliances rusting in his yard." He only had three sheets of plywood, so they had to lay two down, push the appliances, then pick two sheets of plywood up and do it all over again, until a rising slope stopped their efforts. With a last, disgusted look from Eric, they headed back to the house.

"I guess I should give you the full tour," he said as he held the door open for her. "Living room, kitchen, dining room, obviously. Making them all one room makes the whole place seem bigger. That's the master bedroom up there at the top of the stairs, with a little balcony. From the kitchen, this hallway goes to the guest room here, and the laundry room and mud room is at the end of the hall. Here is the bathroom. I made it a lot bigger to have a nice shower. That took room away from this bedroom so I made what was left of it the pantry."

Dani's eyes bugged and her jaw dropped open when she saw the pantry. It was huge, with floor to ceiling shelves stacked full of boxes and cans and bottles. Actually floor to ceiling, with a step ladder to get to the top shelves. And not just food, but a wide variety of items: cleaning supplies, ammunition, toilet paper, candles, batteries, and boxes and boxes of other things.

"Did you *know* there was going to be a plague?" she blurted.

"No, if I had I'd have constructed a Faraday Cage, and…" he paused for a long time. "You never know what's going to happen. I was just trying to be prepared."

Damn it, I didn't want to make him sad, Dani thought. "Can we heat some water? I'd really like to take a bath," she asked, to change the subject.

"Sure, I have a grill out back. Oh, I didn't show you the lake."

Behind the house was a wooden deck, then the yard, then a lake. It was about 3 acres and would provide cooling breezes in the summer as the wind swept across it. Dani stood on the deck and was once more entranced by this place.

I could live here the rest of my life, she thought. *No, that's the wrong word. I want to live here the rest of my life!*

"Let's have something to eat, too," she suggested, thinking *We might need some strength soon.*

Eric fired up the grill and pulled out every pot and pan he owned to make spaghetti and heat bath water. He filled a couple of plastic buckets partially full of lake water, which they mixed with hot water until the temperature was good, then carried them into the bathroom.

Dani went through the house more slowly, noting that it was not huge but neither was it cheap. All of the fixtures and trim and appliances were high quality, maybe not top of the line, ludicrously overpriced industrial stuff, but not the cheap builder's grade, either. And the books! Under the stairs and all along the walls were shelves crammed with books. Most were paperbacks, but at least a third were hardbacks. She scanned the titles and while many were for entertainment, there were plenty of instructional ones on construction, engineering, math, astronomy, ballistics, metalworking, plant guides, and more.

He's a Marine and a scholar, she thought.

While Dani bathed, Eric heated some more water for himself and sat and thought. He had been so mission-intent on getting here that he hadn't thought about Dani. Not much. Well, not a lot. Fine, not all of the time.

So what happens now? Do I offer her the guest room? Do I just make a move? She was almost raped a few days ago, so I can understand if she's traumatized. Except she doesn't seem traumatized, and she wasn't actually raped.

I would love to have sex with her. She's beautiful and has a smokin' hot little body. Not an ounce of fat. Beyond that, I like her. I like her a lot. She's smart. Adaptable. Brave. Strong. Tough. I respect her. Don't screw this up.

While Eric fretted, Dani took her time with soap and shampoo and conditioner and a razor. One advantage of her shorter hair was the reduced effort it took. When she was properly prepared, she wrapped herself in a big towel and headed upstairs. The master bedroom had a balcony in the back that overlooked the lake. She walked out onto it in her towel and called down to Eric, "I'm out of the bathroom," then turned and ran back inside, giggling that she was just teasing him at that point.

Eric bathed, still deep in thought and still clueless as to what was going to happen. He did make sure to shave and make himself as presentable as possible. He exited the bathroom in a pair of shorts and a T-shirt and didn't see her downstairs.

"Dani?" he called.

"Come upstairs," she invited.

He came through the doorway, hopeful, and saw a sight that stopped him in his tracks. Dani was on her side in the bed, propped up on one elbow. She had a sheet partially covering her, but he could see from her uncovered shoulders and leg that she was wearing only a red bra and panties. The effect was much more erotic than if she'd simply been naked.

She was also wearing a little bit of makeup. She normally wore eyeliner, but this time she had added some eyeshadow and a little color to her cheekbones, and a subtle lipstick. She was naturally beautiful, but now she was way more than that.

"Wow!" Eric said, mesmerized. "That's what I thought the first time I saw you, but now... WOW!"

She smiled and looked down demurely, then right back up and tossed her head a little while she was at it. Demure wasn't really her style at all. Eric walked around the bed and slipped between the sheets, putting his arms around Dani. He had some practice at kissing, and he usually started slowly and worked up. He intended to do that now, but she was in no mood for that and their first kiss was hot and wet and deeply passionate. Their tongues didn't lightly play with one another; they fought for dominance.

After a while they came up for air, just enough time for Eric to murmur "we need to do that a lot!" Dani replied with an "Um hmm" and they locked lips and went immediately into a deep French kiss again.

The third kiss, he brushed her hair back on the side and started kissing her neck, working his way down to her cleavage. Dani was panting. Eric unhooked her bra and she shrugged out of the straps and tossed it away somewhere. He moved his lips and tongue to a breast and Dani felt like she was going to jump out of her skin. She was about to pull her panties off herself if he took any longer, but he reached a finger under the elastic on one side. She grabbed the other side and pulled them down as far as she could, then kicked them down into the foot of the bed.

Eric stopped for a second to suggest "Why don't you get on top?"

"I've never done it like that," she replied, but started moving that way. Eric helped, and when she lowered himself down on him, she almost came right then. After a moment she got the motion going, hard and fast. She didn't keep it going for long, since she had been so hot to begin with. Eric helped by continuing to kiss her neck, and with both hands free, he had one on a breast and one on her tight little ass. He took a moment to whisper in her ear "Scream if you want to. Scream as loud as you want to." Her orgasm came quickly, but it was intense, and she did scream. She started low and got louder, "Oh God, oh God, oh GOD, oh GOD, OH GOD, OH GOD, OOOOOOOOoooooooooooo."

She collapsed onto him, panting. Eric was glad she was so quick, because he knew he was going to be, this first time, and he was. He moved in and out of her only a few times before he came.

They lay there, holding each other, his chest hairs tickling her face, his muscular arms around her shoulders. Eric was trying not to doze off when Dani pulled the sheet close to her face and dabbed at her eyes and sniffled quietly. He was instantly alarmed.

"Are you okay? Did I hurt you?" he asked.

She cleared her throat and replied "No, no, it's good. It's very good." *Oh, my God, it's good*, she thought. *My life now is a thousand percent better than what it was*. The fact that her family was gone started to loom up like a dark cloud and she forced it down. *I will mourn them forever, but that is done, and I cannot undo it. I have to live my life looking forward.* She cried a little more, this time for them, gently.

He was still concerned because she hadn't looked at him. She almost always looked people in the eye when she spoke to them. On the other hand, sometimes women did weird shit and it was better not to bug them about it. He did know that much.

A little while later she was looking him in the eye and moving her lips closer to his. "I want to try this position out some more," she purred huskily. "Are you ready?"

Chapter 27

They slept late the next morning, since they were up most of the night, engaged in vigorous activity. The first couple of times had been almost frantic until they sated the pent-up sexual frustration they had built up during the journey. Then they did it more slowly and with more foreplay, getting accustomed to what the other liked as they explored their lover's body.

Eric rolled out first and brewed up some coffee with the butane stove and brought it upstairs. He set Dani's mug on her side table and started back down to get some food. Then he spotted her red bra on the floor. He scooped it up and leaned over the balcony railing to toss it onto the ceiling fan blades for the living room fan. Later on, he could tease her about it.

He was back in a minute with a load of candy bars, cookies, and other vending machine snacks. Slipping between the sheets, he ran his hand slowly down her back, then leaned over and kissed her on the cheek.

"Hey, Sleeping Beauty," he said softly.

She opened one eye for a second and grumbled some. "Oh, God, I am sore!" She opened both eyes and fixed them on him. "You ravaged me."

"*I* rav — I seem to remember that you were on top most of last night."

She looked down and said, "I was young and innocent, and I was seduced by an older man."

Eric had just started to take a sip of coffee, and he almost spit it all over everything. He managed to swallow and then laughed out loud, saying "Oh, what utter bullshit! We know who seduced whom. The same one who threw her red bra so far away that it caught on the ceiling fan!"

She had been laughing at her little joke, but now she went wide-eyed and sat up to look. Her mouth dropped open when she spotted her bra, then she closed her mouth and her eyes narrowed as she calculated the distance from the bed to the fan. Her head swiveled so she could give Eric a stern look and she said "You threw that up there. There's no way I could have tossed it left-handed and had it go that far away." She crossed her arms and ostentatiously turned away from him.

Eric laughed at her antics. "I have cookies and candy, little girl," he teased, waving a pack of chocolate chip cookies. She turned her head just enough to see the cookies so she could snatch them away from him. He moved close enough to put his arm around her waist, kissed her shoulder, and murmured in her ear "I never want to hurt you, so let me know when you're no longer sore. I would love to make love to you again."

Dani broke into an ear to ear smile at that. She was so glad he had said "make love" instead of "fuck" or "hit it" or something like that. And she was glad that she had her back to him so that he couldn't see her smile. *You don't want to let your man know he's pleasing you too much or he'll back off of it, or he'll do something bad because he thinks he can get away with it,* she thought, remembering some words of wisdom from her older sister. The phrase "your man" seemed to bounce up and hit her in the face, softly, but with force behind it, like a heavy pillow. No sharp edges or hard surfaces, but with weight, with momentum enough to rock her back.

Did I just refer to him as "my man"? Is that right? Should I? After all we've been through together, shouldn't I? What's going through his mind?

She put those thoughts on hold for a moment as she leaned back into him and slid her hand back to rake her nails across his thigh. "You'll be the first to know." They snuggled for a minute, until she excused herself to go to the bathroom. She slipped into her red panties (*How did they end up* there?), and rifled the chest of drawers until she found the T-shirts. While she went through them, she commented "You know you'll have to get my bra off of the fan, don't you?"

"Oh, no, no, it'll make a great conversation piece.

Somebody will comment on it and I'll tell them how you lured me up here, all innocent and unsuspecting, and ripped all of my clothes off and violated me repeatedly."

"VIOLATED?!" she interrupted, eyebrows raised in mock amazement. She had unfolded a T-shirt, decided against it, and refolded it. Now she rapidly folded it one more time and threw it overhand like a football, to smack right into Eric's face. He laughed, sitting back and enjoying the view of her firm little ass and toned legs.

She selected an old Marine Corps T-shirt, washed so many times that it was thin and soft. It was faded now but had started off a deep yellow, as close to gold as possible with fabric dye, with "USMC" on the front in red and the Eagle, Globe, and Anchor outlined in red on the back. It was a large, and came down almost to her knees. Eric knew she'd laid claim to that T-shirt and he'd never get it back, so he said "Looks good! Consider it yours." She flashed him a smile and went downstairs.

Dani sat in the dark bathroom for a while, thinking, but she knew what she had to do. She just had to work up the courage to do it.

Chapter 28

Back upstairs, she sat in the bed but stayed on her side. "I need to tell you a couple of things."

Oh, shit, those are words that terrify men Eric thought. *She can't be pregnant. Does she want to break up?*

"Now that our... relationship seems to be... progressing to a new level..." Dani was picking her words with care, "I need to tell you some things, two things, about myself. One is, I was raped when I was 12 years old."

"Oh, damn, I'm sorry!" Eric reached out to take her in his arms but she held up a hand to stop him.

"We couldn't do anything about it. The man was a member of a Mexican gang, and some men came to threaten my Father. He had to be afraid for the whole family, not just me. So there was never a police report or anything. But I don't think I am traumatized by it. I think I'm pretty normal." She had been looking down, but now she brought her head up to look into his eyes. "Although, if I see a gang member, I'm going to kill them. If I see gang signs, gang colors, gang tattoos, I'm going to kill them."

"I'll help."

"Thank you." She looked down again, took a deep breath and let it out, then looked him in the eyes again. "I lied to you. I apologize. I shouldn't have done it, and I will never lie to you again. I swear!"

He looked at her questioningly.

"I told you I was twenty-one years old. Do you remember?"

"Sure, right when we met, you told me your name, said you were twenty-one, and went to San Jac."

"I exaggerated. I'm eighteen. But I'm legal. Eighteen is an adult."

"Dani, that's fine. It doesn't matter." He held out a hand to her.

"You're sure?"

"I'm sure." She snuggled into his arms and laid her head on his chest.

He waited a moment before he asked, "You're not fourteen, are you?"

"NO!" Dani sat up enough to slap his chest.

"Fifteen?"

"Stop! Eighteen!"

Eric figured it really didn't matter. She was of legal age, if maybe a little young for him, but she had shown a maturity far beyond her years. *I guess we* are *in a relationship now.* He thought about that for a while, then *That's a good thing. Probably exactly what I need. Right now, though, we need to get to work.*

"We have a lot to do," he told Dani. "Tonight, I'm going to try to shoot a hog and get us some fresh meat. Today I need to go around to the neighbors and check on them. There are cattle ranches all around my property. We need to keep those cows alive. We need to get crops planted. We need to get things like tractors running again. We have a million things to do."

"What do you need me to do?"

"Come with me. You need to meet people, get the lay of the land."

They got up and Dani thought of the few clothes she possessed, now dirty from sweat and dust during multiple wearings and asked "Can I borrow some clothes?"

They got her outfitted with jeans and a shirt and socks that were all way too big for her, but a lot of rolling up of pants legs and sleeves and tucking in of shirttails made her look more ladylike. Definitely not form-fitting, but not too tent-ish, either.

They also strapped on their combat gear, a full load of weapons and ammo. That was probably going to be the way of this world for a long while to come. At least their packs were light, just enough food and water for the day.

They made a circuit around the property that day. The neighboring properties were two ranches, a tree farm, and a large hunting property that was only used occasionally by a rich family from Dallas. As they rode their bikes, Dani asked about his intentions.

"What is your long-range plan? Are you going to take over the ranches if they're... um, abandoned? I mean, it wouldn't be stealing. If the owners are dead, you ought to be able to take them over."

"I really hope they're not dead. I don't know how to take care of cattle. Don't know how to farm, either."

"There has to be a rancher and a farmer alive somewhere. Can't you get them to teach you? Or even better, there must be plenty of refugees that fled the cities. Gather some of them, get the rancher and farmer to teach them, and they work for you. On your farms and ranches."

"Once they're taught, why wouldn't they just go off and find an abandoned ranch and take it over themselves?"

"Protection, for one. You're a Marine, you have combat experience. You protect them. The other thing is to get the deed to the property. Get legal paperwork that says you're the owner."

"How am I going to do that? I don't have the money to buy the ranches, and besides, money's no good now. Anyone can go into a bank and blow the safe or crack an armored car and have millions of dollars in cash. My money wasn't even in cash, just a number in a digital system that doesn't work anymore. It's gone."

"On the way up here you were talking about the government giving the land to the people that were farming it."

"Yeah, but we wouldn't be the ones that were actually doing the farming."

Dani didn't miss that he had used "we".

"No, but with your protection, you would allow the

farmers and ranchers to do their work," she replied. "We would have to set up and run the infrastructure, everything except the actual farming. We need experienced farmers and ranchers as teachers. Get some people with military or police experience to provide security. Find electricians and mechanics to try to fix the trucks and equipment that stopped running. We'll need a doctor, a dentist, and a priest. Create a community. Have people go out and gather supplies and bring them here. That way the farmers can farm and they don't have to try to find all of those things themselves.

"That's called division of labor. Like a blacksmith can't eat what he produces, but he can trade his products to a farmer for food. The farmer can't do what the blacksmith can without a big investment in time and equipment. It's cheaper for him to buy things from the blacksmith than do it all himself." She smiled and looked very bright-eyed.

"Yeah, but I guess I just never took the next step mentally, to think that land would be granted to someone other than the farmers."

"Think of it like a factory. You own it. The people that work there don't. They may come and go. As a matter of fact there may be something in farming where you could rotate the farmers around the fields. Like during harvest time, all of the farmers work field A, then field B, and so on, versus this farmer does everything on field A and that farmer does everything on field B. That would raise questions regarding who has farmed where. I'm not trying to screw anyone out of what they worked for, but there has to be some consideration for the people that are making bigger things happen."

"You've given this a lot of thought."

"You were kind of intent on getting us here, so I started planning beyond that."

"I was thinking about taking over the nearby ranches and farms if they were abandoned, at least keeping the livestock alive until the ownership can be worked out. How many are you talking about?"

"If Hexen killed off ninety percent of the people, that's nine properties you can take over at least. In theory. But why stop there? Forty, fifty, a hundred." *Oops, maybe that was too fast,* she thought. *He looks like he's turning a bit pale. He needs some time to get used to the idea.*

"That's... ambitious. I never thought about being a cattle baron."

"Would you rather tend cows when you're seventy years old, or sit in the air conditioning and have someone tend the cows for you? Do you want to be rich or merely survive?"

He considered the whole proposal for a minute, not just her last questions, and replied "Easy answer. The guy in the air conditioning. The problem is getting to that point."

"I have confidence in us." Dani did look confident, and happy, and determined. It gave Eric confidence even though his thoughts mainly centered around "Holy shit!" He didn't know if her idea was even remotely feasible but it definitely had an attraction. For all that he enjoyed the outdoors, he didn't want to be a farmer or a rancher. He remembered a neighbor saying "You don't own cattle. Cattle own you."

He had had enough of the military after four years but that was because of the bullshit coming down from above. If he was in charge, then that would be a whole different story. He could run it any way he wanted. He did miss the Corps, truth be told. Creating his own definitely held an appeal.

Dani kept her mouth shut to give him time to think it through while she enjoyed the scenery.

***

Of the closest neighboring properties, only the owner of the smaller ranch, Curtis, had survived. He was also tending the livestock at the other two nearby ranches but the workload was more than he wanted. He needed help. Eric decided to float Dani's idea and see how well it went over.

"Curtis, how does this sound? What if I got some refugees

from the city, good people, you know I wouldn't bring any trash in here, and you teach them how to tend cattle? You manage them. Show them what to do, then you just sit and point, tell them to do this or do that. How would that work?"

"Well, I got to do something. I'd hate to just let those cows die off or turn them loose, but it's going to get to the point where it's either them or me." He shrugged, pondering the idea for a minute. "Where they gonna live?"

"The farmhouses on the other ranches. We'll turn them into bunkhouses. Or that'll be their first job, to build housing. I'll be honest, I might look into taking over those ranches and some other properties, but I don't want you to think that I cheated you in any way."

"No, no, I don't want 'em. I got this one. This is all I want. I was just over at the other ranches so the animals don't die."

"Let's see what we can do. If I can find an electrician, I'll put him to work, too. There was an old car that some guys got running, a 1970 model. It can be done, apparently. I'll keep you informed."

Chapter 29

The next day they toured the surrounding properties in a widening circle, evaluating what was where, what was abandoned, and how that would fit in with their ideas. They made notes and drew maps. They found another rancher and three farmers who were willing to train people. Not only willing, but desperate. They all jumped at the idea. Now they needed the people.

Back at the house that night, Eric and Dani discussed the situation.

"It looks to me like there is a definite need," Eric stated. "All of the people we talked to were armed. All of them were cautious when we showed up. And we have two ranchers and three farmers that want some hands. Plus there are a half-dozen ranches with cattle that are abandoned, and maybe a dozen farms or fields that could be farms. I think this might be feasible. It'll take a lot of work but let's do it. Let's take that next step."

"I have confidence," Dani said. "People have to eat. Once the cities run out of food, they're going to need a supply. If we get a good head start on building a base, we can work up from there. There are no natural barriers here so we ought to be able to grow in every direction."

"I guess it would be a good idea to get into the cities fairly quickly and establish ourselves as a supplier of beef. I'm sure someone will run a grocery store or butcher shop or a distributor that would buy beef in bulk and distribute to the smaller shops. Of course, it would be damned nice to have vehicles for that.

"Anyway, tomorrow is Saturday," Eric noted. "We have to go to the rendezvous point on Saturday. That will be our first recruiting effort." They allowed themselves a romantic evening that night, with fresh pork loin, a little bit to drink, and a long session of scorching hot lovemaking. They took their time and were slower and gentler, which was erotic in its own way. Eric was almost surprised that the sheets didn't catch on fire at the height of their passion.

Afterwards, Dani lay naked beneath the sheet, too spent to locate her panties and slip on a T-shirt to sleep in. *Oh, God,* she thought. *Everything is balanced on such a razor's edge! It looks like things are moving in the right direction but that could change radically in the blink of an eye. But I guess the same could be said about Hexen and the EMP. The flu took about eight weeks to burn through the world and the first week it was just simmering in Asia. That's the blink of an eye, realistically. And the EMP literally only took a second. Please, no more disasters for a while.*

She thought of all of the things that could go wrong until she fell asleep. She showed Eric nothing but confidence and then she worried herself to death at night after he was asleep.

***

On the road by dawn, they biked the eight miles to the rendezvous point with ease, hid the bikes in the woods, and stealthily approached. The R Point, as they called it, was just a little intersection of U.S. Highway 79 and a county road with a convenience store and fast food restaurant. There was a scattering of houses and trailers within a mile, but nothing else actually at the intersection. Dani and Eric were both in camouflage and they crept forward in the trees and underbrush to a vantage point where they could survey the situation with binoculars. The fast food place was a burned-out shell from a long-ago fire but the convenience store was active. They watched a fairly steady stream of people doing business there, including a man that brought in a dead hog in a wheelbarrow, then butchered it right there in the parking lot and started grilling the meat. Another was boiling water to purify it in a couple of huge pots usually used for frying turkeys or boiling shrimp or crawfish.

"This is better than I thought. I feel safe with both of us going in. We can even get the bikes."

They pedaled up and chatted with the men, finding out that there was a steady stream of refugees going back and forth. Basically, people didn't know what to do. They had fled the cities to get away from the plague. Once they figured out that they were apparently immune, some went back, only to find that the cities were barely habitable due to the lack of food and electricity. The cities that were habitable were the small towns or the fringes of larger ones where it was easier to get food transported in from the countryside.

However, some of the smaller towns were closed to refugees by the local population, or closed to certain people based on their difference from the locals. Nobody was enforcing any nondiscrimination laws these days. Even someone who was acceptable to the locals was on their own if they couldn't feed themselves or lacked a useful trade. Unfortunately, when a digital population is suddenly forced into the nineteenth century, very few people have useful skills. Sure, a refugee could take over an abandoned farm or ranch, but what were they going to do with it when their expertise in steak or vegetables ended at the grocery store? There were no more YouTube videos on how to farm.

The good news for Eric and Dani was that there was a population that had to eat and lacked the skills to grow their own food. That was exactly what they needed. The second piece of good news was that there was a connection board on the side of the store. This was a four by eight foot sheet of plywood that had messages written on it. It was like a free-form want ad section, with things to trade, jobs, and people searching for others. It took Eric only a second to see a hand-drawn Marine Corps emblem down in the corner and read the message that started with his name and "text received" and gave directions to a house a quarter mile down the road. It was signed "Shaker."

"Shaker!" he cried, with a big grin and a victory punch at the air. "Fuckin' Phillip!" They read through the rest of the messages but none of the others interested them. They jumped on the bikes and followed the directions.

"I guess 'Shaker' is a nickname? A call sign? What was yours?" inquired Dani.

"Notdoc."

"Huh?"

Eric smiled. "Not doc, but you have to say it like it's one word. Since my last name is Marten, they wanted to call me Doc Marten. You know, like the boots. But doc is a reserved word in the Marine Corps. That's what we call the Navy corpsmen. They're our version of medics. Just think — some guy goes into the Navy and becomes a corpsman. He thinks he's going to be in an air conditioned hospital, eating good chow and flirting with pretty nurses all day long. And what do they do? They assign him to a Marine unit. 'Here, go march with these guys out in the swamp and sleep in the mud and eat MREs'". He laughed.

"Anyway, since they couldn't call me 'doc', it became 'not doc'. Shaker got his nickname because he likes girls a whole lot, and he was up on the dance floor in every bar we hit, shaking his ass. He thought that attracted the ladies."

"Did that work?"

"Well, I guess it depends on how you define success. If it's just a question of getting a girl, then he was pretty successful. Of course, some of them weren't too cute by any measure. But Shaker had standards. I mean, they were awfully low, but he had standards."

They were at the house in minutes, an older brick house, and a couple of dogs tuned up, barking and wagging their tails. A bearded man came to the door, squinted, and said "Eric! Hey, man!" He ran out and put Eric in a bear hug, rifle and bike and all, both of them whooping and laughing. Finally he stopped and looked Eric in the eye, still gripping his shoulders. "How have you been, man — aww, never mind. Stupid question. Everything has sucked." He looked off to the side at Dani. "Well, maybe not everything. You dog!"

"Ha! *You* dog!" Eric nodded at the two women that had appeared on the small porch. "And what is this shit?" He grabbed Phillip's ponytail. "If this is a ponytail, then where is the horse's ass? You know, I got a knife right here, we can get rid of this thing for you, Madam."

"Hey, hey, stop running your fingers through my flowing raven locks."

"Oh, God! I need to wash my hands now."

***

Introductions were made all around and they ended up in the kitchen drinking coffee. Dani asked the girls about themselves and they said they had been roommates and were beauticians.

"Beauticians?" Eric almost choked on his coffee. He pointed at Phillip. "And two of you couldn't do anything with that? Hell, I'll hold him down and you can try to gang-beautify him."

"Oh yeah, you just love to hold men down and force things on them, don't you?" retorted Phillip, then they both laughed.

Eric noticed Dani and the other two girls were looking a bit worried that the men were going to start throwing punches at any moment. He spread his hands out, palm down, in a peace gesture. "Don't be alarmed. This is how Marines talk to each other. If we're not insulting each other, then something is wrong. But we do need to be serious and talk business here.

"I have a house and property and there are cattle ranches and farms all around me. Dani and I have talked to ranchers and farmers who will teach people to tend livestock and farm. We should be able to get refugees to do that. What we need you for is that good ole Marine Corps experience. Security. Guard duty. We take care of the farmers, keep them safe, they keep us fed. We're also going to see if we can get title to the properties. I don't know if that will work or not. We want to do something more than just keep ourselves fed. We want to feed the cities. There's no reason why we can't build a little empire out here."

Phillip nodded. "You always did have big plans. Good plans. I've been telling the girls that."

"The big stuff, the good ideas, are from Dani. She gets all the credit, but I'm not dumping the responsibility on her. We have to make it happen. Let's do it. Let's get on the road."

Fortunately, Phillip and his companions had acquired bikes and as they rode, Eric and Phillip caught up some more. "I've been doing construction since I got out," Phillip said. "I was working for a smaller company but that's good since I got to do everything. You know, with a big company, the only thing you might do is put in windows or paint or whatever, but I got to do a bit of everything. "

"How about electrical?" Eric asked. "I have solar panels."

"I never worked with solar panels but I can take a look. There's not much to it."

"Don't burn my house down. I'd rather have no electricity than a burned-down house."

"I'm not gonna burn your house down."

***

Once back at the house, Eric got everybody together. "It's only late morning. Let's get the grill going and cook the remaining pork from the hog I shot last night. We'll eat lunch, and then Phillip and I will go out to the highway and see what refugees are coming by. We'll take the leftover pork to feed them. Dani, if you could stay here and get things settled in? We'll be back in a few hours and maybe see if we can catch some fish in the pond for supper."

Chapter 30

Back out on Highway 79 after lunch, Eric and Phillip found a shady spot under an oak tree by the side of the road.

"Bruce and his wife Janice didn't make it," Eric stated, flat out, looking down.

"Ah, Bruce, man." Phillip sighed and they both sat in silence for a moment before he asked "How do you know?"

"I was there. We'd arranged a get-together, me driving down to see them, right when it hit. If we'd been lucky, it would have been the other way around, them coming up here. But then I guess Hexen would have gotten them up here, too. You're either immune or you're not, apparently."

There was another long silence, both men deep in their thoughts, until Eric came out with the whole story.

***

Eric didn't notice anything unusual about the traffic. There was always a huge rush of cars out of Houston for the weekend and this didn't really look any different. He worked his way down into the bedroom community subdivisions west of Houston. If he hadn't had GPS he would have been completely lost. He had a pretty good inherent sense of direction, and he had been here before, but the houses and everything all looked the same.

Finally on the last turn he recognized the street and pulled into their driveway a minute later. Bruce heard the truck and came out to greet him. They man-hugged and whooped and pounded each other's backs and then backed off.

"You okay?" Eric asked. "You look concerned about something."

"Have you been keeping up with the news? This thing they're calling 'Hexen'?" he replied.

"That new virus of the month in China? I haven't paid much attention to it."

"Yeah, it's here now. Apparently it's deadly as hell and there are a lot of people saying to keep away from crowds, you know, evacuate the city and that sort of thing. This just came up. If I'd heard about it earlier I'd have told you to stay at your place. Hell, we'd have bugged out and come up to your place."

He got on his phone for a moment and then handed it to Eric. "Read this."

The Centers for Disease Control and Prevention (CDC) is working closely with Health and Human Services of the United States and international partners as they investigate an outbreak of HXN2 in widespread areas of the United States and overseas. The US government declared the outbreak after 70 cases were confirmed by laboratory testing at multiple facilities. CDC is assisting the US government and local and international partners, including the World Health Organization (WHO), as they identify priority areas of support, including establishing an outbreak response platform; implementing surge support for deployment of personnel, supplies, laboratory materials, operational support, logistics, and transportation; and identifying communication needs to support the partners and the response.

"It can't really be that bad, can it? The news people love to take something and blow it all out of proportion. You heard of Covid 19, right? And how many times have they predicted catastrophic floods and it barely rained?" Eric waved a hand dismissively.

"I hope so. Let's get your shit out of your truck and crack open some beer." Bruce was acting cheerier but Eric got the impression that it was a false front. When they got in the door, Janice had the same look, cheery with a cloud of concern in the background. He'd met Janice previously; they'd visited back and forth several times over the past couple of years.

Bruce had hunted on Eric's land but he hadn't been there since the house and pond had been built, and Eric had plenty of photos to show and tell. Janice's phone rang in the middle of that, and she said "Mom" and went into the bedroom to talk. A few minutes later, Bruce's phone rang and he apologized to Eric but had to take it.

Eric began to wonder if there was something to this disease after all. He pulled up the news on his phone and started getting worried after reading the top stories. It sounded like what they were calling "Hexen" had started in China a week or so ago and rapidly spread through the population, and killed plenty of them, all reports unconfirmed by officials, of course. Then China cut off all forms of communication and instituted a complete travel ban. Videos posted to social media before the blackout showed mass confusion, riots, bodies stacked like cordwood, and troops firing on civilians. That was bad enough, but it seemed suspiciously like the rest of the world was going through the same thing, just a few days behind China.

His cell phone suddenly started screaming out an emergency tone and he almost dropped it in surprise. There was a message from the National Emergency Alert System: "FLU EPIDEMIC. SHELTER IN PLACE." Before he could read any more, Bruce came back into the living room, silencing his own shrill emergency alert signal. "That was my sister," he explained. He found the remote and switched on the TV, which had the same alert running across the bottom of the screen in a constant loop. The local news people had reporters wearing surgical masks, live from places like grocery stores to show the empty shelves, gas stations to show the long lines, a hospital to show a standing room only emergency room, and a traffic helicopter to show the jammed highways heading away from the Houston metro area. The highway patrol was heading out to turn the highways into contraflow, which was something they did during hurricane evacuations. What this did was turn all lanes into an outflow from the city, so all lanes of Interstate

45, for example, would be turned into northbound lanes, including the lanes that were normally southbound. Of course, this was the direct opposite of the "shelter in place" broadcast so there was obviously some confusion between the state and federal governments. Nothing new there.

Janice came back into the living room at some point and they muted the sound. "My parents," she explained. "They want us to come out to their place but I was watching the news on the bedroom TV and I don't think we can get out of town. This is going to be like the evacuation for hurricane Irma. You remember my friends from Pearland? They tried to go around Beltway 8 to I-10 and they gave up after eight hours. That's normally a twenty, maybe thirty minute trip and they couldn't get halfway there in eight hours."

Bruce was shaking his head. "The roads are already a nightmare. I don't think we have a choice. We have to stay. Like they're saying on the news, shelter in place."

"I guess I don't know much about diseases," Janice mused. "If I think about a flu going around the office, some people get a bad case of it, some get it mild, and some don't get it at all. But what actually happens to the germs? They pass through an area and then die out or what?"

Bruce took a stab at it. "I think it's like a tomato plant. Birds eat the tomatoes and then later on the seeds pass through their system. Some places the seeds fall, they grow a new plant, others fall into, I don't know, water or a parking lot and they die. People are the soil where these plants can grow. As long as there is a plant somewhere, the germs can keep coming, but I'm sure we're working on a vaccine. The problem is that the flu keeps mutating so the vaccine that works this year may not work next year. Right now, this one is deadly, like the one in 1918 or around there, killed twenty million people or something like that."

"You're saying if we stay in the house for a week and don't come into contact with anyone, we'll be safe?" Janice asked.

"That might be a good start." Bruce looked at Eric. "Let's

take an inventory of what we have in the way of supplies and weapons."

"Well, I feel like a dumbass because I'm so unprepared," Eric admitted. "I have a Glock 19, three magazines, knife, multi-tool, a couple of flashlights, and not much else. I brought a case of beer and an ice chest full of frozen pork."

"No, that's great. That's a lot of pork. We actually ought to be pretty good on food. Let's treat this like a hurricane. Eric, let's get anything you need out of your truck in case we have to seal the doors. I have duct tape, plastic sheeting, and a staple gun if we need to do that. We have canned goods, candles, propane, and a bunch of containers we need to fill up with water. I don't know if anything will happen to cut off the water but I'd rather have them full than empty. We'll be okay."

Eric was afraid that might be false optimism. He thought the important thing to know was the incubation period of this flu. That was the factor that could kill them all. The incubation period was how long the disease took from the time a person was infected until they began to show symptoms. If that period was a week, then they could all be infected already. Anything they did now would be useless. He wasn't going to say that, of course. It would be better for them all to take precautions that weren't needed rather than not take ones that were. The incubation period may be hours, for all he knew, in which case they would all be safe if they could avoid becoming infected in the next few days. He started, realized that Bruce was trying to get his attention.

"Let me show you where everything is." He followed Bruce through the house, to the gun safe in the master bedroom to the gear closet upstairs to the garage. He had a lifelong association with firearms so he could operate anything in the safe with a good to excellent degree of expertise. Bruce's uniforms and gear were the right size for him to use, as both were about 6 feet and 180 pounds. The garage held a few tools, like the tape, staple gun, and plastic sheeting Bruce had mentioned earlier, plus some small propane bottles for a single burner camp stove.

After about an hour, they had done everything they could do to prepare, so they started some coals burning in the grill and popped some beer can tops. Bruce slumped in a patio chair.

"I don't know what else we can do." He looked Eric full in the face and asked "How can you look so calm? Aren't you worried?"

"Yeah, I'm worried for you and Janice. Some other people, but not many. The only family I had was my father and Ashley and I've already lost them both. Dying just doesn't mean that much to me. You've got Janice, so you have a much bigger stake in things than me."

"You were always like that. You just never really seemed to give a damn if you lived or died."

Eric saw an opportunity to lift Bruce's spirits, so he started in with the war stories. "That reminds me. Do you remember that time… "

They resolved to turn the TV off and stay off of the Internet for the evening, and just enjoy the cookout and some adult beverages. They almost succeeded. Janice had a couple of sisters in other states, plus her parents in the Hill Country of central Texas, and was almost constantly on the phone with one or more of them. She basically left the boys alone to drink and tell war stories about their time in the Corps.

The phones, though. The emergency alerts kept going off every half hour or so. Eric powered his off, but Bruce felt he had to keep his on in case his family called him.

Chapter 31

When Eric came downstairs the next morning, Janice was already up and had the news on. It was all the same thing, just different channels, different talking heads, and different experts. She looked terrified.

> *"This just in. All active duty military personnel are instructed to report to their units immediately. This includes Air Force, Army, Navy, Marine Corps, and Coast Guard. The Army and Air National Guard and all Reserves are being called up in New York, California, Illinois, Texas, Pennsylvania, and Arizona. There is also a long list, too long to read here on the air, a long list of other states that are putting their Guard and Reserve units on alert for activation. All active, Guard, and reserve military personnel are advised to contact their assigned units for instructions."*
>
> *"I'll repeat all that... "*

"You're both out, right? I mean, Bruce served out his enlistment. They can't call him back in, can they?" Janice was wide-eyed.

"No, we're out. We don't have units to call. Technically, they could call us back to active duty but that would take a long time and a lot of paperwork. Weeks, months. They're not going to do that in this situation."

She still seemed skeptical. Every channel was nonstop gloom and doom.

> *"... and is an expert on infectious diseases. Dr. Foster, thank you for agreeing to talk to us on such short notice. What can you tell us about HXN2, or Hexen, as it is being called?"*
>
> *"Well, of course. These are very serious times, don't*

you see? This pathogen, HXN2, has simply exploded to worldwide pandemic proportions in a matter of days, so obviously it's being transmitted person to person. Earlier strains of Asian avian influenza were transmitted almost exclusively from poultry to humans. Although, let me point out, we have seen an upward trend in human to human transmission as different strains of the flu have appeared."

"Dr. Foster, what can we do to protect ourselves from getting this flu, and what can we do if we or a loved one does get the flu?"

"Hmpf. Well, if a disease is transmitted between humans, then stay away from humans! At minimum, wear a mask, but I can offer no guarantee that that will be an effective prophylactic. As far as treatment, well, the CDC has released no effective guidance at this point. It appears to be highly virulent with a high mortality rate."

"So, you're saying, and please correct me if I'm wrong, Dr. Foster, but you're saying that it spreads easily and it is very fatal?"

"Yes, yes, that's precisely what I said."

"Should people go to the emergency room if they detect symptoms?"

"That won't do any good. There is no effective treatment at this time. Stay home."

"Dr. Foster, that's… actually… very frightening."

"Yes, well, this may be it. This may be the end, don't you see?"

***

"… have confirmed that Los Angeles County General Hospital has put out a call for refrigerated semi-trailers. What we have not yet confirmed is the reason for these refrigerated trailers. Logically, these would be for an overflow of bodies from the morgue, and the cause for such an overflow would be deaths from the Hexen epidemic. Officials at the hospital will neither confirm nor deny… "

***

Eric looked at his phone while Janice channel surfed. One of his friends had posted a YouTube link that supposedly showed a bulldozer with the driver in a full biohazard suit, burying bodies in a mass grave. A truck backed up and dumped a load of full body bags into a big trench while the bulldozer lengthened the trench. He figured it was a fake. It was grainy and jumpy, reportedly shot from long distance, and enlarging it just trashed the resolution. All he could really tell was the driver was wearing something light colored, probably a faded khaki jumpsuit and a white hard hat. Or maybe it was genuine but old, like the Chinese burying bodies from the Tiananmen Square massacre, or even the U.S. burying Iraqi bodies in the First Gulf War. Who knew whether it was relevant to Hexen?

"What do you think is going to happen?" Janice asked.

"I don't know. I don't know enough about diseases or epidemics to make an intelligent prediction. I mean, I had training in biological warfare, CBR they called it: Chemical, Biological, and Radiological, but the main thing was to look for similar symptoms in a number of different people and then report who, how, where, all that sort of thing. There was no training beyond that."

"But historically, we've been through plagues before and here we are. We survived. Let's look at the Black Death." He pulled up the Wikipedia article and started to read "one of the most devastating pandemics in human history, created a series of religious, social and economic upheavals, which had profound effects on the course of European history, estimated to have killed thirty to sixty percent of Europe's total population, took two hundred years for the world population to recover. That's bad, but that means that forty to seventy percent of the population survived."

"How about the 1918 flu — let's see — killed three to five percent of the world's population. Later on it says ten to twenty percent of those who were infected died, so that means eighty to ninety percent survived."

Janice had a thousand yard stare on her face, apparently running those odds and finding them not to her liking.

Eric tried again. "The good thing is, think how far our medical knowledge has advanced since then. During the Black Plague, they thought that the alignment of three planets caused bad air that caused the disease. They had filth in the streets, no sewage disposal, so they pretty much spread the disease themselves. The 1918 flu, seems to be some controversy about the origin, but that was a hundred years ago. We didn't even have penicillin or probably a thousand other drugs that we do now. I think this is going to be bad, but we'll be fine. We'll get through this."

He didn't think that helped either, but Bruce came into the living room and saved him. He looked at Eric and asked "How are you so bright eyed and bushy tailed? My head is pounding and you drank more than me. As usual."

A spike of fear made Eric's throat clutch up. The two main symptoms of Hexen were pounding headaches and a fever that got worse until it basically boiled the brain, causing death. He wasn't a praying man but he prayed it was just a hangover.

"My head hurts, too," Janice sighed. "I only had a little wine but my tension level is way up in the stratosphere."

Eric sat still for a moment and mentally checked himself out, ran a systems check, so to speak. No headache, not hot, no aches and pains, maybe a little dry from drinking the night before, but that was all. "Water would be good for you." He jumped up and walked into the kitchen. "Gatorade? You have anything to replace electrolytes? Nothing with sugar. How about breakfast? Can I fix y'all something?" *Slow down, slow down,* he told himself. *You're panicking. Take a deep breath.*

He made omelets for everyone while they sat on the couch and channel surfed and talked on their phones to various people. And that's pretty much how the entire day went, except that everything got worse. The phone circuits were the first to go, fairly early in the morning. A call was met with a "cannot be completed" message, then "all circuits are busy," then calls just didn't go through at all, not even getting as far as a recorded message. Text messages just timed out. The emergency alerts even stopped.

The Internet slowed drastically, slowed some more, and then locked up entirely. There was no indication that the government had cut it off or something sinister like that, it simply petered out. Maybe it was simply jammed with people trying to communicate.

The news shrank. The big stations had started out with reporters on site in far-flung locations, and they stopped reporting in, one by one. The traffic helicopters stopped flying. The civilians that lived for the opportunity to submit their cell phone video about a breaking news story weren't posting anything. The experts weren't available except via phone, and later, not at all. The news shrank to the studio, and then that shrank. Cameramen, directors, assistant assistants, and the talking heads themselves disappeared from the newsrooms and the screen, either put down by Hexen or deciding that family came before fame. If you stayed on one channel for a while, you could tell that the amateurs were running the show. Feeds got switched way prematurely or at random, cameras were badly operated, and sound went in and out. Then midafternoon all of the channels went to an emergency broadcast, a recorded message telling everyone to remain in their homes until further notice, do not travel, dusk to dawn curfews.

Bruce and Janice were sleeping on the couch and loveseat by that time, overdosed with ibuprofen, aspirin, and shots of Jim Beam, anything that would help to dull the pain. Their headaches were getting worse and worse and their foreheads kept getting hotter. As the drugs wore off and they woke up, Eric helped them to bed, dosed them again, and kept up a continuous series of ice and washcloths on their foreheads. He still took a moment every now and then to do his system checks — *how do I feel? Not feverish. Headaches, yes, as a matter of fact, I'm under a lot of tension here. My friend and his wife have Hexen and there's not a fucking thing I can do about it! SHIT! SHIT! SHIT!*

He threw together a sandwich for his evening meal, eating it with one hand while he cranked up the coffeemaker and got a cup and sugar out. It looked like it was going to be a long night. He didn't know what he was going to do when the ibuprofen ran out.

Chapter 32

Eric had just put a cold washcloth on Bruce's forehead when he died. He just gave a little kick with one foot and his body slumped, seeming to melt into the bed. His eyes rolled back in his head.

"No!" yelled Eric. "Come on, man, don't do that to me!" He pulled Bruce off of the bed to the floor to start CPR. It's not very effective on a springy mattress. He tilted his head back and stuck two fingers into his mouth to make sure there was nothing there and that he hadn't swallowed his tongue. He did compressions and breaths, compressions and breaths until his arms burned, and then did some more. Later, much later, he had to stop. He had to. He was spent. There was still no pulse. He sat back against a dresser and caught his breath, his vision clouded with tears. Almost immediately, he realized that he hadn't checked on Janice, so he lurched to his feet and moved quickly around the bed to her side.

She was gone.

Her death was almost worse than Bruce's. He was the warrior; he was the one who had volunteered to risk his life, not her. He had written his will at the age of eighteen, not her.

Eric manhandled Bruce back up into the bed beside her, and pulled the sheet and comforter over their faces. He just stood there helplessly for a minute, his head down, then turned and walked to the kitchen. There was a full and a partial 12-pack of beer in the fridge. He grabbed the partial — the box, not just a beer — and sat on the couch.

I hate this life, he thought. *I don't know how much more of this I can take.* He could feel the Glock behind his hip. He had thought about checking himself out every day, multiple times a day, for months. He thought about it less frequently as the months since Ashley's death had passed, but it was still there. It came roaring back with a vengeance now. *What would it matter? Who would care?*

He started in on the beers, one after another, slamming them down. He briefly turned on the TV and flipped the channels. Emergency broadcast, emergency broadcast, emerg—wait! There's a guy in front of the camera. "Is this on? Yeah? Okay, hey, I'm, like, an intern here. There's only three of us here. Usually there's like ten times that many. I dunno if anyone is going to see this but at least I can say I've been on national television. Coo coo kachoo. Okay, so back to the scary warning." He gave a weird look, something between a wistful smile and a grimace. The emergency broadcast started up again so he turned it off. If he had tried the Internet, it was back up. Enough users were sick or dead so the traffic had dropped off.

He didn't want to think about anything, but his mind was racing. He pulled out his phone and selected a group to text, a group composed of his old Marine buddies, and added a few more names. Then he just said "screw it" and selected everyone in his phone list. He broke the news that Bruce and Janice were dead from Hexen and invited people to bug out to his place. If they knew where it was, they should come straight in, otherwise, he gave them an intersection that was about eight miles from his place and said that he would check that intersection every Saturday. Maybe that was paranoia, but he didn't want to put his address or directions out in a text. No telling who was going to read that. Hell, no telling if it was even going to go out. Nothing had for hours.

In a few seconds, there was a noise from the bedroom and Eric jumped to his feet, moving swiftly. A few steps in, he realized what it was and slowed. He didn't enter the bedroom, just peered in from the hallway, and could see Bruce's phone on the dresser. Of course he had been in the group that Eric just texted.

Eric closed the door and went back to the couch and the beer. He was through the partial box, so he packed the empties back into the box. There were beeps as a couple of texts came in, but he was on a task and didn't drop everything to view a message the instant it arrived. It was interesting that texts were working now. He tried to put the box in the trash can, but it was too full, so he had to take the trash out. He carried the bag out the back door and heaved it up and into the big plastic can-on-wheels that goes out to the curb. In the middle of that motion the bag caught on a snag and ripped, spilling something wet and smelly on his jeans. A lot of wet and smelly. Eric could feel it already soaking through onto his leg. He didn't know whether to scream loudly or just let it go.

He did believe that action was always better than fretting over something, so he stepped over to the garden hose and sprayed off his pants leg and boot so that he didn't drip the wet and smelly in the house. The boots were waterproof, so he took them off just inside the house. Then he headed in to the guest shower, stripping off his Glock, phone, belt, knife, and other junk in his pockets and tossing them on the bed. He ended up in the shower with his jeans still on, and lathered and rinsed the spill a couple of times. Then he removed the jeans and bathed himself. He planned to throw the jeans in the dryer.

Dried off, he stood naked in the guest room, pulling clothes from his backpack, when the world went black. No transformers blew, no lightning struck, the lights didn't flicker, nothing dramatic happened — but everything electrical died in that instant.

Seriously? What the hell now? Eric thought. He picked up his phone to use the screen as a flashlight until he got the flashlight app running. It was dead. A jab of fear speared into his consciousness. *Shit.* He dropped the phone and ran his fingers across the bedspread until they hit his keys. He found the Streamlight Nano on the keyring, a tiny but bright flashlight. It was dead. *If the power went out, the flashlight would still work. The phone would still function. Maybe it wouldn't connect, but the screen would light up. It would have some functionality. I don't believe both batteries are dead. EMP? Shit!*

He raked his fingers across the bed again to find his watch and tried to make out if the second hand was moving. He walked around the bed to the window and peered through the blinds. Everything he could see was dark. Suddenly there was a flash of light. He reacted instantly, spinning around and dropping to the floor, his feet towards the flash. The Marine Corps trains its people to react exactly that way in case of a grenade or explosion. Better to take any wounds in your feet than in your head. You can even learn to walk without feet, but you can't do much without a head.

Also, since he was thinking of EMP, he had nuclear weapons on his mind. EMP is Electro Magnetic Pulse, which can be caused by nuclear weapons, and fries unprotected electronics. Eric had also been trained in nuclear weapons defense, and the first rule is to not look at the flash, which can blind you. The second is to count the flash-to-bang time, which tells you how far away the explosion is from your position. The flash travels at the speed of light, so arrives virtually instantaneously. The sound travels at about 1,100 feet per second. Count five seconds and that's 5,500 feet — about one mile. Ten seconds is two miles and so on.

The next thing Eric thought of — all of these things in the space of a second or two — was to get away from the window. The glass shards could be deadly if blown in by an explosion. At some point, when he'd had time to think about it, he wished he had a video of himself at that moment — stark naked, low-crawling down a hallway, counting "one thousand one, one thousand two, one thousand three." It was the right thing to do at the time but must have looked pretty ridiculous.

He got onto the stairs and figured that was a pretty safe place. Lots of thick lumber in a staircase. Besides, he never heard an explosion, never felt a blast wave. He waited a couple of minutes, then went back upstairs, crouched and ready to fall to the floor if needed. He looked out the window again and saw a fire, a pretty big one considering how far away it had to be. Visualizing a map of the area, he wondered if that was an aircraft that went down. There were no refineries or other large, explosive things that he knew of in that area. *Could have been heading into Hobby Airport, dropping altitude, electronics went out, not much you can do to save it. Damn, that may have been a hundred and fifty or so people dying right there.*

Eric got dressed by feel, found his keys again, and went out to the driveway. His key fob did nothing to his truck. He couldn't even open the door. He knew there was an actual key in the fob but trying to deal with it in the dark would just be frustrating. Today had already sucked enough. He didn't need more of that.

He went back inside and managed to find the refrigerator and then the couch without slamming a toe or shin into anything. He laid into the beer hard and fast. He was getting a hellacious headache. *If it's Hexen, then fine, fuck it, do it, let's go. I just want this day gone, by whatever means necessary.*

He woke up sometime, dehydrated and hungover. Or infected. He didn't care which one, but considering how quickly Hexen killed, probably hungover.

His phone was still dead. He drank a bottle of water and tried to take a shower. A little bit of water dribbled out and then stopped. He got a bottle of water out of the pantry, stood in the tub, and poured it over his head.

He fired up the grill on the patio. Fortunately it was gas. He preferred charcoal or, to be really hard-core, actual wood, but today he wanted quick and easy. He made a big breakfast of bacon and scrambled eggs. He had to improvise with the coffee, boiling water in a pot and then pouring it through coffee grounds in a filter.

He figured out how to get into his truck with a dead fob and pulled out a Texas map. He spent a little time with it, measuring the distances between cities and planning a route back home. It was over two hundred miles. A few hours, maybe four, depending on traffic, in comfort and luxury in his truck. Hot? It was air conditioned. Cold? It was heated. The seats were comfortable. There was music for entertainment, hands-free telephone capability if you needed assistance or were simply lonely. It was dry, if the weather was rainy, and shielded from the wind and the dust and the bugs. It was an intensely engineered and controlled shell that kept the occupants completely shielded from the environment through which they sped.

At least, that's how he had traveled down here. The trip back up was going to be slow and done from a bug's viewpoint, down in the weeds and the wind and the rain and everything. He'd camped out all of his life. He'd been in the Corps. He knew what it was going to be like. Plus the two hundred and some miles to travel on foot. Via LPC, Leather Personnel Carriers, also known as "boots."

***

Next he looked at food. The stuff in the refrigerator would stay cool for another day or two, maybe, so he'd eat that first. After that was food that didn't need refrigeration and didn't have unnecessary weight or bulk. Cans of tuna and ham were in, cans of soup were out since they were big and heavy for the protein they offered. Instant mashed potatoes, peanuts, candy bars, and pasta were in, pasta sauce was not. Bottled water and electrolyte drinks were in, soft drinks were out because the sugar made you thirsty.

He stacked all of his supplies on the kitchen island and then started whittling down the pile. It was too much to carry so he had to prioritize. He couldn't carry enough for the whole trip and he'd simply have to find a way to get more on the road.

He drank a cold Coke, probably his last, while he thought about Bruce and Janice. They deserved a burial, but he didn't know how to do that. Their yard was the size of a postage stamp, and covered half with a patio and half with a jungle of trees and plants, with cables, power lines, an irrigation system, and God knew what else beneath what little soil there was. There wasn't anywhere in the subdivision that he had seen that would work — it was one of those intensely landscaped and over-manicured areas, nothing like a farm where the family could bury Grannie in the back forty up near the tree line when her time came. If his truck ran, and if the roads weren't all jammed, he could move their bodies to a suitable burial site, but he couldn't do it otherwise.

He thought of coffins, but he'd have to find the materials and the lumber and try to transport everything here, and his carpentry skills were probably not up to the task anyway.

Cremation was out. That takes a surprisingly large amount and intensity of flame, and a failed cremation would just be a disgrace to the person. He growled in frustration — a low, animal sound in his throat, and snatched the Coke bottle up off of the counter. He wanted to throw it, but he wasn't going to disrespect Bruce and Janice's possessions.

***

"There was nothing I could do," Eric told Phillip, as they sat on the road, two weeks after the event. "I had to leave them in their bed." He took a long, shuddering breath.

"Dude, you're good," Phillip assured him, but his eyes were brimming with tears. He stood and walked around, almost in a circle, tossing away a twig he'd been toying with. Abruptly he stopped.

"Damn, there's a guy right there."

Chapter 33

It was a tall and skinny teen, probably still in high school, and he was armed. Everyone was armed these days if they knew what was good for them. He had his rifle at the ready, but not pointed at them. He had stopped in the road, less than a hundred yards away.

"Hey, it's fine, man," Phillip called. "Come on. We're friendly."

Eric could understand that they probably looked like a pair of intimidating characters. He made a mental note to get the older one of Phillip's friends, Emily, on duty here. Apparently Phillip and Emily were an item, and Jamie was mourning her lost boyfriend. And family, too, but everybody was doing that.

"Cover me," he told Phillip. "But don't be real obvious about it." He left his rifle and rode his bike slowly towards the skinny kid, waving when he got within easy talking distance. "Hey, we're friendly. We're hiring people. You need a job? Food?" The kid looked bruised, maybe a black eye and fat lip?

"What kind of job?" the kid asked cautiously.

"Cowboy, ranch hand, farmer. Maybe something else if you have training or skills. What can you do?"

The kid shrugged. "I was in advanced math and chemistry classes. And JROTC."

"Good skills. I don't know that we can put you to work using those skills right now, but if you can work, you can eat and have a roof over your head."

"Okay."

"Cool. My name is Eric. This guy over here who needs a shave and a haircut is Phillip. Would you believe he's dating a beautician and looks like that?" The kid laughed a little. "What's your name?"

"Mark."

"Did you eat? Phillip has some pork we just grilled a little while ago."

That was generally how it went with hiring refugees. They were tired, dirty, hungry, and above all, shell shocked. Not that ninety-eight percent of the remaining fragment of civilization wasn't shell shocked, but this was two weeks past Hexen and people should be rolling up their sleeves and getting on with what lives they still could. People like Curtis who had never left his ranch and didn't have any family to lose were rock-solid. Hexen was almost a non-event for them. Eric and Dani had had a couple of days of shell shock but got their feet back under them quickly. Others may be off for the rest of their lives.

They hired two late teens/early-twenties guys riding bikes together, and then a young girl came near on a road bike. She was maybe fifteen, whippet thin, with long corn-silk blonde hair in a ponytail. She rode up, U-turned, and stopped, looking at them over her shoulder. She wanted to talk but was poised to run. One thing Eric noticed right off was that she had no gear, no pack, nothing beyond the clothes on her back, sunglasses, and a ball cap. *That either means she's living around here or she's stripped down for speed*, he thought. *And if she's with someone, they would be smart to have a rifle sighted in on me from somewhere back in those trees.* He had been standing at the side of the road but now he sat down, figuring that would be less intimidating. There would be less chance of him catching her before she could get away, so she should feel safer.

"Hi! My name is Eric," he called to her since she was forty or fifty feet away.

"My name is Taylor," she replied. "Do you, do you have any extra food?" Eric wasn't sure at that distance but he thought she was trembling. Her voice certainly was.

"Nice to meet you, Taylor. We do have some extra food. Tell you what, we were just about ready to leave for the day. How about you ride off down the road a little bit and I'll put the extra food out in the road where you are now? Then we'll go home and you can come back and pick it up?"

"Thank you." She started to push the pedals down.

"Taylor, wait just a second. We're friendly. We're hiring people to work on farms and ranches. Food every day and a roof over your head. And we'll protect you. Tomorrow morning I'll bring my girlfriend back and you can talk to her, okay?"

Taylor nodded and took off as fast as she could pedal, a scared little bunny scampering away from a predator.

There wasn't as much pork left over as Eric would have liked, with three teenaged boys gnawing on it, but he wrapped it back up in the aluminum foil that they had brought it in and placed in it the road. Then he waved at Taylor, about a quarter mile down the road, and they went back to the house.

He realized that he had called Dani his girlfriend. A barrier — milestone — event — something — had been reached or breached or whatever. He mulled that over on the trip back and decided that he liked it.

***

Dani had not wasted the afternoon. She and Emily and Jamie were cleaning the houses on the ranches. Curtis had buried the dead occupants a day or two after Hexen, so there wasn't a terrible smell, but a good cleaning never hurt anything. While they were at it they had inventoried the contents to see what they had to work with, and made a list of what they needed. They were all in the same situation with clothes and other items. They only had what they had carried with them when they evacuated. Nothing much, in other words. A trip to town was in order. And Dani was going to have to find a church nearby.

When Eric and everyone arrived, he had the boys set up their tents in the yard and found a bucket in his workshop for them to use as a temporary toilet. *Need to look up latrine construction*, he thought. Then he put them on a rotation that included fishing in the pond, splitting wood, and boiling water to wash their clothes. Phillip examined the solar panel system while Eric stood ready to find tools or whatever.

By sundown the boys had caught enough fish for supper, and Eric was showing Phillip the best spots to hunt hogs. They shot one and dragged it back for breakfast, lunch, and food for Taylor.

After supper, Eric called a meeting. "Tomorrow is Sunday and I would like to make it a day of rest, but I can't. I don't think we're going to get a day off for a while. There's just too much to do. Later on, when we get things up and running, yes. Now, no. Mark, Mike, and David, I'm going to get you up bright and early and get you over to Curtis so you can start learning to be ranch hands. At the end of the day, come back here and then we'll get you settled in one of the houses.

"Phillip, I need you to build bunk beds in the ranch house, research digging a latrine or an outhouse — I have a book around here somewhere — and select the site. Oh, but before you do any of that, come with me tomorrow morning to meet Curtis and see if there is anything electrical you can fix for him. Make a list of what you need.

"Dani, Jamie, and Emily come with me to hire ranch hands and I think Emily will take that over at some point. Jamie, you said you were interested in becoming a nurse but it was too expensive to go to school. I have at least two books in the house on first aid. Why don't you find one and study that while we're recruiting?"

"Let's plan a trip into town the day after tomorrow. Make lists of everything you need and what store. I want to take Dani, Phillip, Mark, Emily, and Jamie."

There was some discussion of details and Eric went to bed. "I have to get up at zero dark thirty to butcher that hog and cook breakfast. We're going to be running hard. The easy part was that leisurely trip up here."

Chapter 34

They were back at what they were designating the Hiring Point, or H Point, by midmorning, equipped with plenty of pork. Eric and Dani both stood in the middle of the road for a little while, then moved back into the shade. The weather was turning warmer, and the air was not really moving yet. A few minutes later, Taylor rode up and did the same U-turn maneuver as last time. Dani walked out into the road without any weapons and sat down.

"Hi! I heard your name is Taylor. I'm Dani. How old are you?"

"I'm fourteen. Almost fifteen."

"Well, I'm not that much older than you are. Are you hungry?"

She nodded. "We're out of food."

"How many people are hungry?"

"I'm not supposed to say."

"No problem. I have a bag of food for you over there. Why don't you ride off and I'll put it there and you can come back and pick it up? And read the note that I put inside, okay?"

Taylor nodded and they went through the drill to let her pick up the food and ride off safely.

Dani watched her go, let out a long sigh, and said "Oh, God, that could have been me." She hugged Eric tightly.

***

A man came along after a while and stopped to talk, but he was trying to get home to Kansas City. They gave him a pork chop for an early lunch and wouldn't accept anything in trade for it.

Next up was a man on horseback, all in BDU camouflage and heavily armed. Eric didn't like the vibe, and just exchanged a "good morning" with the man, who was courteous enough but didn't even slow down to talk. About a hundred yards behind him was an identical figure, but female, fairly stout and with gray streaking her hair and a bandage on the side of her face. A minute or so behind her came the third man, going a little faster to catch up to the first two. All were courteous but curt, intent on their mission.

Eric watched them go, turned to Dani, and asked "Did you see what they were doing?"

"Yeah, they were doing a bounding overwatch. The third guy was watching us when the first two went by. Then the first guy stopped and was watching us from up the road somewhere."

Eric grinned widely. "Excellent. Let's see how the other student is doing. Jamie!"

"Sir?"

"What are you reading about?"

"CPR."

"Tell us the procedure for CPR."

She went through the steps pretty proficiently, and Eric upwardly revised his estimate of her.

"Emily. I see someone coming this way. I want you to talk to them, see if they have any special skills, that sort of thing. Size them up. See if you think they would be a good addition."

The man was in his late thirties, early forties, and looked like a deskbound middle manager suddenly thrown out on the streets, which is probably exactly what he was. He was pulling a suitcase with wheels. They exchanged hellos when he got close enough, and he followed it up with "I don't suppose you have any food I could trade for, do you?"

Emily looked him up and down and issued a challenge: "We're hiring for ranch hands and farmers but you don't look like you'd last a day."

The man swallowed, then straightened his back and replied "I played football in high school and college! I know I've gotten fat working behind a desk, but it's coming off, believe me! I don't know anything about ranching or farming but give me a chance! I'll work hard! I have noth—" his throat clenched up on him as he remembered his losses, and he turned his face away, wiping tears from his eyes.

Emily looked horror-stricken. She ran up and hugged him, trying to soothe his pain, looking at Eric and Dani wide eyed, seeking help. Eric waved a "come on" gesture and Emily led the man to the side of the road where they gave him water and pork and allowed him to compose himself.

"I might have a job for you," Eric told him. "Right now, all it pays is room and board and safety, and right now it's just hot, dirty work, but we're going to try real hard to push that into something better as quickly as possible." He talked to the man some more, getting a feel for his skills and experience. He also asked about proficiency with firearms. Nobody asked questions about spouse, kids, or things like that. Everyone knew the answers and no one wanted to bring it up. That did no one any good.

While he was talking to the man, Dani kept an eye on the road, and Taylor rode up. Dani waved and smiled and sat down at the edge of the highway. Taylor hadn't done the U-turn thing, she just stopped, took a few deep breaths, and then slowly moved the bike closer to Dani, pushing off the pavement with her feet and not pedaling. She had a backpack on this time, too.

"Miz Mitchell wants me to come with you tonight and go back and talk to her tomorrow." She said it all in a stream with the words run together. She reached into a back pocket and handed Dani a note with a hand that trembled.

"Here, come sit down beside me while I read this," Dani instructed. The note was brief:

> *Dear Dani, thank you so much for the food! As you can understand, we must be very cautious. There seem to be more bad people than good now, and there is no law to stop them, but Taylor is a very brave girl. I would like for her to stay with you tonight and come back to*

*me tomorrow. Can we talk after that? Thank you! Liz
Mitchell.*

Dani put her arm around Taylor. "We're not going to hurt
you. Calm down."

"I'm just scared."

"I can understand that, but you're safe now. Do you think
it would be a good idea for you to take more food back to Miz
Mitchell now?"

"I... guess. They don't have any."

"Let's pack up what we have left."

When Taylor returned from dropping the food off they all
headed for the house. Eric was discouraged that they had
recruited only the one man. He had wasted a lot of man-hours
for not much return, but tomorrow was the trip to town, so
maybe they could find some workers that way. He also had to
do something about them all eating tonight.

These damn people have to eat every *day!* he thought,
trying to make it a joke to cheer himself up. *I know one thing
that will help: delegating some of the chores.*

"Emily, you are now the house manager. I want you to take
care of keeping us fed, with adequate firewood, fresh water,
clean clothes, haircuts, whatever. I don't expect you to do it all
yourself, but I need you to manage it. You will get others to
do the actual work. What the military does is draw up a
requirement and ask for people to fill it. The companies then
release people from their usual duties to perform the required
task. Suppose you need firewood cut. You tell Curtis or
whoever that you need one man for one day to split wood and
he has to supply someone. I imagine you'll have two or three
people working for you every day. I'd rather the tasks be done
by everyone on a rotating basis rather than having one guy just
split wood every day, for example. We need to cross-train so
that people can perform multiple tasks. I have confidence in
you." She looked kind of wide-eyed but nodded.

He turned to the ex-jock ex-businessman. "Ted, you are

going to go to the ranch in the mornings. Come back after lunch. In the afternoons I want you to experiment and learn how to make beef and pork jerky. You said you'd been deer and hog hunting, so you're on hunting detail in the evenings. I'll show you some good spots when we get back. And we'll find you a rifle. My philosophy is to keep military calibers for defense and use other calibers for hunting."

That eased some of the pressure in his mind. He didn't need to fritter his time away with everyday crap. He had to step out of the sergeant's role and get into the lieutenant's. No, more like the captain's, with a freer hand to run a company as he sees fit.

That evening, he really enjoyed directing some questions to Emily. "Ask Emily. She's the house manager." She would look at him and he would smile and very deliberately turn his attention elsewhere. Then she would make a decision and he would ignore the hell out of her. He might not fully agree with what she said but he was going to let her make her own mistakes as long as they were not catastrophic ones.

Dani stayed close by Taylor, who finally seemed to calm down some. Eric mainly stayed away. He figured Taylor was afraid of men, and he didn't want to intimidate the poor girl. He didn't know Dani would get the same idea. After they ate, Dani plopped down in his lap, put her arms around him, and gave him a kiss. "Why don't you and Phillip have a boy's night with the ranch hands? In the bunkhouse? Tonight?"

His face fell. "You're kicking me out?"

"It's for Taylor. It's not just her and Miz Mitchell. There are some other kids there, too. I don't know how many yet. Just think, if we save those kids, this could be your ticket to Heaven, you heathen."

He sighed dramatically. "Don't stay up late. We're on the road tomorrow to town." Phillip walked up about then, looking forlorn. Obviously Emily had just given him the word that he was kicked out for the night, too.

"Let's go so the girls can have their little sleepover," he

moaned, hamming it up, sticking his lower lip out in a huge pout and hanging his head.

"Oh, get out!" Dani cried, laughing. "Go! Two grown men acting like five-year olds."

Eric and Phillip play-stomped out, pouting, heads down, acting like the most put-upon creatures in history.

Chapter 35

In the morning, Taylor took off in one direction with a smile on her face and a backpack that had more in it than when she'd arrived. Eric assumed it was full of food and that there would be more mouths to feed by nightfall. Emily would stay to manage the household, and Eric, Dani, Phillip, Mark, and Jamie headed to Henderson, which would be about four hours round trip at most. Coming in on Highway 79, they would run into a grocery store, two auto parts stores, a Tractor Supply Store, a drug store, a few places for clothing and boots, and a Wal-Mart. Eric gritted his teeth when he thought about the Wal-Mart, but maybe he wouldn't have to shoot his way out of this one. At least he'd have more backup if he did.

The trip in was uneventful. All of the stores they wanted to get into had already been scavenged, so they had no problem getting in, but finding some items was difficult. Of course anything remotely related to food was gone. Fortunately, they weren't looking for food, and they managed to find most of what they wanted. Dani was especially happy to get some clothes and footwear. She only had a couple of changes of clothes and one pair of boots, so she multiplied her wardrobe several times over on this trip.

The real gold, though, was at Tractor Supply Company. Phillip was at the auto parts stores and the girls were clothes shopping with Mark designated as their security and beast of burden. That left Eric to go alone, which was fine with him. There were several small groups of people and singles in the parking lot, and inevitably a couple of them begged him for food. He stopped and said "I can't give you anything, but if you want to work, I'll feed you and give you a place to stay."

He was almost mobbed.

The dozen people in the parking lot tripled in size in no time at all, all of them clamoring at Eric to choose them. He was dumbfounded. *Where the hell did all of these people come from?*

"HOLD IT!" he yelled, trying to get them to be quiet for a minute. "I —" he started, then hesitated, then decided to just go for it. "I have enough positions open to take everyone." Cheers went up, and some thank yous. "That doesn't mean I'm *going* to take all of you." Some groans. "The work is ranching and farming. There may be some other jobs but count on those for now. It's hard work in the hot sun. If you have a skill that we need, then you'll do that. I don't care what color you are, or what sex, or religion, or any of that. You work, you eat. It's that simple. I am not running any fucking social experiments. I don't owe you anything. If you're lazy, then go away. No one is going to lay on their ass and bitch because they aren't getting their welfare checks. No one is going to lay on their ass because they used to be rich or important. That was yesterday, and yesterday is gone. This is today. And today, if you want to eat, you work."

"That's fair," a big guy in the crowd replied. "That's all we're asking for."

Eric nodded at him. "First, any military?" Three people put their hands up or stepped forward. Eric made a "follow me" gesture and walked away. "First person stand here." He pointed at the pavement and walked another four steps. "Second person stand here." He walked another four steps and stopped. One was with him and the others were spread out where he'd put them. They'd all gotten that right, at least. The one near him was a black woman, about 5'8" and built like a truck. Not fat, but broad shouldered and muscled, with hair worn tight against her head. A good sign of her competence was that she regarded him with cool, unintimidated eyes. He was willing to bet she'd stared down officers before.

"Tell me your branch, rank, and MOS" he said.

She came to attention and stated "United States Air Force, master sergeant, retired, Security Forces."

He stepped off to the side a little, out of her direct line of vision, to see if her eyes would follow him. The position of attention requires that the eyes remain forward, so cutting them over to look at someone standing to the side breaks the position. Her eyes remained straight ahead. Eric started a rapid fire series of questions, sometimes not giving her the chance to fully answer one before he hit her with the next. That, too, is a military trick to throw someone off of their game.

"Where were you stationed?"

"Basic was San Antonio —"

"What was your service pistol?"

"M-9."

"Where is Keesler?"

"Biloxi, Mississippi."

"What is a C-130?"

"A four-engine turboprop —"

"What does an AC-130 carry?"

"Guns. It's a gunship. 105 millimeter cannon and, uh, Gatling guns —"

"How many B-52s loaded with nuclear weapons are on standby at Barksdale Air Force Base?"

She stiffened even more and replied "Sir, I have no knowledge and can neither confirm nor deny —"

"Stop." He stepped back in front of her, smiled and put out his hand. "You are definitely hired, and not to be a ranch hand. I want you to run my security forces. My name is Eric Marten."

"Thank you. I'd prefer you just call me Brennan. That's my last name." She was still formal but looked relieved.

Eric pointed at the nearest man who claimed military experience. "Interview him. Was he really military?"

He wasn't. He fumbled her questions, and the more he fumbled, the harder she pressed. She told him to stop and turned to Eric and looked at him inquisitively.

"Do what you think you should do," he told her.

She turned back to the man and said "No, we can't use you. Don't lie about military service."

"No, wait!" the man cried, grabbing Brennan's arm. Mistake. She drove the heel of her hand into his nose twice, then caught his arm, twisted it, and took him face first to the ground. She was holding his arm in a position to break it if he resisted. "If you ever touch me again, I will tear your arm off and beat you to death with it. DO YOU UNDERSTAND ME, MOTHERFUCKER?"

"Yes, ma'am! Yes, ma'am! I'm sorry!"

She released him and he got up and took off running. She looked at Eric, unsure if she was about to get fired. She started to assume the position of attention again.

His expression hadn't changed one bit. "You're also on instructor duties. I want the girls — hell, I want *everyone* — to be able to react like that," he said. "Talk to this next guy, who looks like he's about to piss his pants, and I'm going to ask for medical personnel. You find out if anyone is an electrician, mechanic, engineer, that sort of thing."

"I may not know what questions to ask them."

"Fake it. I don't know that much about the Air Force."

Eric turned to the crowd and pointed out a teenaged boy on the edge and called him over. "Are you here with anyone?"

"No, sir, I was riding with some people but I'm not related to them or anything."

"We're hiring you, so you're good. Your first job is to go look in those clothing stores down there. Find a girl named Dani. Dark hair, Latina, five foot two. Ask her to please come here and talk to me." *We're going to be able to carry more stuff back with us*, Eric thought. *We're going to need it.*

***

Dani's jaw dropped when she saw the crowd. "Wow, it's all about location, isn't it?"

"Yeah, it kind of makes up for only hiring one guy yesterday. The good news is that now we can carry more stuff back. We're gonna load these guys up. I need you to choose what we load them up with. The bad news is that we have to feed these people."

Dani's eyes went wide. "They're... *all* coming with us?"

"Yeah. We're gonna strip all cargo off of Mark. I need him to haul ass back and tell Emily about this crowd coming in. We need to butcher a cow and start cooking. We probably need stew. These people are malnourished. They'd get sick if we slapped a big steak down in front of them. We need — hell, I better just start writing up a list."

***

In the end, they took almost everyone. The rejects were the drunks and meth heads and a couple of others that had attitude problems. The highlights were a motorcycle mechanic, a carpenter, and a guy that had flunked out of the fire academy. Despite flunking out, he knew more about fire safety than anyone else around.

"Listen up, everybody!" Eric called to the crowd. "We are going to leave in a half hour. If you can come with us today, then stay here. If you need to go somewhere and get your stuff, then be here tomorrow morning and I'll send someone to get you. Either stay here or come back tomorrow morning." A few people hurried around the building to the big patch of woods behind it, struck their tents, and returned within minutes. No one else budged.

Next problem is that only about a third have bikes. Most are on foot, Eric thought. He found Phillip. "I have to get back soonest and prepare for this influx of people. I need you to bring them in. You're the only one I trust to find the way back. Dani and Jamie have never been this way before. Once we get back I'll send out guides."

"I paid attention on the way in. I can get back to your place."

"That's why I trust you. You might want to get some shovels at Tractor Supply so they can dig those latrines when they get there. I guess a lot of them are going to have to sleep in tents until we can get them parceled out to the other farms and ranches. Bunk beds, we're gonna need lumber and stuff to make more bunk beds. Are we gonna have men's and women's bunkhouses? How are we — why are you laughing? God, I'm losing it, aren't I? I am truly bouncing off of the walls."

"You're losing it like an adolescent girl when her prom date is late."

"I am going to treat you like the Marine Corps NCO that you are. Corporal, get these troops in to the company area and get them housed."

"Aye aye, sergeant."

Back home, Emily introduced the newcomers: Taylor had brought in Liz Mitchell, two girls about nine or ten, and a boy about five, none of them related. Liz had just gathered them in along the way. The best thing about her was that she was a nurse. Apparently she had a Bachelor of Science in Nursing, which is better than being a Registered Nurse. Eric was too busy at the moment to appreciate the distinction.

"I am overjoyed that you're here," he told her. "And your first task is going to be taking a look at the ten or twelve people that came in with me. Check for lice and whatever, you know better than I do. Then we have another twenty people walking in, another two or three hours for them to get here. We're going to put them to work so we need to have plenty of water purified for them. I have a description in a book that shows how to build a water purifier. You know, charcoal, sand, whatever. I need you to head up getting those built. Team up with Emily to get some hands to help. Jamie wants to be a nurse, so use her as an assistant. If you need another assistant, choose one. If you think something needs to be done, do it. You don't have to come to me with everything to get my approval. Do it and tell me about it the next time we talk." He mimed using a sword to knight her. "You have the authority."

Chapter 36

They muddled through.

The refugees didn't complain, yet, because now they had more food and better security, but most of all, now they had a safe home. That went a long, long way towards making other difficulties less irritating. Emily almost tore her hair out for the first week, but Phillip and Eric both brought her along in delegating and managing people, and she threatened to quit less and less frequently. The ranch hands got some much-needed help, and the farmers thought they might even be able to eat this year. Eric wasn't about to let the ranch hands get lazy, though. He and Dani went out in every direction, finding new ranches, farms, and woodlands to take in. They made another trip to Henderson for more labor, and tried to hit the rendezvous intersection every Saturday, but no one else that Eric knew showed up. The last time, they posted a note on the bulletin board to go to Tractor Supply in Henderson.

Dani also launched into what Eric thought of as her Marine Corp basic training. Not that he stood her at attention and yelled at her, but she started a regimen that involved physical training and military studies. They continued what they had started during the journey, transferring all of Eric's military knowledge to her, and she read from his large collection of military-themed books and technical manuals. She had worked out religiously pre-Hexen, and she continued that now. Eric had weights and a kick-boxing punching bag and they both went at it early every morning. Dani worked with Brennan extensively, soaking in hand-to-hand combat knowledge like a sponge. She groaned in the mornings from the sore muscles, but she gritted her teeth and got up and did it all over again. Taylor went through it all, too. She had glommed onto Dani and was a constant shadow to her, earning the two of them the nickname "Salt 'n' Pepper" for their hair colors.

Eric had a three hundred-yard rifle range, and if they needed a shorter distance, say for pistols, they just moved closer to the targets. Dani practiced everything as much as she could. Eric wanted to conserve military caliber ammo but there was plenty in other calibers available. Every house they went to had at least several boxes of ammo. Dani didn't like shotguns since even a twenty gauge beat her small frame up, but she became absolute hell with rifle or pistol. They found some ARs in odd calibers so she could practice on that platform with iron sights, but scope or irons, she was deadly. Taylor was even better.

***

The big news was Phillip's electrical successes. He got the solar panels working, so Eric's house had electricity. The lights worked, the air conditioning worked, and the well and therefore the shower worked. Eric wasn't keen on actually running the air conditioning, though.

"I don't want us to be the lord and lady in the palace with the cold air while all of the peasants are out sweating their asses off," he said. Fortunately, he would allow the use of the shower, so they had hot running water as needed.

Phillip and Bear, the motorcycle mechanic, an enormous black man who probably went 6'4" and three hundred pounds, also got trucks and tractors and motorcycles to run, provided they were old enough that they didn't have anything that was EMP-fried beyond their capabilities to replace or bypass. The collection parties they sent out changed from a group on bikes returning with whatever they could carry on their backs to scouts on bikes, and then motorcycles. They found things and then gave the address to a group in an old truck. That increased their cargo-carrying capacity immensely, and made it practical to get heavy things like lumber and concrete blocks, and bulky items like mattresses and furniture. Eric's house got a new freezer and refrigerator and his garage got turned into a meat locker, with rows of freezers and refrigerators full of beef and pork.

Since lumber and building materials were now more available, that made housing easier, and Eric gathered Phillip, the carpenter, and a couple of others with construction experience.

"The real heat of summer is going to slam into us in a couple of months, as you guys know. Now, there were plenty of people living in Texas long before air conditioning was invented, so it can be done. I know some theory but I don't have the experience here. I do know that we need shade and airflow. That means we need to put the bunkhouses in the shade of trees and have big windows. What else?"

"Tall ceilings help, and put a cupola on top. Let the hot air rise and flow out the cupola and draw cooler air in the windows."

"You need porches or at least a roof overhang to shade the windows and also keep out rain."

"In south Louisiana, they have shotgun houses. They don't have halls. All of the rooms are in a line, with the doors and windows all lined up so that breezes go right through them. That's why they're called shotguns. You can open all of the doors and fire a shotgun from outside all the way through the house and not hit anything."

"Yeah, a dog trot house is like that, but they separate the rooms under one roof. You have a living room and kitchen on one side, then a gap of eight or ten feet, then a couple of bedrooms. "

They ended up with a quick and dirty design that reminded Eric of a screened-in pavilion or porch. The flooring resembled a wooden deck, covered with plywood. Over that was a wide roof supported by four-by-four columns, with screens in between. This allowed maximum airflow to blow through the structure but kept the mosquitos out. The houses were sited amongst the trees to take advantage of the shade they provided. Eric never could understand why someone would want to build a house out in the middle of a bare field, with no trees in sight. When the temperatures turned colder, they could see about building walls in between the columns.

"And flags," Eric said. "Every house will fly the American flag. Texas flag is optional, but *every* residence will fly the Stars and Stripes. That's one of the things we're going to fix when we rebuild this country." Eric's house sported twin flagpoles in front that carried both flags every day. As a typical Texan, he flew the state flag at the same height as the U.S. flag.

The story goes that since Texas was once an independent nation, it is the only state that can fly its flag at the same height as the U.S. flag. That's not entirely true. All states can fly their flags at the same height as the stars and stripes, it's just that they don't.

Except Texas.

***

Dani and Eric lay in bed together after a long day. They had the door closed, since there were about four other people in the house currently. People were up at all hours of the day or night, hunting hogs, shooting coyotes and domestic dogs-turned-wild that preyed on the calves, cooking, boiling water for purification, guarding against rustlers, an endless list of chores to keep life going in a world that was only slowly beginning to move back from the early to the late nineteenth century.

"Big picture," Eric said, lying on his back and staring at the ceiling. "We are doing good with the properties that we have. We've scouted more properties and we're starting to manage them. We at least had someone open all the internal gates so the cattle can roam any field on the property. What next? It's been a little over a month since Hexen hit. I think any canned food that people may have is going to be gone soon. We need to get cattle into town and establish the connections with butchers or whoever."

"Yes," Dani agreed. "We need to meet people and set up agreements with them. Let them know that we are going to be an ongoing operation and not someone who is just bringing in all the cattle from a ranch and then abandoning it."

"I'll talk to Curtis tomorrow. He's going to have to teach me how to do this. Or teach someone."

"Which town are you thinking? I looked at the map and Tyler is definitely bigger than Henderson or Jacksonville."

Eric didn't answer immediately. "I guess we need to explore the situation in Tyler at some point. It's a hundred thousand people. Well, before Hexen. Ten thousand now, maybe, minus those that might have fled, plus refugees that came in. Henderson and Jacksonville were both about thirteen or fourteen thousand, so just over a thousand now. Tyler is obviously the best market to get into."

"And shop!" Dani was smiling and gazing off in the far distance, imagining what treasures she might find. Although in a few short weeks, her shopping habits had changed radically. Before Hexen she wanted cute, trendy clothes. Now she wanted some necessities like underwear, plus hiking boots, athletic socks, and well-made pants and shirts that would stand up to her current lifestyle. She may not have been tilling fields and working cattle but she seemed to rarely walk on pavement any more and her clothing needed to be sturdy. Sleeves and pants legs that could be rolled up helped, cargo pockets were in, and belt loops meant that her pants would stay on when she loaded up with a pistol, extra magazines, knife, and other items.

Chapter 37

They loaded eight cows into a trailer and towed it with an old truck, with two other trucks and smaller trailers in their convoy.

Curtis drove, with Dani in the middle and Eric riding shotgun. Phillip, Mark, Bear, and David rounded out the other truck crews. They were all fully armed as a matter of safety but intended to trade and shop.

They wound around to Interstate 69, coming into Tyler from the south. There were a number of dead cars on the road but there was one clear lane open all the way, if not two lanes. Cars had been pushed off to the sides. It had taken machinery to move a lot of them, since many newer cars can't be shifted into neutral unless the engine is on. That obviously wasn't an option, so many of the cars showed marks from having been shoved by a bulldozer or bigger vehicle. Whoever had cleared it, Eric was thankful. He had taken horseback riding lessons as a kid but he had absolutely zero illusions about his ability to be a cowboy. If they had to herd these cows from horseback, he would just turn around and go back now.

Maybe they should have turned back.

They saw the roadblock from a ways off and stopped to examine it through binoculars. Afterwards, Eric and Phillip looked at one another, shrugged, and got back into the trucks. They hadn't seen anything that screamed "Stay away!" There were some young guys in ball caps sitting and standing under the shade of a pop-up canopy, one of those cloth things with a folding aluminum frame. Certainly they had weapons but they weren't in their hands. They rolled forward and stopped at the canopy. The young men were on their feet now, holstered pistols on hips but no long arms in their hands.

Almost everyone got out of the trucks, too. Better to be free of the confines of a truck cab if something bad goes down.

They took their cue from the roadblock crew, holstered pistols but the rifles stayed in the trucks. Dani got out but stood by the truck with the door open and her rifle within easy reach, muzzle down.

"Good morning" Eric greeted the men, although there was no cheer in his voice, just neutral, neither friendly nor hostile.

One of the men replied in the same tone *"Como estas"* and raised his sunglasses up. He looked Eric up and down carefully, evaluating him. Eric was wearing his usual hiking boots, jeans, and a plain black T-shirt. He had on a normal leather belt with a holstered Glock 19, a double-magazine pouch, a Becker Combat Utility knife, and a utility pouch. Although the man couldn't see it, it held an M-14 magazine and a QuikClot packet. He could see Eric's tattoos, including the Marine Corps Eagle, Globe, and Anchor.

He nodded to himself. What he saw was not a man merely wearing the trappings of war, but a man of war. This was a man to be treated with a certain amount of respect, otherwise he might leave this earth this morning. His brothers might avenge him, but he would take no pleasure in that. He would rather remain where he was for now. He removed his sunglasses entirely and looked Eric in the eye.

"We are *Los Pistoleros De Oro*," he said. "This is our territory. We provide security for you to come here and trade. You have cattle?" He didn't wait for a reply but strolled down the length of their little convoy, looking into the trucks and the trailer, and checking out the people. Dani got back into the truck as he approached her, and rolled up the window. She had had to be shown how to roll the window up, since it was manual. The man stopped and peered into the window at her, smiling. She flipped him the bird and ignored him. He laughed and walked on.

He returned to his original spot. "We also have things for sale, little pleasures of life. Girls. Drink. Various herbs and chemicals and whatever you want. Just a mile from here, at the Buckingham Hotel."

"I think we're good."

The pistolero smiled and dipped his head in acknowledgement. "A man of steel," he mused. "You have eight cows. Our tax is twenty-five percent, so we require two cows. And I can probably say that we would like to trade with you if you can bring in a steady supply of beef."

Eric's temper started to flare. He glanced around at the other men around the roadblock, evaluating their readiness.

The man smiled and wagged a finger. "No, no. I see what you're doing. We could shoot it out here, your men and mine, but that would do no one any good. You may even kill us all, but we are not the only ones. We have many more. My brothers would hunt you all down. Much better to pay the tax and trade safely and securely here. Hasn't there been enough death?"

Even through his anger, Eric knew that he should try to gather some intel. "You say this is your territory. How big a territory? Where exactly are you providing security?"

"All of Tyler. We are huge in Dallas, and we are expanding our operations."

"So you have more than the five guys here?"

"Of course! We have many men here in Tyler."

"Fifty guys, then?"

The pistolero had been getting angry with the questions, the challenge to his power and authority, but now he paused, realizing he was giving up maybe too much information. He smiled instead.

"Many. *Numeroso.*"

"Where's the boss?"

"At the Buckingham. He likes to be close to the little pleasures I mentioned."

"You think he'd be interested in trading for some cows? After you take your tax?"

"I do. He may even invite you to a barbeque."

***

Lighter by two cows, the little convoy headed deeper into Tyler to a hospital. Eric sat and seethed anger. Dani was about to bounce off of the walls herself, but she kept quiet for the time being. No sense in irritating him further, but once they stopped, Eric gathered everyone around.

"You know what went down back there. Basically, we got robbed by a gang. This gang says Tyler is their territory. I want to get a look at their operations, gather some intel. I hate like hell to deal with them, but otherwise we'll be blind. We have to know something about them in order to deal with them. I'm going to have to smile and be my charming self. We're going to get the things we need, maybe not all of them, because I'm going to take two cows to the gang and talk to their boss. See what I can find out."

"Shit, that means we're going to be out half of our load! They stole two and now you're going to *give* them two more?" Curtiss was usually totally calm, but this had gotten under his skin. Eric had known him since he was just a kid and he'd never seen him this mad.

"No, I'm going to trade. Hopefully they have something useful. But either way, it's a small price to pay to get a look at their headquarters."

"Shit!" Curtiss kicked a tire and stomped off.

"After we get our stuff, I want Mark driving the truck with the trailer. He and I will go to the gang HQ. Just us."

Chapter 38

Inside the hospital, they found a single doctor and almost no other medical personnel. "The disease has apparently burned itself out," he related. "Everyone is either dead or immune to it. That really cut down on the number of children and elderly we've admitted, and we've had an upsurge of injuries and conditions that we don't usually see as frequently. Heatstroke and heart attacks brought on by working in the heat, cuts and broken bones from people doing work that is unusual to them. Imagine a forty-year old man, sedentary lifestyle, and suddenly he has to forage for food and chop wood. He's unfamiliar with the tools and unaccustomed to the heat. It's a recipe for disaster."

"Those are exactly some of the same problems we are having with our workers," Eric replied. "Which is why we'd like to trade for some medical supplies." He presented the list. "We have a woman with a Bachelor of Science in Nursing. She made that list and signed it at the bottom."

The doctor read through the list and handed it back. "I'm afraid I can't really spare any supplies. We may never get any restock, and some of these drugs listed are prescription-only. I can't simply give away cases of it. Despite the world situation, I may lose my license and even go to prison if I authorized that."

"How is your patient nutrition?" Eric asked.

The doctor snorted. "Poor. Almost exclusively canned foods loaded with salt and sugars, and dwindling supplies of that."

"Well, I guess we'll take our thousands of pounds of beef and get back on the road, then."

"What? Beef? You didn't say anything about that!" The doctor leapt to his feet.

***

They left the hospital with most of the supplies they'd listed, including the drugs. They'd bargained to trade one cow for the supplies. When they were ready to turn the cow over to the doctor, Dani looked at Eric and held up two fingers. He looked at her for a few seconds, until she said "It's the right thing to do." He sighed, nodded, and walked over to where Curtiss was handling the movement of the livestock.

"Dani is negotiating for our entry into the Pearly Gates," he told him. Curtiss looked at him uncomprehendingly. "Let's give him two cows."

"TWO?" he looked at Eric, then turned to look at Dani. She was smiling beatifically. He looked at Eric, looked at Dani, and finally shook his head and bent to the work of herding another cow out of the trailer, muttering under his breath.

Eric walked back to Dani. "Tell the doc what you did."

She looked embarrassed. "No, no, I don't want to take credit for it. You go and tell him. I'll stay here."

Eric walked over to the doctor, who was sending a messenger off to find a butcher. "Doc, we bargained for one cow in return for those supplies, but we're giving you two cows."

The doctor looked amazed, then questioning. "But —"

Eric nodded his head in Dani's direction. "Dani's suggestion. I think she's hiding behind the truck there. I guess she's a better Christian than the rest of us. She wanted to make the donation."

"And she's embarrassed by that?"

"Well, you know how it is. You don't want to do a good deed and then throw it in someone's face so they have to praise you."

"What a remarkable young woman. Please convey my heartfelt thanks to her, and thanks to all of you. Everyone please have a blessed day."

***

They made several other stops, restaurants for large pots for communal meals, drugstores for minor first aid and bath supplies, an auto parts store for things needed to get some more old trucks running, and several stores where they could find work boots and clothing. They didn't need to trade for the most part, as the stores were chains that had been abandoned, but they did part with some ammunition for some needed boots from a local shop owner.

The last stop was the last stop on purpose. It was at a Lowe's, and they intended to use the cattle trailer to haul the hardware back. They found someone in a Lowe's red employee vest that claimed he was the manager. Whether he was or not was impossible to tell, but they weren't going to just steal the items if he claimed them, so they traded. They offloaded two cows and tied them up in the parking lot. Eric and Mark took off in the truck with the two remaining cows and headed to the Buckingham Hotel. The others stayed there and gathered the hardware and items they needed. They got cases of nails and wood screws, and smaller quantities of nuts and bolts, large stacks of PVC pipe with the appropriate fittings and adhesive, plywood and MDF, chain, rope, window screening, vegetable seeds, insecticide, and a selection of hand tools.

***

After staging all of that in the parking lot for easy loading into the trailer, Phillip started roaming. He saw an older model eighteen-wheeler, actually just the cab, at the far end of the parking lot and thought *why not*? It was unlocked and there was no one dead inside, so he jumped in and tried to start it. His mouth dropped open when it actually fired up. He looked out at the others and gave a victory fist in the air. Bear wandered over.

"You know how to drive that thing?" he asked.

Phillip looked around at all of the gauges and switches, turned back to Bear and said "No."

"Scoot over." Bear hopped into the driver's seat and proved he could drive it, running it up and down the parking lot, doing figure-eights, and testing the brakes, which almost threw Phillip through the windshield. "Brakes work!" he observed.

"Awesome! We're taking this sucker. I have some ideas for this thing."

Chapter 39

On the way to the Buckingham, Eric told Mark "When we get back, I want you to be able to sketch the hotel, the parking lot, and everything around it. Don't be obvious; don't make any notes or sketches while we're there. Just casually look around at everything. And watch the people. See what they do and how they do it."

They found the Buckingham, no problem. It fronted onto South Broadway and they had actually passed it earlier. They circled around in the parking lot and got out. There was one guy at the door, apparently stationed there since he didn't move from that spot. A couple of other guys came out and waited for Eric to approach.

He nodded at them. "I understand you are *Los Pistoleros de Oro*. I want to meet with the boss, what do you call him, *El Jefe?*"

"*Eres un ranchero?"(Are you a rancher?)* one of them asked.

Eric understood it, since his Spanish was improving under Dani's tutelage, but he didn't want to give that away. He'd rather be able to eavesdrop on their conversations. He turned a hand up. "*No habla, señor.*"

"Rancher. Do you have more cattle?"

"Yes, I do. And I understand that I might be able to keep you boys in a steady supply of beef."

The man almost smiled but seemed to restrain himself. "Come inside," he invited. He went through the lobby to the bar and to a table in the back where a bearded, well-dressed man sat. He spoke in rapid-fire Spanish to the man, who nodded, then retreated to stand a few feet to the side.

"A drink?" the man asked.

Eric was tempted to ask for an ice-cold beer, but his host could not provide that, and so would be embarrassed. He would have to forego the pleasure of being an asshole in order to get in their good graces. "I would love a drink. Bourbon, perhaps?"

"An excellent choice." The man standing nearby walked to the bar to get their drinks.

"I am a captain of *Los Pistoleros de Oro*," the man explained. "We have a military organization. I am in charge of the city of Tyler."

"That's a large territory." Eric hated kissing the man's ass.

"We are growing. The recent difficulties have suppressed the police and allowed us to operate relatively unimpeded. Which has actually created the difficulty of feeding my men. I understand you are a rancher?"

"Yes. We have gathered some workers to us and have taken over some ranches south of Jacksonville." They were actually east of Jacksonville by a number of miles.

"Can you offer a steady supply of beef?"

"That is our intent, but that remains to be seen. Fires or a drought or disease or who knows what could interfere with our plans. Excellent bourbon, by the way. Thank you."

The captain nodded graciously. "My pleasure."

"So a steady supply means how much beef to you?"

"How much can you supply? I have a large need."

Damn it, he's going to be cagey with the numbers. That's okay. I guess I couldn't expect him to blab everything to me right at first. I am in the enemy's camp, after all.

"I have two cows available right now, just outside. Plus I paid a tax of two cows coming in. Why don't you sample those and I'll come back in three days? If you want, we can set up a steady supply run. For an appropriate trade, of course."

"Of course. Everything has a price. What would interest you? A lovely lady for your pleasure? Cases of that excellent bourbon? Money has no value now, of course."

"Ammunition would be high on my list, .223 mainly, plus some .308."

The captain's eyes grew suspicious. "Isn't .223 too light

for deer? A man-killer?"

"Oh, for dogs. The countryside is overrun with them. Millions of them. Cats, too. The owners died and the pets went wild. They attack anything — calves, chickens, pigs, deer. It's only a matter of time before they start attacking grown men. A pack of big dogs can tear a man apart. Even a single bite can give you rabies. I hear that is an especially agonizing death."

The captain looked uneasy and glanced at the door as if a pack of slavering wild dogs would materialize at any moment and start hurling their bodies against the glass in an attempt to attack him. He had apparently grown up in a city and wild animals terrified him.

Eric decided to lay it on thicker. "I have people out every night shooting the dogs down, and coyotes, too. I'm surprised you don't have packs of wild dogs running the streets here at night. If you don't now, you will soon."

"Then allow me to assist you in this effort," the captain said. He spoke in Spanish to the man nearby, who hustled off and soon returned with three others. Eric and the captain had spent the time in small talk, speculating about the plague and power outage. The men all had heavy boxes of ammunition, three thousand rounds of .223 and five hundred of .308. Eric was delighted. He didn't have to fake that at all. The men stacked the boxes in the bed of the truck and directed them around the southeast side of the parking lot.

There was grass there, and a corral made up of cars. The gangbangers had pushed dead cars into a huge circle, bumper to bumper, to form a fence. There was a normal gate supported by posts set in concrete, and they fed the cattle simply by tossing hay and grain over the hoods. Eric was taken aback by the herd. He tried to get a quick count but didn't want to be obvious about it. There were dozens, maybe a hundred. He looked at Mark and muttered, "How many damn cows do they need?"

***

As that was going on, the captain was issuing orders to two young men. They took a good, long look at Eric's truck and trailer from inside the building and then hurried out the back.

Chapter 40

Returning to Lowe's, they loaded the now-empty cattle trailer with the building supplies and hit the road, Eric deferring all questions until they were back home. He did pull Phillip aside for a brief conversation, and made some rearrangements with the seating. They took a different route out, for two reasons. One is that Eric didn't want to go through the first roadblock again and have them "tax" him on the way out. Secondly was to see if all of the routes were covered with roadblocks. He doubted they had enough manpower to cover every back road but wanted to check.

Heading north with Bear in the lead in the eighteen-wheeler cab, the convoy took Shiloh Road east, continued east on Old Bascom Road when it turned south, and eventually worked their way out of town and back home. They didn't see any of the *Pistoleros*.

Eric and Phillip did, though briefly. They were riding together in the last truck, looking for the perfect spot. They found it about a quarter mile down Old Bascom, where the trees are close to the road and it curves to the left. As soon as they got around the curve, Phillip slammed on the brakes and skidded to a stop. Eric already had the door open and was running into the trees at the curve. They were going to watch to see if anyone was tailing their little convoy. A follower would fall back on straightaways, speed up when the convoy went around a curve, but then slow or stop once at the curve to prevent running into the back of the convoy if it stopped.

Laying an ambush at a curve was the perfect spot because a follower would be going as slow as they ever would. This curve was especially good because there were straightaways both before and after it with no turnoffs, which allowed a long shot if needed.

They spotted them within seconds, two motorcycles with quiet mufflers, speeding up to the curve and then braking. Eric stepped out into the road and leveled his Scout rifle. One of the riders braked hard and tried to turn. He lost all momentum and most of his balance and Phillip had an almost stationary shot. He fired a load of double-aught buckshot into the guy's back. He slumped, tried to straighten back up, and Phillip racked the slide of the 870 and hit him again. He and the bike sank to the pavement.

Eric had a more exciting time. The other rider full-throttled it, bringing the bike up on the back wheel, straight for him. He got off one hasty shot and then dodged out of the way. The biker roared past him but there was nowhere for him to go except straight down a long road, or go into the woods and risk smashing into a tree. Before he had time to make a decision, Eric took careful aim and put a round into his back. Rider and bike tumbled down the road.

Working quickly, Phillip and Eric threw the bodies into the truck and Phillip rode one bike into a nearby subdivision and left it in the street with the keys in it. That was the tried and true method of getting rid of a stolen vehicle: make it easy for someone else to steal it. He fired up the other bike, intending to keep it, and they took off after the convoy. They stopped once again at another curve but no more followers came along.

They made one more stop, a few miles south of Whitehouse. They turned off into a powerline cut, drove down it a little way, and dumped the bodies. They figured the chance of the *Pistoleros* finding the bodies was miniscule, that far away from Tyler. A couple of days in the sun and some attention from scavengers and the bodies would be unrecognizable anyway.

They had burned a bridge with the Pistoleros. Now they had to either hide or do something about it.

Chapter 41

Back home, Dani was happy that more gangbangers were dead, but miffed that she hadn't been invited to shoot them.

"I needed to give Phillip a shot. That was his first kill. Look at him," Eric nodded in his direction, where Phillip was recounting his shooting for an appreciative audience with sound effects and an air shotgun: "... so he raised back up, and I thought he needed another dose of Mr. Twelve Gauge — clickety-click BOOM! And he went down."

"See how happy he is? You have to share some."

Dani cut her eyes back at Eric without turning her head. "Okay, you're right."

***

After they ate that night, Eric gathered up everyone that was available, the security and predator control teams being out, and related the events of the day. He ended with "Obviously, I don't trust them. They attempted to follow us back here. I might have a suspicious mind, but I can only think of one reason why they would want to do that. That reason is for them to attack us, to steal the cattle instead of trading for them, and to steal whatever else we might have. Kidnap the females, turn them into prostitutes. Murder anyone who stood in their way. I don't want that to happen. How about you?"

"Can't we just call — well, not call, but alert the police or state troopers or something?" came from the crowd.

"I don't remember the last time I saw a single cop," Eric replied. "Much less the thirty or so it's going to take to put these guys out of business. Besides which, they are operating right out in the open. If there were enough cops to do something about it, I think they would have done so. They haven't. That means they can't. There's also the possibility that the cops or their bosses are allowing the gang to operate. As in payoffs. They're being bribed. I hope that's not the case. I imagine they're just outnumbered."

"Should we at least talk to the police? We could maybe team up with them to go after the gang."

"Under normal circumstances, I think that would be a great idea. Now, I have two concerns. One is that they may be on the gang's payroll and would alert them. The other is simply finding a cop. I guess we could go by the police station, but I just don't think it would do any good. We need to hit them with a surprise attack and I really want to keep this in-house to prevent any leaks. That would be a disaster."

That meeting broke up after some more discussion and the inner core remained: Dani, Phillip, Emily, Brennan, Mark, who had become something of an aide de camp, and Taylor, who seemed to be moving into Eric's house. Eric contemplated kicking her out for this discussion, but decided against it.

"My analysis of the situation is that we have to do something about it. This is a gang that steals and murders, sells drugs, turns girls to prostitution, and I don't know what all. Like I said earlier, I haven't seen any cops of any type anywhere, no military, nothing. No vestige of authority. So I think we have to take matters into our own hands, just like we have with everything else we've done here. I mean, no one else has stepped up and crushed these roaches yet. If we don't do it, they're going to grow stronger and take us over."

What I'd give for a squad of Marines, he thought. *Even just a fire team. Instead, I have one Marine, a Junior ROTC kid, an Air Force military police type, a couple of National Guardsmen, and not much else. And Dani, of course, who just might be tougher than any of us.*

"I have an idea where we won't have to fight them one on

one. An advantage. I need to gather some more intel on them but I don't see why I can't do that."

At Eric's direction, Mark taped a large sheet of butcher paper to the dead flat screen television. The furniture was pointed at it anyway. "This is a sketch that Mark did of their headquarters. It's a four story hotel. Looks like eighteen rooms per side, thirty-six per floor. I don't know who's on what floor yet, but this is an older hotel and the windows do have at least a portion that opens. I imagine the higher floors get more breeze, so I'd bet the *Pistoleros* are all on the upper floors."

"The bottom floor is the only one I got a look at. I don't know what is on the west end. Here is the office, then the lobby, bar and restaurant. Kitchen has to be on this end. Consulting with our former fireman, there would be fire stairs at each end of the building. Of course the elevators are out, so the fire stairs are the only way up and down."

"To the west is South Broadway, multiple traffic lanes, then parking lots and businesses. To the east are some trees and I don't know what is on the other side of them. Southeast, they have a corral made up of dead cars in a circle, and it's full of cows. To the north there are some businesses nearby. Like next door, maybe fifty yards away. To the south is a big parking lot, then more parking lot and some businesses. This is a hundred fifty to two hundred yards. The ground floor from the front desk all the way through the bar slash restaurant is glass. Also, there is a small patio to the north. That's all we have right now, but we can refine the numbers and fill in the blanks."

"My first thought was, if they have three to five man groups out at the main roads, we ambush them one by one. But I don't think that would work because we'd have to move all around the city and there would be a huge opportunity for one of them to escape and get back and warn the others. My next thought was to hit the headquarters and sit there in ambush, waiting for the teams to come in. That won't work because I don't want to be inside with them outside. They could just fade away and escape easily, to come back at us at some future time. So my idea now is to hit them just before dawn. Catch them all, or most of them, asleep. Trap them on the upper floors of the building and burn them out.

"Phillip, do you remember Field Expedient Munitions? Or explosives, whatever it was called?"

"Sure! Homemade napalm, Molotov Cocktails, all of that fun stuff." His eyes lit up and he started rubbing his hands together like an evil genius in a bad movie.

Dani looked at them questioningly. "The Marine Corps taught us how to make napalm and explosives from things you find in a hardware store or on a farm or whatever." He turned to Phillip. "Let's run some tests. I'm thinking something that's more liquid than napalm but thicker than just gasoline. Mix in some diesel, thirty-weight oil, maybe some soap flakes to thicken it up if needed. With that in mind, I want the scouts to find some tanker trucks of gas and diesel and get Bear to haul them back here with that eighteen-wheeler cab. And motor oil. It can be used, I don't care. Maybe a quick change oil place has some big drums of used oil."

"How much are you going to make?" Dani looked concerned, thinking *Boys and their toys*.

"I don't know. Couple hundred gallons. Maybe four hundred." That didn't reassure her. "We'll be safe. We're professionals." Phillip choked and spit his drink all over the table and himself. That *really* didn't reassure her. She stared at Eric intently.

"We'll be safe. I promise," Eric tried. She sighed and looked away.

I'm going to have to watch these two like a hawk, she thought. *Obviously they need adult supervision. Chronologically, I'm the youngest one here except for Taylor, but apparently the only adult.*

"Sunday afternoon we'll hold a rifle range challenge. Two hundred yards. We need to identify the four or five best riflemen or women. We need a lot of containers like milk jugs and five-gallon gas cans, two-liter Coke bottles. I want an inventory of rifles, magazines, and ammo. We're gonna need a way to block the fire doors. Lights. If we hit them at night, we're going to have to be able to light them up somehow. This would be an excellent opportunity to put flashlights on our weapons if any of the flashlights worked."

Phillip looked thoughtful. "I might be able to build flashlights with auto or motorcycle turn signal bulbs and motorcycle batteries. It would be heavy as hell."

"Define hell."

"Seven, eight pounds at the lightest."

"That's way too heavy. There's no way you could swing a rifle with that. You'd have to hold it in your left and use a pistol in your right. That might work. But still, eight pounds in your hand, swinging around... "

"Backpack it," suggested Phillip. "Put the battery in a backpack and run wires to the light."

"We need something. High priority. Can you have a working model tomorrow night?"

"Ask and ye shall receive."

Eric rubbed his eyes. "There are a million things I need to think about but I think the thing that would do me the most good would be to take a break from it. I'm going to bed."

Dani jumped in the shower for a quick rinse and went upstairs and made sure he didn't think about a single one of those million things for the rest of the night.

Chapter 42

The next day, Eric and Phillip got together with Mark, Mike, and David. They filled them in with more detail on the gang's headquarters, and Mark knew how to get there. "What we need is information on what they do and when they do it," Eric said. "I want you three to set up in one of the buildings to the west or the south and just watch the building. Take binoculars and a notebook. Write down everything you see. If someone walks up, write down the time and how many men, what they're doing, anything you see. Candlelight in a room, note what floor, what room. Someone needs to be awake and watching them at all times. Stay there today and tomorrow, and then the next day, watch what they do in the morning and then come back here about noon."

"Yeah, be very stealthy," Phillip added. "If they think you're spying on them, they'll kill you. No joke. Be quiet, don't show any lights, don't let the sun reflect off your binoculars, nothing. I guess if they did find you, you could claim you just wanted to watch the setup before you went to go rent a girl."

"Hmm, that might be a great way to gather some more intel, but..." Eric shook his head. "If I condoned someone getting with one of their prostitutes, Dani would — well, let's not go there. I've watched her kill men."

Phillip smiled at that, looking satisfied like he had just gotten confirmation for something he had heard previously. The other three gaped at Eric with open mouths.

"Dani... has... killed men?" Mark stammered. "I mean, I know she practices shooting all the time, and martial arts, but... she's so tiny and... nice... I never would have thought..."

Oh my God, Mark has a crush on Dani! Eric thought. *The kid is — well, hell, now that I think about it, that 'kid' and*

Dani are virtually the same age! That makes me feel as old as Methuselah. Almost ready to shuffle off to the old folk's home. Of course, maturity-wise, Dani is eighteen going on thirty and Mark is seventeen going on about fifteen.

Aloud, he said "Maybe I shouldn't have said anything, but yeah, Dani and I got into three gunfights coming up here from Houston. We took out, oh, I think fourteen men. Well, thirteen men and one woman who tried to stick a big freakin' revolver in my face while some guys sneaked up behind me. Dani saved my ass. Shot the guys coming up behind me. One guy pointed a shotgun at her and tried to kidnap her. She shot him about fourteen times with a 9 mil and then kicked him in the balls until he bled to death. In one gunfight, Dani ran out of ammo so she had to go hand-to-hand with a guy. He tried to strangle her. She cut his throat from ear to ear, got absolutely drenched in his blood. She doesn't carry that Gerber Mark II for show. She's used it. Hell, she took it off a guy she shot."

Phillip was now grinning broadly. He was delighted. Like true warriors everywhere, he respected another proven fighter. Mike and David were awed and excited about knowing such a badass as Dani. Mark looked like someone had taken away his puppy.

"We'll tell war stories later. Let's get you men set up with the gear you'll need and get you a couple of ATVs."

***

Dani found them while the surveillance team was still getting ready and before the two older boys started playing with fire. They were tying ATVs down on a trailer which they could take in closer to the city and then slip into the city itself on the ATVs.

"You guys be careful," she told them as they got on the road. "We want you back here safe and sound." As they left, Eric turned to find her staring at him, hands on hips.

"What?" he asked.

"Mark was acting weird, and the other two couldn't stop grinning at me. Neither will Phillip. Why is that?"

"Um, well, I kind of let it slip, and then had to give them a summary of our adventures coming up here from Houston."

She cut her eyes at the disappearing truck for a second while she thought about that, then back at Eric. "Oh. Mark doesn't think I'm so sweet and innocent anymore, huh?"

"I think he has a crush on you."

"Well, yeah, he does, but I have my man, and I'm here to make sure he doesn't set himself on fire." She directed a stern look at Eric.

"We can do our experiments with cups of gasoline instead of gallons."

Dani rolled her eyes, sighed loudly, and replied "Good idea."

Even using cups, it was frightening to her. Gasoline has a lot of explosive power in a small package. She had to give them a couple of verbal kicks in the butts to stop having fun and get the work done and in a couple of hours they had decided on a formula. It was liquid enough to pour easily and soak into a carpet, but thick enough to burn for a long time. As a bonus, it gave off a heavy, black smoke. They called it good, and just needed enough material to make up the several hundred gallons that they needed.

That task done, Phillip went off to work on the weapon light prototype and Eric and Dani started working on the million things in addition to their normal duties that this operation demanded.

***

Bear was from the local area and started bringing tankers of gasoline and diesel back from a distribution facility not too far away. He spread them out, one here, one there, and not close to any housing, for fire safety. Other items started to pile up — empty milk jugs, oil, medical supplies, some fire extinguishers, motorcycle batteries, small backpacks, glow sticks, and the list went on and on.

***

Once it got dark, Phillip demonstrated his weapon light. He had the battery in a lightweight backpack, with wires running over his shoulder to the light duct-taped under the rifle barrel. "It's ugly, it's clunky, it's not elegant," he admitted. He turned it on and swept it across the yard, illuminating the trees. "But it works."

Eric, Dani, and Brennan all tried it out themselves. "Good work. This isn't something I'd want on my rifle all the time, but for this situation I think it's great. Now we need twelve or fifteen more."

Chapter 43

A day later, Mike, David, and Mark returned unscathed on schedule. Eric gave them the afternoon off and sent them back that night, to explore the north and east sides this time.

Their work over several days of surveillance showed that the *Pistoleros* were pretty confident. They didn't run any patrols and only had three men working on the ground. They were, basically, a drug dealer, a pimp, and a guard. There was a slow trickle of people that crept in under cover of darkness to partake of the drugs and girls. It appeared they were doing a bigger business with recruiting, with a number of young refugee men showing up and being given a meal. Gang members talked to them throughout the meal, and they ended up staying in the building overnight.

In the evenings, the whole crew ate in the restaurant, and then they would hang out in the bar and the parking lot, drinking and smoking. They had collection teams that pulled up to the north side of the building to unload. It appeared they were using the conference rooms as storage. Lots of the loads were simply anonymous cardboard boxes, but there were some interesting items they could make out. The green military cans were obviously ammunition, but a number of them were painted gold for some reason. The rifles in long boxes were easy to pick out, and the cases of liquor had labels that were easily legible through binoculars. Interestingly, they didn't seem to be stockpiling the items for their own use. They were banding or plastic-wrapping the items to pallets, which seemed to indicate that they intended to ship them somewhere. And they had a running forklift to handle the pallets.

The boys filled in the sketch of the surrounding area. To the east, the patch of trees was only about forty yards away and then there was a subdivision.

"That's good. That's what I hoped. Tonight I want you

guys to take me and Phillip there. I believe you but I need to see the ground for myself. We won't stay there. We'll just spend a few hours on recon."

***

The main thing that troubled Eric was their estimate of the *Pistolero* manpower. They were estimating thirty-five or forty men. "It's hard to tell. They look a lot alike. They have the same haircuts, most of 'em. They wear the same clothing." Mike shrugged. "Unless they all stand out in the parking lot at the same time, I don't know if we can get any better count."

"That just seems high," mused Eric. "I mean, if this is a gang out of Dallas, and they have thirty-five men here, then that was a gang of three hundred and fifty before Hexen. If half of the gang is still in Dallas, that's a gang of seven hundred pre-Hexen. I don't have any experience with gangs but that seems way high." He looked at Dani.

She looked a little irked. "Right, ask the girl from the *barrio*, huh?" She exaggerated the roll of the double r. "You'd be surprised. Some gangs are huge, with thousands of members."

"No offense intended. That's not good news, but if we slap their hand hard enough in Tyler, then maybe they'll stay in Dallas. The cops can deal with them when they get reorganized." He turned things over in his mind for a minute. "That just makes it more important to not fight fair."

Dani was looking at nothing, deep in thought. "I think the *Pistoleros* in Tyler is an outpost feeding the main group in Dallas in a gang war. Well, let me start at the beginning of my thought. The police have been ineffective or nonexistent, from what we've seen so far. We can figure ninety percent of them died, and the rest are just trying to find food for themselves. Even if they are on the job, they don't have radios any more, so they are really crippled. The streets of Dallas are jammed with stalled cars, I'm sure, same as Houston, so they are on foot or bicycle. If they go out alone, they are truly alone, with no backup coming to their assistance. If they go out in groups, then that is effective only in the area where they are right then. They can't stop crime in any other area if they are bunched up in one area.

"That's basically a free-for-all for the gangs. The gangs can put more men on the ground and outnumber the cops anywhere they choose to do so. If three cops come up on thirty gangstas, the cops can either go away or die. That's no choice. Or, on the other hand, the gangs can do whatever they want while the cops are somewhere else. There are no cell phones and no 911, so the cops won't even know there's an issue. What I'm saying is that the cops are not even a factor in the equation.

"All gangs want to grow and take over more territory and make more money. With no cops around, the gangs are going to go after one another, and I'm not talking about a drive-by shooting here and there. I'm talking full-scale, military-style assaults. What's to stop them? They probably figure the government will come in at some point with the Army or state troopers or something, so they have to act now to grab anything they can get their hands on. If they can wipe out their competition, then even if law is restored in the future, they will be in a better position.

"So, Tyler... I think the *Pistoleros* sent out groups to outlying cities to gather resources to assist in their war effort. Or maybe they only sent the one group to Tyler. The point is that these guys are gathering things and feeding them in to the Dallas *Pistoleros*. They seem to be recruiting young men. They have a corral for cattle, far more cows than they can eat, and they want more. What are they doing with them? They're bringing in pallets full of guns and ammunition. They gave you three thousand five hundred rounds of ammunition without batting an eye. How much ammo would they have to have on hand that that many rounds is an insignificant number? They're collecting items and packing them on pallets for shipment. Something is going on."

"That makes me think that we need to hit them as soon as possible," Eric said, not looking happy about it. *People are going to get killed*, he thought. *Our people. My people. My responsibility. Now I know why officers get gray hair at such an early age.*

***

They had a big barbeque meal together that evening, getting as many people in from the outlying farms and ranches as possible. Before the meal, Eric stood and called for their attention.

"I'm not good at making speeches, so apologies in advance," he started. "You all know that when we took cattle into Tyler we were stopped and robbed. They called it a tax, but it was robbery. A gang called *Los Pistoleros De Oro* has established itself in Tyler and is stealing things from people going into the city. Now, when the government taxes us, they at least provide something in return, security in the form of the military and the police, streets and highways, inspections to keep the food and water safe, things like that. These thugs don't do that. They just steal, and they're selling drugs, and they have some girls that they are putting out for prostitution.

"If we just sit back and let that happen, then I don't think that says good things about us. We can just wave our hands and say it's not our problem, but when will it be our problem? What if they gain power and come here? What if they want to take our cattle, and kidnap the women? They've already tried to follow us back here. I can only conclude they want to know where we are so that they can steal everything from us. I think we have to put a stop to this now, before they get bigger. And before anyone asks, no, the police aren't going to handle it. When was the last time any of you saw a police officer? State Trooper? Any military?"

Silence.

"So I think it's up to us. We have to take them out. What I don't want to do is to go head to head with them. I don't want to fight fair. I'd like to fire an artillery mission at them and blow them away while we all stay perfectly safe a few miles away, but that's not possible. I do have a plan to make things as safe as possible for us. I want to not give them the opportunity to shoot at us.

"In order to carry out this plan, we need several different teams. Let me tell you what those are and then I'll ask for volunteers. In some of these teams, you will need to be able to shoot at men, and I mean shoot to kill. If you don't think you can do that, that's okay. Please volunteer for something else.

"The first team is the snipers. The distance is about a hundred fifty yards so I think you'll be pretty safe, but you may be shot at. You won't have to move around a lot. Next team is the Gunslingers." Eric didn't particularly like that name, but Dani suggested it as a selling point. From the way the faces of the younger men lit up when he said it, she'd been spot on.

"They will have AR rifles with a lot of ammunition and may have to shoot at fairly close range but I want us to overwhelm the enemy with firepower. Then we have the engineers. Engineers may carry pistols but that's optional. The Gunslingers will protect them. The engineers will need to be able to carry things, push wheelbarrows full of stuff. We need muscle. And last but certainly not least, the medics. Besides the ones who are training to be nurses, if someone wants to assist them, please volunteer.

"Tomorrow, you will carry out your normal work in the morning, then come here at lunch and we'll shoot targets and do some fun things."

Chapter 44

That night, Eric walked the ground to the east of the hotel with his scouts. They checked out the four houses that were closest to the hotel, prying open the doors and opening the windows to air them out. There were bodies in two of them and they sealed those bedrooms off with duct tape. There wasn't much moonlight but Eric could make out the American flag that flew from the front of one house. His throat clutched up.

Nice brick houses on a beautiful little tree-lined street. Why did all of this have to happen? He took a sip of water from his canteen to give himself a moment, saluted the flag, and then carried on with his grim work of preparing to inflict death.

He made sure they drew a map and wrote directions so they could get back here, their staging area, without fumbling around in the dark. They were going to have a convoy of trucks and trailers and he knew that trying to get that monster straightened out if they got lost would be a nightmare. He'd played that game before in the Corps. He tied yellow engineer's tape on the street signs at the corners. Tie it on the right to signal a right turn and vice versa.

***

The next afternoon, Dani ran the rifle range, with targets at a hundred fifty yards so that the snipers could get their scopes adjusted. Phillip ran a course for the engineers, showing them the napalm and letting them light some off themselves to see how flammable it was. Eric was with the Gunslingers, making sure that they were all familiar with the controls on an AR rifle and getting them all equipped with whatever gear they had that would carry extra magazines. It ran the gamut from new high-speed MOLLE chest rigs to ratty Viet Nam-era cotton web gear, to repurposed camera bags and laptop backpacks. Liz and her nurse trainees loaded medical supplies and gave first aid classes with an emphasis on stopping the bleeding and treating for shock.

Anyone not doing something else mixed napalm, filled containers with napalm, loaded magazines, or loaded equipment into trucks. Bear and a couple of assistants were busy replacing mufflers on a couple of the trucks. Eric wanted them to be as quiet as possible. That hurt Bear's soul, since he loved to hear the unmuffled roar of an engine, but he complied. He used clamps and didn't weld any of the mufflers, though. He could take them back off.

***

Brennan and some of her security team were going to stay to guard the homestead. Half of them were in the assault team. She'd pulled in the boundaries. If they lost some cattle to thieves or wild dogs tonight, they would deal with that. Also, Eric was just paranoid enough that he had had her set up roadblocks so that no one could run to the *Pistoleros* and warn them. He really didn't think anyone would, but a healthy dose of caution is a good thing.

"If we don't come back, I know you'll do okay. You're a survivor," he told Brennan.

She made a tight little grimace, nodded once, and replied "I'd rather you came back, sir," Then she stepped back, came to attention, and saluted.

Eric hesitated a moment, surprised, before he also came to attention and rendered a salute, an officer's salute, up and down, while Brennan, the lower rank, held hers. Once he cut his salute, then she was free to cut hers.

"Although you outrank me," he pointed out.

She gave a small but definite shake of her head. "That was in the last world. This is this one."

***

Eric found Mark and called him over. "I have an important task for you. I want you to guard the *Pistolero* guards that we are going to take down. Now, don't think that guard duty is not important. It could be critical. We cannot let them get away and warn the others before we're ready, and, if they got weapons, they could attack us from behind. We could lose the battle if they did that." Mark gulped and nodded.

"You know how every movie has guys that are tied up or in jail or whatever, and they trick the guard into coming close and they disarm him and get away? We cannot let that happen. For one thing, they'll kill you. I mean that literally. To prevent that, remember two things. One, do not approach them under any circumstances. If one of them has a fit like he can't breathe, then he dies. Heart attack, epileptic seizure, whatever, I don't care. If he dies, he dies. Oh, well. You will have a rifle. The rifle was developed to give you some standoff distance. That means you can kill someone from a distance. Do not give up that advantage. Do not approach them. The second thing is, if they give you trouble, then shoot them. Plain and simple. If they try to break their restraints or whatever, shoot them. Now, I'd rather not make that noise until our attack is under way, but do not hesitate to shoot them if they try anything. You probably won't have to do that, but we need you to be able to do it. Understood?"

Mark gulped again and got out "Yes, sir."

***

Almost show time. Dani and Eric were in their bedroom, gearing up. He held her in a long hug, burying his face in her hair. Finally she asked "Are you all right?"

"I'm scared shitless," he replied. "Not for myself. I don't want to get our people killed. Or, maybe even worse, maimed.

We have to do this, but I hate it."

"Your plan is based on trying to keep them alive. Don't fight fair; don't give the *Pistoleros* a chance, right? If someone gets killed or wounded on our side, you did the best you could. That's the most you can do."

"Maybe I do need to see if we can find a couple of artillery pieces for the next problem." He stared into her eyes and said "I love you."

She put her finger on his lips. "No. Don't tell me that tonight. Tomorrow, after this is all over and we've won a great victory. Then, if you want to, then you can tell me that." Then she hugged him so he wouldn't see the tears coming to her eyes. After she had blinked them away, she pulled back enough to look at him.

"We'll be fine. We'll survive. We'll take our losses and move on. Haven't we survived everything life has thrown at us so far?"

He smiled a little, a sad smile, and kissed her long and hard, and then they had to get ready. Dani began by kneeling by the bed and praying, making the sign of the cross when she was finished.

He didn't have a lot of gear to get together since he was going in disguise, so to speak. He wore civilian clothes more appropriate for a date than a gunfight, with a Glock in an IWB holster at the five o'clock position, and carried his rifle with the light taped on and a small butt pack for the battery and a couple of magazines. He needed to be a leader, not just another rifleman.

Dani, on the other hand, would be in full battle rattle. She donned a black T-shirt, tiger stripe camouflage top and bottom, and hiking boots. When they got to the staging point she would don the remainder: MOLLE plate carrier with front and back plates, four ammo pouches with three 30-round magazines each, first aid kit, knife, water bottle, and rifle with the battery and light. She also had zip ties and a roll of duct tape. She felt like it all weighed about as much as she did, but she had worn it for the better part of a day, even running in it a few times, getting used to it, moving or taping down or adjusting anything that rattled or rubbed or got knocked out of place. Eric had insisted on her wearing the plates as soon as a collection team had found them in an abandoned house. The same place had yielded several tiger stripe uniforms in Dani's size and a lot of other gear, stockpiled by a prepper who apparently didn't survive Hexen.

Chapter 45

Ahead of the convoy, Phillip, Mike, and David rode into Tyler and into the subdivision staging area, taping glow sticks on street signs to mark the route. Eric rode with the convoy, a long line of pickup trucks with trailers. They drove slowly and made a stop at about the halfway point to make sure that there were no issues, no mechanical failures, no one fell out, that sort of thing. Lacking radios or cell phones, they had to stop to talk. After everyone had the opportunity for a bathroom break, Eric called everyone together.

"Y'all don't need to hear me make another attempt at a speech, so I'll be quick. I have confidence in each and every one of you. I deeply appreciate what you are doing, what you volunteered to do. I think it is necessary, it is moral, and it is the right thing to do. Lord knows we've been hit hard, terribly hard, so we have to rebuild. But we are strong, and we can rebuild, and this is part of it — taking out the trash. I was in the Marine Corps, I was in the war in Afghanistan, I've been in gunfights here on American soil, and I say, without any reservations, that I am proud to stand with you men and women here tonight!"

There were cheers and applause, and shouts of "USA!" that buoyed Eric's spirits and made him smile for the first time that day.

***

They did have one vehicle go down and ended up leaving it, piling the cargo and people into other trucks. Eric's plan had been to take as many trucks as possible, so that a breakdown did not leave a serious gap. Fortunately, one of their major efforts had been to locate pickup trucks of the right vintage that they could be brought back to life. Once they were running, the mechanics went through and replaced anything that was worn. After they got enough of them on the road, Eric figured they would start doing thorough rebuilds, bumper to bumper, but that was on his list of the next million things to do. Tonight, he had a different problem to focus on.

***

As they rode, Eric looked at the map in the dashboard light. They had issued one to every driver, and without a copier, they had to be manually copied. Taylor had taken on the task, proud of the responsibility, and had written a note at the bottom of each one: "Please be careful and come back safely!" with a heart at the end.

If I live through this, I'm going to frame this and hang it on the wall. Maybe she'll be famous one day, like Betsy Ross, Eric mused.

Mike was standing in the road about a half mile and a couple of turns from the staging point, waving a glow stick of his own. That was the point to turn off the headlights. From there, they just idled forward, trying to not even hit the brakes if possible, although the brake lights had been covered with duct tape so that only a fraction of their original size showed. They did have to brake when they met David at the "engine off" point. There was one more turn and then they would be headed straight in to the staging point, about a quarter mile away. All drivers shut down their engines at that point and the trucks were pushed the rest of the way in or left where they were, depending on their intended use. Liz and her medics took over two of the houses as their first aid station and waited for customers, hoping they wouldn't get any.

Mike and David guided the snipers out to their positions, one taking the north side teams and one the south side. The ones closest to the east were actually less than a hundred yards from the staging point but the ones to the west took longer to get into place. Bear went with the north side sniper team so that he could come around the building from the west. The engineers and the Gunslingers holed up in the other two houses, with a couple of scouts in the woods to wait for the signal to approach. They had done the whole 'synchronize watches' thing, with the few wind-up watches they'd been able to find, but the operation didn't depend on split-second timing. That never worked, anyway.

Chapter 46

The *Pistoleros* had all gone in for the night. The customer traffic had pretty much died down, a furtive druggie now and then, going no further than the drug dealer standing just outside the front door. He had a rolling suitcase behind him which held his product. There were two security types at a table in the bar, from which they could keep an eye on the dealer and the front door.

Dani went in first. She had her full battle gear on, her AR rifle slung. She bulled her way in and glared at the two guards when they catcalled her.

"I hear you have girls here. I'm looking for a nice young one. The younger the better." The guards broke into laughter and slapped each other's shoulders. "You gonna rough her up?" one challenged.

"Yeah. But she'll get better. She may even enjoy it." Dani brought a hand up to her face, split her fingers apart in a V, and then lewdly ran her tongue through the V. That brought more laughter and backslapping.

"How you going to pay?"

She pulled a pistol from one of the pouches, placed it on the table, and stared at the speaker. It was a race gun, a 1911 that had been modified for shooting competition, with a flared magazine well for fast reloading, extended controls, and a big compensator on the barrel to cut down on recoil. It was something they'd found in one of the abandoned houses they were taking over.

One of the men picked it up, played with it for a minute, and said "Sure. Come with me." He stood up.

Dani felt a spike of fear. *Damn, that was too quick and easy. I need to stall!*

"Hang on, now, cowboy," she said. "What are the terms?"

"Terms? You get an hour. I'll knock on the door when your

time is up."

"Is the door locked? I mean, can I lock it?"

"No, the doors don't lock. And don't try to block it or jam it. If I have to break in there it's gonna be your ass."

She was frantically trying to think of something else to ask when the pimp looked past her and asked "What you want?"

Eric had come in and was dressed for the occasion in low-top hiking boots, jeans, and dress shirt, and a navy blazer. He was going for a "respectable businessman" look, and topped it off with a pair of glasses which were actually shooting glasses with clear lenses. He looked around uncertainly, and stammered "I, uh, I heard you have... girls here."

Dani cast a disdainful, sidelong glance his way and stepped off to the side as if trying to distance herself from him. In reality, she was getting out of his line of fire and putting herself in position to bring fire on the guards from the flank.

The pimp was saying "Yeah, we have some fine young ladies —" He never finished because Eric initiated the action. He pulled his pistol out from under the blazer and covered the two guards. Dani brought her AR up and snapped off the safety with a click that was loud in the sudden silence. The fat guard froze, not even breathing, while trying to look at Dani by rolling his eyes as far to the side as they would go. The pimp started talking, since that was what he did.

"Oh, you people are making a very bad mistake. Don't you know who we are? We —"

"Shut up, asshole. Get down on the ground, face down. Now!" Eric had his sights aimed at his chest and injected his command authority voice into the order. The pimp took his time getting down, but he knew that things like Miranda warnings, plea bargains, and lawsuits for alleged police brutality were a thing of the past, so he complied. Next they got the fat guard down.

Meanwhile, Bear had been taking care of the dealer out front. He had come in on Eric's heels, slinking in and making a beeline for the dealer. He had an excellent view of Eric and

Dani through the window, so he knew just when to make his move. As they pulled their guns, he just hauled off and punched the dealer in the stomach. As the man bent over, gasping for breath, Bear punched the man in the jaw and he went down. Bear was a veteran of numerous bar fights. He knew exactly what to do to put a man down and out.

He dragged the dealer inside with one hand and worked with Eric and Dani to bind the *Pistoleros* with zip-ties and duct tape, and taped the mouths of the dealer and the fat guard. They had other ideas for the pimp. They dragged the guards into the kitchen to get away from the floor-to-ceiling plate glass panels that exposed the lobby, bar, and restaurant to view from the street.

Eric cracked a glow stick as he stepped outside and spun it around at the end of the string he had tied to it earlier. Phase II started as a small army rushed forward into the lobby with their equipment. They went to all of the stairways and climbed them to the third and fourth floors. Opening the doors quietly, they uncapped their cargo of five-gallon cans of gasoline thickened with diesel and laundry powder, and dumped them upside down on the floor so the improvised napalm would soak into the carpet and baseboards.

The next step was to close the doors and lock them down. They had some home security devices which consisted of an adjustable-length steel tube which went against the doorknob at an angle and then down to the floor. A rubber pad gave it traction, so a push on the door would be transferred through the bar to a push against the floor, which, of course, would not move. They backed that up with a similar but bigger device made of lumber that went against the door and the opposite wall of the stairwell. Once those devices were in place, the occupants of the third and fourth floors were locked in unless they wanted to jump out a window or down the elevator shaft.

While that was going on, Dani and the pimp were having a little heart-to-heart talk. He was currently on the kitchen floor with his legs spread, each ankle zip-tied and duct taped to the leg of a large stainless steel work table. There was also a paracord noose around his neck, tied off to another heavy table, to prevent him from head-butting Dani if she got too close. She lit a few candles for light, since what he saw might be almost as bad as what he felt.

She pulled on some heavy leather work gloves and started slicing his pants off with a big butcher knife. "What girls have a guy in their room right now?"

"Fuck you!" He spat at her.

She dug the knife into his leg and sliced it as well, opening a six inch gash along one thigh. The pimp squirmed away from the blade. "You bitch! You fucking bitch!"

Dani looked up at Bear. "Tape his mouth, but so I can take it off when I want him to talk, please" she asked sweetly as she smiled. She transferred the smile to the pimp as she continued to slice his pants off, digging the blade in here and there, and then cutting off his underwear.

"Small," she said derisively as she tossed the underwear away. She took one of the candles for a walk around the kitchen, rifled through a couple of drawers, and came back. "Look what I found!" she said excitedly as she held up a cheese grater. The pimp began to look less defiant.

She reached between his legs and grabbed his penis. "What's the matter, can't you get it up for a girl?" she asked. "But I guess you *were* the girl when you were in prison, weren't you?"

She brought the cheese grater closer. "I understand the head is the most sensitive part. Is that right?" She raked the grater across the head of his penis, hard and fast. It dug in and scooped flesh from the organ, sending little shreds out the other side. Blood welled up immediately.

Mark muttered "Oh, Jesus Christ!" and turned his head away, unconsciously covering his crotch with one hand. He couldn't even watch, so he didn't see Bear in the same position, automatically protecting his own family jewels. The pimp howled, muted by the tape, but loud anyway. He squirmed and bounced, trying to rip his legs free from the table. He also peed and defecated himself.

Dani stood up and kicked the pimp in the ribs until he stopped thrashing. She knelt next to him and ripped the tape off of his mouth. "Which girls have a guy in their room right now?"

The pimp took a few deep breaths through clenched teeth and spat back "I'm not telling you shit. I would give my life for those guys!" He took another deep breath and screamed "HELP! HELP!"

Dani was ready for something like that. She kicked him in the stomach to take his breath away and she and Bear got his mouth taped again. She went to work with the cheese grater again. She raked it across the head again but over to the side. Fresh territory. New nerve endings. Muffled screams and curses and thrashing.

"Ready to talk yet? Just nod when you are." *Rake.* Muffled screams and curses and thrashing. *Rake.* Muffled screams and thrashing. *Rake.* A sound like a cat mewing.

"Oh? Ready to talk?" The pimp nodded, tears streaming from his eyes. She ripped the tape off.

"Three rooms," the pimp panted. "Three rooms. 208. 210. 218."

"What rooms are the girls in?"

"There's a chart, on the clipboard, on the table."

Eric entered the kitchen about that time, having seen to other activities and gotten his rifle from one of the engineers.

They found the clipboard on the table where the pimp and fat boy had been sitting and drinking. It was a simple graph with the girl's name, room, and a column with hash marks, obviously a tally of customers. The last occupied room, furthest down the hall from the stairs, was 218.

Eric drew Dani, Phillip, and the three other members of his rescue team together to go over the plan one last time.

"Okay, the first priority is to get the girls out of here, next is to wipe out the gang, but the conference room is loaded with their stash of ammunition, guns, and liquor. I'd like to grab as much of it as we can. It'll be good for trade goods.

"As far as the girls, the plan is simple. If there are no locks, then we go in with the lights, find the males in those three rooms, and shoot them. Go in quickly, blind them with the light, and shoot. Shoot them in the head. If they're awake, say something to distract them. Tell them the captain is pissed off or something. If we do it all at the same time, then there will be no warning to the others. Then we evacuate the girls. Right now we have the snipers outside, making sure no one looks out a window. We have teams in each stairwell, making sure they don't breach our blockades. That means that the bulk of their troops are trapped."

Upstairs, each chose a room and watched Eric as he did a one-two-three countdown with his fingers, snapped on his light, and entered the rooms. The doors made quite a bit of noise when they closed automatically behind them. For Phillip and Dani, it was not a problem. The men in those rooms had been drinking and smoking marijuana and didn't react at all to the noise or the light in their faces. They never saw the rifles that were fired from less than two feet away into their heads. They died without ever stirring.

Eric had one that was in the bathroom. He got two steps past the bathroom when he heard "*Que mierda*?" coming from inside. He backed up and blasted two rounds into the man sitting on the toilet. He fell to the floor with shards of the toilet tank clattering around the bathroom. In all three rooms, the girls woke up and started screaming.

Eric grabbed the girl's arm, pulling her out of the bed and away from any weapons that may have been handy. He wasn't sure whose side she was really on. "Go stand at the door," he commanded. He dragged the sheet off of the bed and tossed it at her. "Put that on and go out into the hall." She sniffled and wiped tears from her eyes, but did as he ordered.

Oh God, she's young! he thought, as his light briefly illuminated her face.

Liz and a couple of the medics, women, were in the hallway now, herding the girls to the stairs and rousting the ones who were still asleep out of their beds. Dani came out of room 210, supporting a girl who leaned heavily on her. She was very drunk or on something pretty heavy and could barely stand on her own.

Then a fourth guy came out of a room, awake and armed.

Chapter 47

Phillip had chosen that moment to sneeze… for the rest of his life. It was a big, full-bodied sneeze that took all his attention. He never saw the guy. He never even knew about the .45 ACP bullet that hit him in the face and smashed into his brain.

Dani started to turn at the sound of gunshots, and as she turned, it put the girl she was supporting in between her and the fourth guy. One slug slammed into her back plate at an angle and ricocheted off. The next two hit the girl. She dropped like a rock, overwhelming Dani, who ended up on the floor with the bigger girl on top of her. Other bullets sped past, hitting people further down the hallway.

That cleared the sightline for Eric to engage. He knew that accuracy usually beat spray-n-pray so he took the extra moment to get the sights aligned before he started firing a steady stream of bullets. One solid hit from that big .308 would do the trick, but he wanted this guy down completely and immediately. There was a muzzle flash, two flashes, incoming fire from the fourth man in the dim hallway, and then Eric's bullets were impacting. The man was twisting, falling, wiping his left hand down his chest like he was wiping the bullets away, but that proved very ineffective. Then he was on the floor and Eric pumped a few more bullets into him. He advanced, keeping the muzzle on the bad guy, terrified that Dani was hit. She was squirming, maybe wounded, he couldn't tell.

He grabbed the girl's arm and dragged her roughly off of Dani. "Are you okay?" he asked, probably screaming, he couldn't tell. Everyone else seemed to be screaming at the top of their lungs, repeatedly.

That's fine, just so it's not gunshots, he thought.

"I'm good, I'm good," she replied. "The shit's going to hit

the fan now!" She came up swinging her rifle up to her shoulder and scanning the hallway. "How is she?" she asked, with a nod of her head to the side.

"I think she's gone," Eric replied. He really didn't have time to care at the moment. She had taken two .45 caliber wounds to the back, so he figured her chances of survival were somewhat less than his chances of being canonized as a saint. He moved up to Phillip. He got some light on him and shook his head. He didn't need to check any vitals. A half-inch hole in the bridge of the nose, only slightly off-center, was not survivable even in the world of medicine they had left behind.

He put Phillip's death in a little box in his mind, shoved it in and slammed the lid. He couldn't deal with it right now. There were too many other things that required his attention, too many other people relying on him. When he had the time he would open the little box and mourn his friend. Soon, but not now.

"Stand guard here for a second," he requested of Dani, before he turned and ran down the hall. She was standing there, openmouthed, staring down at Phillip, but she snapped out of it and stood her post as ordered.

Liz was in a cluster of girls, trying to give first aid to a girl with a gunshot wound in her back. There was another one with a bloody face nearby. Eric's temper went off the scale. "GET OUT!" He screamed at the top of his lungs. "GET THE FUCK OUT OF HERE! OUT THE FRONT DOOR, TURN LEFT. GO TO THE WOODS!" The reaction was mixed. Most of them took off running. A couple, drunk or high or something, leaned against the wall and stared at him. Liz and another ignored him and continued to try to save the girl on the floor. Eric could see her struggle to breathe with a lung with a hole in it.

Goddamnit, it would make it easier if she was dead, he thought, and kicked himself for thinking it. *I mean, she's dead, she just hasn't stopped breathing yet.*

"Pick her up, drag her, whatever. Just get her out of here.

This building is going to be on fire in about two minutes." He turned away. He was done with them. Either they would survive or they wouldn't. He couldn't waste any more attention on them, especially when he heard the gunfire one floor up.

He ran back to Dani. "Who's in that room?" he nodded towards the room where the fourth guy had been, his body limp and leaking blood on the carpet in front of the door.

"No girls were supposed to be in that room. The furthest one was 218 and that's 222 or 224."

"You take the right side. I'll take left and make entry." He moved to the room, opened the door about a foot, and called out "Come out *now*. We're going to throw a firebomb in there in five seconds." He let the door go, but caught it when he heard muted noises inside. He looked at Dani and shrugged. Easing the door open, he crouched low and duckwalked in, rifle at the ready. He checked the bathroom on the way, based on his earlier experience.

He stopped when he saw the naked guy tied to the bed. He looked back at Dani, who had come partway into the room. She saw the look on his face and moved up to see. Satisfied that no one else was in the room, he untied the gag and the guy started asking "Who are you guys? Thank God you're here! Can you untie me now?" He spoke perfect English, with none of the slang and poorly pronounced words and attitude that were indicative of thugs and gangstas and their wanna-bes. Eric moved to pull a knife and cut him loose, but Dani stepped up.

"Wait!" she said, running her rifle light over the man's back. "Step back," she commanded Eric. He trusted her. He stepped back.

"Hey, now, you don't need to be doing all that. Everything's good. I'm just a guy that got caught like those bit — girls down the hall. It ain't nothin'." He looked at Eric. "Can you tell your woman here —" he never finished the sentence. Dani swung her rifle to a point about two inches away from the man's temple and fired a hollow point into his skull. The blast was loud in the small room but they could still hear a wet *smack* as a large quantity of blood and brain matter painted the wall. The man slumped.

Eric glanced at her, turned, and started out of the room. As far as he was concerned, that was one less problem.

"He has gang tattoos. Prison tattoos. He was one of them!" Dani said, sounding defensive.

Eric stopped and turned. "I believe you. I think you did the right thing. He was fooling me to begin with. You did good. I may keep you around."

Dani was starting to smile at the praise and then the last comment hit her. "You asshole!" she called at his back as he went out the door.

Chapter 48

When the gunfire broke out on the second floor, people started waking up on the third and fourth floors, getting their guns out, and going to investigate. As is frequently the case, the first ones into the situation were the first to die. At the south stairwell, three men tried the door and found it blocked. They tried brute force, slamming into it with their shoulders and feet, but it was a steel door with bracing that took their blows and transferred it to a concrete wall and floor. In other words, there was no effect. One of them decided they needed light to see what was blocking the door, so he fired off a cigarette lighter, a nice gold-plated one he had looted from a jewelry store.

The world erupted into fire around him and the other two men.

The homemade napalm had enough gasoline that the fumes burst explosively into flame, igniting the diesel, and then both ignited the oil. The men's bare feet were coated with the stuff, and as they instinctively ran from the flames, the one in the lead fell and skidded on the carpet, covering himself in sticky, flaming napalm. The other two tripped over him and also got a napalm bath. The third one was the luckiest, as he got the least, but he was still aflame from the waist down, plus his forearms. He thrashed in the hallway and got the flame extinguished with the assistance of a couple of other *Pistoleros*. The other two couldn't find a way out and they rolled around in it, screaming until their lungs were seared out.

The other hallways were ignited by the engineers when Eric shouted at them to "Burn the bastards!" Enough napalm had leaked under the doors that the blockers just had to drop a match into the puddle on the landing and it burned under the door and into the hall. Each hall had about sixty gallons of napalm dumped into it. Under normal circumstances, that would create a formidable problem for a fire department to handle. In the current world, it was immensely deadly.

The sprinklers still worked since the activation is mechanical. The sprinklers held glass bulbs filled with a glycerin-based liquid that expanded when heated. At a certain temperature, the bulbs shattered and caused the sprinklers to activate. They dripped a little bit of water on the flames and promptly quit. The problem was that there was no electricity to pump water from ground level up to the sprinkler heads. The sprinkler heads were open, there was just nothing available to come out of them. There were some fire extinguishers on the floor, but even if they had been competently manned, they were woefully insufficient for the task.

That left escape as the next option. The stairs were blocked by both the fire and the barriers. Most men went to the windows, to look out and see if three or four stories was really that much of a fall, or if enough bedsheets could be tied together to climb down. Either of these options required that the windows be broken, and as they were, the snipers went to work. Deer rifles started to take their toll of anyone who looked out a window. Even with the darkness limiting accuracy, a missed shot was almost as good as a hit since it kept the *Pistoleros* inside a burning building. The gangstas fired back, but their targets could be anywhere, and could move between their shots, while they were limited to shooting out of the same predictable windows. The odds did not favor them in this gunfight.

Frustrated, the thugs next tried the elevators. They finally got one set of doors pried open and looked down. When the power had died, the elevators stopped where they were and stayed there, which happened to be on the ground floor. Eric's people had the roof hatches in the cars open and were waiting for the bad guys to show themselves. The fire in the hall backlighted them perfectly, and they were met with a hail of gunfire. One of the thugs took a hit in the leg and fell down the elevator shaft screaming. He smacked into the top of an elevator and the person inside fired a few rounds up through the elevator roof and into him to make sure he was out of the fight. The gangstas pointed their weapons down the shaft and blazed away, but they were firing blindly down into total darkness. The odds did not favor them in this gunfight, either. They weren't going to climb down the elevator shafts and then crawl through the roof access panels one by one into the waiting guns.

***

Meanwhile, the girls had been escorted off of the property, through the patch of woods and into the subdivision. Dani had seen them off, sending Bear to carry a wounded girl, then walked over to the three thugs they had zip-tied and duct-taped earlier. Mark had stood across the room as ordered, covering them with a rifle.

She marched over to the pimp. He didn't look too good and was probably in shock. He was about to be more shocked. Dani swiftly bent down, grabbed his penis and balls, and pulled them up as hard as she could. The pimp screamed through his gag and arched his back to lessen the pressure. That was exactly what she wanted. She drew her knife and sliced his penis and balls off. It did not all come off neatly in one slice. Most of it did, but there was a piece of skin still attaching it to his body. He screamed and started to thrash about, but was torn between getting away from the blade and not wanting to help her pull his manhood all of the way off of his body. She went in with the knife again and solved the dilemma for him.

She stood, holding the bloody lump aloft, blood dripping and some kind-of tubular things dangling.

"You didn't tell us about the two boyfriends in 224, did you?" she yelled. He probably didn't hear her over his own nonstop screaming. She threw his manhood in his face, unslung her rifle, and shot him in the knee. He writhed on the floor, bleeding profusely from the knee and the crotch, adding to the blood he had already spilled.

She turned to her left and spotted the drug dealer, with his back up against the wall, staring at her wide-eyed. He shook his head violently from side to side and made a noise behind his gag. NO! NO! NO! She swung her rifle up and shot him in the chest, then in the head. The wall behind him was splattered in blood and brain matter.

Mark clenched his teeth and tried not to throw up while his mind screamed *HOLY FUCK! HOLY FUCK! HOLY FUCK!* in an endless loop. He'd seen plenty of shootings and blood in movies and video games and on TV, every bit of it fake, but this was no bullshit like that. Nobody was getting back up when the scene was over. This was real, and Dani had just blown a man's brains out. Literally. Blown. His. Brains. Out. Killed a man. The sheer brutality of it shocked him. Not only that Dani had done it — how often do you watch someone you know shoot a man — but the gory effect of a high velocity rifle bullet on a human body. He'd fired rifles frequently before, but not inside a room, where the noise and concussion were so much greater. Even worse was the sight of a living man immediately turned into blood and bone and dead meat, a split second separating life from death. He was glad that the only light was from candles so he didn't see it in full color and clarity.

Dani turned to the right and saw that the fat guard was on his stomach, trying to get away from her with a motion like a caterpillar. It reminded her of an animated movie she had seen as a child. In one scene, some slugs were frightened and were screaming and fleeing, but of course slugs don't move very fast, so there was a lot of screaming and not much fleeing. She smiled at the memory.

Mark saw the smile crease her face and thought *Dear God, this girl is crazy! I heard she'd killed people, but I've watched her cheese-grate some guy's dick, and then cut his balls and dick clean off, and blew that guy's head off while he was tied up, and now she's gonna shoot these other two guys, too, and* SMILE *while she's doing it!*

He had not been a religious person but he found God right then and there, and prayed to Him fervently. He had a huge crush on Dani, but right now she scared the absolute *shit* out of him.

Dani didn't realize she had made a convert to Christianity. She was busy shooting the fat guard in the back, and again when he was still moving, and then in the head. Some pieces of something wet caught the candlelight as they sailed off into the darkness. The pimp was next. He was rolling around on a floor slick with his blood, screaming through the duct tape. She shot him five times in the chest, rapid fire, and put a more carefully aimed shot between his eyes. A piece of his skull flapped up, hinged by skin, and lay on his forehead. Mark thought it looked like a technician had opened up the head of an android for servicing in a science fiction movie. It didn't make him sick. He was kind of dazed at this point.

When Dani looked around at Mark, she still had the smile on her face, and her eyes were shining. Mark urinated on himself right then. Not a little, but an entire bladder's worth. *Please, God, I'll give up drinking, too*, he prayed. He wasn't sure if she had gone berserk and was going to shoot him, too.

"Come with me," she said. "They don't need to be guarded any more."

"Yes, Ma'am!" he leaped to follow her. He wouldn't dream of doing anything to piss her off.

Chapter 49

Eric was making the rounds of the positions, as any good commander should, boosting morale, correcting issues, and directing operations. Casualties were, so far, light. Phillip was dead. The most serious after that was a man with a bullet track down his forearm, acquired when the thugs started firing rounds down the elevator shaft. He thought at least nine of the enemy were dead or captured.

Eric ran out to the riflemen on one side of the building, risking getting shot by his own people from the front or by the *Pistoleros* from the back. He waved a glow-stick, the signal for a friendly, but he knew how things went at night and in the fog of war. Despite his expectations, he made it without any bullets directed his way. "How's it going?" he asked the first person he saw.

"I think I got two. Then there was one guy that threw those sheets out the window and tried to climb down. He caught a couple of bullets before he let go and fell the rest of the way. The sheets weren't long enough, anyway. Damn, look at that!"

A guy had just gone out a third floor window clutching some cushions. Eric and the rifleman looked to see if he survived the fall but a rise in the ground blocked their view that low down. The important thing, when Eric looked at the building, was that the third and fourth floors were becoming more fully engaged in the fire and thick noxious smoke was pouring out of the broken windows.

"I think that's going to work to burn those rats out of that nest" Eric commented. "Shoot out any windows that aren't broken or open already. Let's get some air in there to help the fire." He sprinted back to the building as the rifleman started putting .30-06 bullets through the glass. He was smart enough to hit the lower portion of the window first and let gravity work against the upper half of the glass to make it collapse and fall out.

***

After the engineers had lit off their napalm, they turned to their next task, which was to raid the stash. Eric had thought about cherry-picking the cache and just taking the good stuff, but there was too much and it was too well-packed to easily sort through. The gang had moved industrial-strength shelving into the conference rooms and stacked pallets ceiling-high. There was no way to open them all to see what he wanted. They just had to take it all. And there was just a little pressure because two of the three floors above them were on fire.

Eric, back from his visit to the snipers, tried to take a quick look to determine if there were pallets of ammunition or guns, but gave it up as a hopeless task.

"Just take it all. It would take longer to pick and choose than it would to just grab everything."

They got the forklift and a couple of manual pallet jacks and started moving the pallets of goods out to the lobby. The driveway immediately in front of the doors was roofed over, allowing customers to move from their cars to the hotel without having the weather inflicted upon them. The engineers rolled stacks of pallets out the door and dropped them under this overhang. Eric wasn't worried about the weather, but was using the roof to shield them from any shooters in the windows above. There were snipers on this side of the building to keep the *Pistoleros* out of the windows but he'd rather be safe than sorry. Somebody could pop up, fire off some rounds, and be back out of sight before the snipers could home in on him. They would pull trucks up later to load the pallets. Right now they needed to get them out of the building and the path of the fire. Immediately in front of the building wasn't great, but it was a start.

Things seemed to be going well, which is exactly when things usually go straight to Hell.

Chapter 50

Dani thought about the situation, the mental picture she had of the area and the plan. They had drawn up a sketch of this building and the surrounding ones. To the south was the parking lot, with an open area of maybe two hundred yards. West was a four-lane street with turning lanes and parking lots, plenty of open area, in other words. Any gang members that tried to flee in those directions would be shot to ribbons by the people they had stationed there.

If the gang made a break for it, they would want to go north, to the cover of the other buildings nearby. She drifted over to that side of the hotel, something nagging at the back of her brain. Something wasn't right. Something was different from before.

Then it hit her: the gunfire had changed.

Instead of a relatively random exchange, the shooting had become more orderly. There was a little patio on the north side of the hotel and she opened the glass door to hear better. And there it was — one of their snipers fired a shot, a whiplash rifle shot, incoming, hitting a couple of floors above her head. And then the return, a massed flurry of shots outgoing, back at the sniper that had just fired.

The sniper screamed in agony.

Dani turned to Mark, her eyes wide. "They're taking out the snipers!" She looked back out onto the patio and saw a flash of white, a sheet tied up as a makeshift rope, falling down from an upstairs window.

"Come on!" she cried.

She ran out onto the patio and craned her neck upwards, trying to see what was happening. The gang had gathered in the center of the third floor, driven there by the flames at either end of the building. More ropes now dropped from the windows in the center, made up of sheets, electrical cords, belts, whatever the men could find and tie together.

No one shot at them. No one tried to stop them. The snipers were all silent. Dani was horrified to realize that their people were in the wrong place and unaware of the danger. She could just see the gang coming down their ropes and rushing into the hotel, catching everyone unaware, and shooting Eric and everyone else to pieces.

"We're going to die," she muttered, with a sinking feeling in the pit of her stomach.

***

Dani stepped up behind one of the wrought-iron tables, with maybe a half-formed thought that it would provide some protection to the lower part of her body. She glanced over at Mark, who stood by her side, wondering if that was the last friendly face she'd see on this earth. And then the *Pistoleros* came pouring out of the windows, one after the other, going hand-over-hand down the makeshift ropes.

She snapped her rifle up to her shoulder and became the embodiment of the Grim Reaper. She didn't have any other choice.

The sun was starting to come up but she had night sights on her rifle anyway, bright green Trijicons. Just put all three green dots in a line and fire.

And fire she did. She fired almost as fast as if she had a three-round burst rifle. First target — three shots, second target — three shots, third target, fourth, fifth, sixth. They started dropping off of the ropes like flies, a steady rain of bodies thumping onto the bricks or crashing into the tables and chairs below. Mark was shooting at one of the other ropes, but they were coming too fast down all three ropes simultaneously. Then the fourth floor threw down a couple of ropes and even more men flooded down.

Their intelligence had been bad. Very bad. There were a

lot more gangbangers here than they had thought.

Dani was firing and reloading, firing and reloading, a finely-tuned, high-performance machine running at full throttle. Adrenaline screamed through her system. Her hearing went out completely, her vision narrowed down to a circle barely bigger than her gunsight, and time slowed to a crawl.

She wasn't even conscious of some of the things her body did. She just found her sights on a man with no realization of targeting him. Her finger moved and the rifle fired three times, no noise, no recoil, and then the sights were magically on someone else and she did it all over again and again and again.

There was a guy swinging a pistol towards her while hanging from a rope. Her sights were already on him, and he was moving far too slowly to beat her. The rifle trembled and the man fell from the rope. Her muzzle followed him down, but he hit the ground like a rag doll, breaking an arm, lifeless, no threat.

Her sights snapped up to another man and she shot him, and then another. But there were just too many of them, and they were jumping now, risking broken limbs to avoid her bullets, their falls cushioned by the bodies of their fellows. Dani sensed bullets snapping by her, could almost see them sailing by, plucking at her clothing. One bullet snapped by between her shoulder and ear, cutting a lock of hair off. Others ricocheted off of the wrought-iron table in front of her, one slamming into an empty magazine that had landed on the table and sending it spinning away.

None of it mattered. She fired and fired and fired and fired.

Chapter 51

The forklift whined as the stack of pallets came down, then the machine reversed and trundled off. With that noise gone, Eric finally noticed the difference in the gunfire. He realized with a start that it was no longer on the upper floors, but right at ground level. An icy cold spike went down his spine as he realized that that was not the plan.

Unfortunately, the enemy also gets to vote on your battle plan.

He turned to the men remaining in the room and bellowed, "GET YOUR RIFLES! FOLLOW ME!"

He raced down the hall, towards the patio and the now obvious gun battle going on there. He saw the mass of *Pistoleros* first, a tangle of bodies, some dead, some alive, with more coming down in a continuous stream. Their landing area was limited, so they were all in a compact scrum, trying to get out from under the men coming down on top of them, slipping and tripping on the blood and the bodies of those who had come before.

Eric swung his rifle up and started blasting away at anything that moved in that cluster, blowing holes in the floor-to-ceiling plate glass windows. He felt, rather than heard, people on each side of him, also firing madly into the enemy crowd.

The thugs who weren't running for their lives were focused on Dani and Mark, so Eric and his shooters came up on their right flank and mowed them down with intense, near point-blank rifle fire. They were so close that Eric wasn't even using his sights. He had his big M1A Scout rifle in his shoulder but held his head up high to see over the sights and take in the whole picture. He swung the rifle from side to side, firing continuously, the 7.62mm muzzle blasts noticeably louder than the 5.56mm that everyone else was using.

One or two thugs threw their hands up in surrender but it was far too late for that. They died of multiple gunshots, riddled where they stood or knelt. The ones that ran got the same treatment unless they were very lucky and very quick.

Suddenly the gunfire dropped to nothing.

Eric's group had all emptied their magazines and there was a pause while they reloaded. There were a few more shots outside and then that died away, too. Nothing was moving out on the patio. All of the *Pistoleros* were down, and no more came out of the upper floors. One of the ropes fell down, the end of it on fire.

Then there was movement.

Dani walked around the table and started shooting the bodies in the head. It didn't matter to her if they were wounded, dead, screaming in pain, or begging for their lives. She shot them all.

For a few seconds, everyone was transfixed by the image of Dani shooting the wounded as the sun came up behind her as if backlighting a performer onstage. She moved like an assembly-line robot: feet planted, shoot target one, pivot at the hips to target two, fire, pivot, fire, pivot, fire, left to right, then raise up to the second row and run it the opposite way, right to left, fire, pivot, fire, pivot, fire. It was precise but quick. Smoke poured through the slots in her rifle's handguard, gun oil burning off of the barrel, hot from the rapid fire. Blood splattered up, the droplets seeming to flash as they caught the sunlight, like some kind of horror show performance art, the soundtrack formed by the whiplash noise and muzzle blast of her gunfire, a rapid, steady drumbeat of single shots CRACK CRACK CRACK CRACK CRACK. The empty brass shell casings arced through the air, also catching the sun's rays as they spun away and fell to earth.

Eric came to and took control of the situation again, grabbing people and assigning tasks. "You, you, and you, I need security out there, a hundred and eighty degrees. You are responsible for this sector, you have the middle, and you have that sector. Put your backs to the hotel and watch out for anything coming into your sector. Go, get in position. You, get out there and watch those windows up there in case any more are still up there. Keep scanning the third and fourth floor windows. Get it done. And I need both of you to go out to where the snipers are and check on them. I'm afraid they're hit, so give them first aid and then come back here and tell me what they need. Go!"

He walked out onto the patio to Mark, who was slumped in a chair, blood flowing from his cheek. His mouth was open and his eyes were wide and focused a thousand yards away.

"Hey, you did good," Eric told him, putting a hand on his shoulder and squeezing. "You have a bandanna? Put it on that wound, hold pressure on it."

Mark's head swiveled in his direction but the eyes didn't change focus. "I'm wounded?" he asked in an emotionless voice, seemingly unconcerned, just mildly curious.

"Yeah, here, use my bandanna. Just press it to your face right there. Looks like you just have a little graze. I've cut myself shaving worse than that." That wasn't true. Mark needed stitches and he'd have a nice scar on his cheek for the rest of his days.

Dani circled around the bodies, now coming near Eric. He tried to intercept her. "Dani? Baby? Can you stop for a second? Are you okay? Is any of that your blood?"

She had quite a bit of blood on her, drops and splotches and smears, pretty much everywhere. She'd been cutting people up and shooting them at close range all night. You don't shoot someone in the head with a rifle at point blank distance and not get blood splattered on you. She'd shot a couple of dozen so far. Two drops of blood were running down the side of her face.

"Busy." She slapped a fresh magazine in, dropped the bolt, and went back to her task. She was in the zone.

Eric sighed. "All right, how about I help you?"

But that got no response. He suddenly had a vision of

himself and Dani as white-haired old people, him telling a pack of wide-eyed great-grandchildren how the innocent-seeming little old lady beside him had stalked battlefields, bullets flying all around her, mowing the bad men down like sheaves of grain. Then his throat closed up and his eyes filled with tears. *Oh, God, I only hope that we should be so lucky as to live to a ripe old age!*

Eric looked around, taking in the whole scene, since he obviously wasn't needed to assist Dani. *I have to count this as a victory. Mission accomplished, despite our losses.* His mind insisted on bringing up Phillip, and he shied away from that thought. *I can't do that right now. When it's time. There's still too much to do tonight. This morning. Whatever.*

He realized, with a start, that they were victorious on several fronts. They had broken the gang threat, and any survivors were probably thinking of nothing but running for their lives, right now. They could bring cattle into the city without being extorted. In the bigger picture, they were successfully feeding people, turning refugees into skilled ranch hands and farmers.

And they were expanding their little empire, taking over abandoned farms and ranches. *It sounds like Dani wants to do a lot more of that. That's a great idea. Security in this world is going to be based on having good people around you, a well-trained, badass army, if needed. In order to have an army, you have to feed them. In order to feed them, you have to have the farms and ranches to produce the food. So yeah, I'm a hundred percent behind this empire thing.*

He could think of a million things that could go wrong, but he shoved those doubts aside. *We'll make it. We'll defeat whatever comes our way. And by "we", I mean Dani and me. I'm going to marry that girl.*

Stay Tuned for the next Hexen Book, due out in later 2024!

In the meantime, join Al Hagan's Fan Group, Hagan's Heroes on Facebook,

For more great fiction, check out Cannon Publishing!

www.cannonpublishing.us